A BLUE ROSE ANTHOLOGY

BY NATANIA BARRON, NERINE DORMAN,
GEORGINA KAMSIKA, RHIANNON LOUVE,
MICHAEL MATHESON, TIFFANY TRENT,
CAIAS WARD, AND SUZANNE J. WILLIS

NISABA
PRESS

TALES FROM THE MOUNT

Tales from the Mount is © 2021 Green Ronin Publishing, LLC. All rights reserved.

Printed in Lithuania

Blue Rose

Tales from the Mount is set in the world of Aldea, the setting for Green Ronin Publishing's *Blue Rose* roleplaying game. Blue Rose is a game of romantic fantasy, where the relationships, friendships, and alliances characters make are frequently as important as their skills with stealth, sword, and spell. For more information about Blue Rose, please visit us at https://blueroserpg.com.

Green Ronin Publishing
3815 S. Othello St. Suite 100, #311
Seattle WA 98118

Email: custserv@greenronin.com
Web Site: www.greenronin.com

10 9 8 7 6 5 4 3 2 1

GRR7302 • ISBN: 978-1-949160-70-3

Editorial Director: Jaym Gates
Authors: Natania Barron, Nerine Dorman, Georgina Kamsika, Rhiannon Louve, Michael Matheson, Tiffany Trent, Caias Ward, Suzanne J. Willis
Editing: Andrew Wilmot
Graphic Design: Hal Mangold & Kara Hamilton
Cartography: Phillip Lienau
Cover Art: Jian Guo
Publisher: Chris Pramas
Team Ronin: Joseph Carriker, Crystal Frasier, Jaym Gates, Kara Hamilton, Troy Hewitt, Steve Kenson, Ian Lemke, Nicole Lindroos, Hal Mangold, Chris Pramas, Evan Sass, Malcolm Sheppard, Owen K.C. Stephens, and Dylan Templar

CONTENTS

Introduction viii

Anchor the Moon 3
By Suzanne J. Willis

A Confluence of Stars 22
By Georgina Kamsika

A Quest for Hope 49
By Rhiannon Louve

Whispers in Shadow & Bone 70
By Michael Matheson

No Turning Back... 89
By Nerine Dorman

Waning Moon 121
By Caias Ward

Faith & Deeds.. 139
By Rhiannon Louve

Like Smoke in My Mind 228
By Tiffany Trent

A Draught of Holly 243
By Natania Barron

The Authors 274

DRUNAC

FALLEN RIVER

R E Z E A

STONE FOREST

FALLEN RIVER
TRADING CAMP

TRIDENT
BAY

REZEAN
GULF

RO

SCATTERSTAR ARCHIPELAGO

THE WORLD OF ALDEA

0   25 50   100   150   250

MILES

INTRODUCTION

The Doom of Faenaria is a part of the tragic history in the *Blue Rose* setting, encompassing the apocalyptic end of a nation of folk who survive as the Roamers of Aldea today as well as the utter disappearance of the enigmatic vatazin of old. While the full-length roleplaying adventure path called *Envoys to the Mount* gives *Blue Rose* players an opportunity to explore not only the legacy of that ancient tragedy but to perhaps also shape its future, the push-and-pull between Shadow-haunted Austium and the last desperate hold-outs of near-mythic Mount Austium begged for more.

It is that which has led to this collection: these *Tales from the Mount*. Two legendary places, set in the desolation of a place like the Shadow Barrens, begs for room to tell stories about them, and that's what we're doing here. Here we explore some of the tales of hope, of tragedy, of grief and of joy that can be found in these realms, told by some of the most wonderful storytellers we could find.

So it is my distinct pleasure and privilege to welcome you to this collection of stories. Whether you are reading these on their own or as part of a bigger exploration of Austium and Mount Oritaun, we hope that you find something beautiful and tragic in these pages, enough to make you sit and dream a little with us about them as well.

Good Reading!

Joseph D. Carriker, Jr.
Autumn, 2020

ANCHOR THE MOON

Suzanne J. Willis

In the basement of the Great Library, among the ruined books and enormous seafarers' globes that had miraculously stayed intact, rhy-owl Raolin and historian Ghiselle watched the spring flowing fast beneath the broken flagstones.

Ghiselle glanced over at Raolin, who was still as a statue. He had not even blinked; he simply peered into the depths with his great amber eyes. It was not unnerving, just . . . well, Ghiselle wished that they were all as patient and *sure* as the rhy-owls. Ghiselle shifted again, the stones horribly hard against her knees.

It won't be long now, Raolin said, not taking his eyes off the water.

Ghiselle didn't reply. Despite Raolin's confidence, she was nervous for Vyleng, who had dived down into the waters without a second thought, his blue skin shimmering as he kicked away and out of sight. Vyleng had volunteered to swim for the Gratling Gate, on the outskirts of the city, thinking that it may be a way out for all of them—Ghiselle, Raolin and his sister Cyrah, Vyleng, the healer

Lane, and Cillian. And anyone else who might have survived the horror of—

There! Raolin's thoughts were interrupted.

Ghiselle reached down into the freezing water and grasped Vyleng's outstretched hand. The moment she touched his skin, she knew that something was wrong. He was warm, in a way that the skin of the sea-folk never was, and so weak that Ghiselle had to pull him from the water. She stroked his hair from his face as Raolin hopped gently around him, looking for any signs of injury. Vyleng's eyes were closed, but his carotid pulse was steady. Then the rhy-owl stopped at his feet.

Ghiselle, he said softly, *something is not right.*

She looked closely at Vyleng's skin, from his foot to halfway up his shin. Where before it had been blue as a summer river, now it was gray and mottled, like something diseased. Reaching out to touch it, Raolin gently stretched out his wing, between her hand and Vyleng's leg.

I do not think that would be a good idea, he said.

"How bad is it?" Vyleng lifted his head, but his voice was weak. Green weed was tangled in his gold hair and stained his fingertips, but other than that he looked as he always did. Except for the terrible color of his leg.

"The only time I have ever seen flesh look like this is when a limb is lost to poisoning." Ghiselle was not given to lying, as much as it hurt her to see him wince. "What happened?"

"At first, it was like nothing down there had changed—as though what had happened in the city didn't touch the spring. Water as clear as the air, even the tiny silver cloud fish in current." He coughed. Ghiselle helped him sit up while Raolin continued to inspect the leg, gently fanning his wings over it as it began to flush red. "At the gate, there was . . . I thought it was waterweed, although I didn't recognize it. As I got closer, it seemed to *wake* . . . it reached out for me, long fingers of shadow. They stretched out and grasped at me. I turned quickly to leave but it managed to wrap itself around my leg."

Leaning forward just in time, he heaved and threw up a stomach-full of water. Ghiselle looked at it in horror as tiny, shadowed shapes in the mess squirmed like worms then began to coagulate. To take shape. Dark tentacles twitched forward, creeping across the flagstones.

Raolin had seen them, too. He rose on his wide wings and headed for the door. *I'll make sure the way is safe.*

Ghiselle hauled Vyleng to his feet, then lifted him onto her back and followed Raolin. Past the giant globes that mapped out the different historical periods of Faenaria, its monsters both imagined and real. Starpoint maps of her skies. Scrolls of secret locations and cities, built layer on layer, like time. How much time had she spent here? What could she have added if she'd had the chance? Unable to bear leaving it all behind, she grabbed two of the smallest scrolls that were bound together and tucked them in her tunic pocket.

"I thought the sacrifice would keep us safe," he whispered in her ear.

But Ghiselle refused to think about that for too long. The sacrifice had already been too great a price to pay; she refused to believe that it may all have been for nothing.

Raolin burst into the second-floor atrium of what had been one of the city's fanciest guesting palace, one that only the most well-connected could afford. The roof was still intact, and so were some of the walls. The staircase still wound up through the ruins, and Ghiselle came up behind him, gently placing Vyleng down before dropping to the floor, utterly exhausted. She was not used to running at the best of times, let alone with the dead weight of a person on her back.

"What was that?" she asked, remembering the ragged creature that had appeared in the twilit skies above them, skimming the air at first then dropping lower and lower, until it nearly took a chunk from Vyleng's flesh.

But Raolin shook his head, then nodded to the bed in the corner.

Cillian, in the last throes of labor, gasped as the child's hand, balled up in a little fist, emerged, followed by her shoulder and then her head—as though she were punching her way into the world. Lane, the va'ta midwife, murmured about how good she had been while exchanging a dark look with Cyrah, now the second and last of the rhy-owls with their little rag-tag group. Cyrah closed her eyes and bowed her head almost imperceptibly in return; anger uncurled in Ghiselle's gut as Lane laid the babe on Cillian's chest.

There are so few of us already, Ghiselle thought. *How can we lose another?*

She stood and moved over to Lane's side. The babe was rosy and perfect, with long fingers clutching at the air. A tiny pool of Cillian's blood was cupped in the fold of her ear. Although Cillian's eyes were closed, her hands patted the swaddling, feeling the child's first movements independent of her mother's body. Giselle remembered Cillian at the gate of the Garden of Sighs, heavily pregnant and wielding her blades against their enemies. And then, fighting a very different battle through labor, to give life to her child. Warrior to the last. She hoped it was something her babe had inherited. It seemed that they would need warriors, more than ever.

Lane left the bedside and Cillian's hand slipped a little from the babe's back. Ghiselle reached out to place it again. As she did, her own hand brushed the babe's back. She felt the promise of new life, beating boldly in the ruins of their dying city. Lane and the rhy-owls had been whispering over near Vyleng. Now the great birds flew over and settled on the end of the bed, as Lane brought Vyleng over. His leg looked almost *dead*, grey and pale and swollen, like a body that had floated in the ocean for days. Ghiselle cried out as Lane placed Vyleng's hand on the baby and then tried to knock it away. But Lane was much stronger and held Ghiselle at bay with their other hand. Vyleng shuddered and dropped suddenly to the floor as Cillian murmured and moaned, tossing her head back and forth, all while the baby lay quiet in their arms.

It might be the only chance to save him, Cyrah said to Ghiselle.

"How do you know it will work?"

We don't. Cyrah's words were heavy.

Ghiselle didn't reply. Who was she to say what was right or wrong? She walked to the window, utterly exhausted and confused and terrified at all that had taken place over the last few days. Meeting up with Vyleng, Lane, and the rest of the group, contacted by underground whispers and desperate messages. Connecting with those who held the same belief as her and convincing them of the truth of the books she had found. Fighting off those who sought to keep them quiet. Then the sacrifice they made before the city fell—

Outside, a shadow passed across the sky. How she missed the sun, the blue sky! Against the gloom, the ruins of Austium showed in relief what this abandoned, doomed place really was. Not just a city, crumbled and torn, but something twisted, taking on a life of its own amidst the decimation.

Cyrah and Raolin rustled and fussed over by the bed, as Lane called softly to Ghiselle. "Come and see! I think it has worked . . ."

She turned toward her friends—the only people, for all she knew, left in the whole city—and watched as Vyleng opened his eyes and looked up at her. The angry red tinge drained from his leg as the swelling subsided. It flushed sea-blue as Vyleng flexed his ankle slowly. Although it wasn't the same as it had been before—perhaps it never would be—at least it looked as though it was no longer necrotizing.

They smiled at one another, small smiles at this bright point in the dark. Cillian opened her eyes a little as she stroked her baby's back. Vyleng leaned forward and gently grasped Cillian's hand, softly kissing her upturned palm. The baby began to wail, thin and urgent. As Ghiselle and Lane helped Vyleng to his feet, their arms steadying him, there was a flutter of wings at the open window. Cyrah and Raolin lowered their heads and flared their wings in defense.

Ghiselle turned. Immediately, she recognized it as the creature that had followed them through the streets. Perched on the windowsill, it looked like a bird of prey. But its shape, its angles were wrong: wing feathers standing out as though the bones beneath were broken, feet splayed so that it squatted rather than stood straight, head cocked as though its neck had been snapped. It eyed the group, crying out with an unearthly squawk when it saw the baby. It flapped once, twice, and rose from the sill, ready to dive across the room. Ghiselle and Lane both reached for their weapons. Before they had a chance to draw, a starblade spun through the air, pinning the bird to the window frame through its chest. It screamed, then made a sound that Ghiselle would never forget: laughter, low, guttural, and sputtering.

Where the bird should have bled red seeped a dark shadow, tendrils of it reaching, exploring.

"I have not lost my aim then." Cillian's voice was a rasping whisper. She smiled. "My daughter's name is Aviarta. At age, give her my weapons . . ."

Lane nodded and stroked her brow, then gently took Aviarta from her as Cillian's breath grew shallow and ragged. "A babe should not know their mother's death rattle," Lane said to Ghiselle and Vyleng, who each held Cillian's hands.

Despite the shadow seeping from the creature, snaking down the wall and toward the group, none would leave Cillian to die alone. Raolin and Cyrah stood watch on the shadow's progress as Ghiselle and Vyleng whispered the words of their people, to sing her into death: Vyleng's, a water song of sluicing away time; Ghiselle's, the turning of a page and the record of life. Two weeks ago, they had barely known one another. Yet she felt the grief deep in her gut; the sacrifice had bound them all as family. None would have made it even this far alone, in the ruins of what was once home.

One last exhalation, then the night was still.

The tendrils of shadow reached the foot of Cillian's bed as they closed the door behind them.

It was as though they had all come from different cities. Vyleng knew every inch of Austium's waterways and the secret underground springs, had drunk with visiting mariners and haunted some of the more *unsavory* back alleys and secret chambers. Lane spoke of knowing the city from its scents: the spring bloom of the Garden of Sighs, stewing meat and spiced tea from the markets, the tannery and dye stores on the outskirts. Raolin and Cyrah had flown its night skies, looking down on streets lit by thousands of lanterns—a perfect, ever-changing constellation. And Ghiselle knew it not from walking its streets but from its books and scrolls and ancient maps, city built on city; the present built on the past.

It is the way of cities—one place is a thousand different places to a thousand different people.

But now, the city belonged to none of them. There was no life here anymore, nothing in these ruins to say that there had ever been. Between them, they could not find a way out. They had made their way out of the atrium, each silently cursing themselves, Ghiselle was sure, for leaving Cillian's body behind. The city should have been eerily silent as they walked its streets, strange weeds already growing up between the great pavers and gray lichen that covered the rubble of its once-magnificent buildings, the stone looking like diseased organs. But there were odd rustlings and cooing sounds in the near distance. Once or twice, they thought they had seen lights in the distance, but when Cyrah flew ahead on silent wings to get a better look, there was nothing there.

"At least there's no more of those *things*," said Vyleng.

"None that we can see," Lane replied.

Finally, they had come to the observatory, which was, amazingly, almost intact. Once inside, they barred the doors. Lane fed Aviarta among the polished wood and brass instruments that Austium's astronomers and scientists had used for so many years. Ghiselle ran her hand over them, wondering how they actually worked. She coughed, her throat dry.

Vyleng opened one of the other doors cautiously, looking out.

"I'll find us water," he said. Before any of them could object, he had slipped outside and was gone.

It felt like the city had turned on them, was purposely leading them astray, keeping them captive. Ghiselle could not help but think it was her fault. After all, she had been the one to find the book detailing the sacrifice. She was a historian—she should have known that these types of things never work out how they are meant to.

Raolin and Cyrah settled by her side. *There will be a way out, child,* said Cyrah. *We just haven't found it yet.*

Perhaps it is time to view the scrolls you brought from the map room in the library. Raolin nodded his head solemnly.

Ghiselle took a deep breath and pulled them from the pocket of her tunic, grateful that she was not given to the frocks and frippery that had been so popular in recent times. She unrolled the first one and Raolin stood on its end, so it would not roll back up again. The three of them studied it intently. It was not a map but a detailed history of the flora of Faenaria: knowledge trees, ghost apples, the healing herbs of Scoundrel's Scythe. Nothing, in short, that would help them leave the city. But the second . . . now, this was interesting. Ghiselle stood, ready to show it to Lane, when there was a knocking at the door.

Ghiselle crept over, while the two rhy-owls positioned themselves on either side of the door, ready to attack with their talons. Lane hid the baby in an alcove then drew their bow. The knocking came again, more urgent this time. Then a whisper: "It's me, Vyleng. I can't open this from the outside . . ."

Ghiselle grabbed the handle and pulled the door open, just a crack. Vyleng scrambled inside, his canteens sloshing with fresh water.

"I don't know if I want to hug you or hit you," said Lane.

Vyleng limped to one of the chairs and sat heavily, his face grave. "I think I may have been followed."

Ghiselle tensed. "Not another one of those . . . *things*?" She shuddered at the thought of the unliving bird, pinned to the wall and laughing grimly.

Vyleng shook his head. "No, this was different. I had no trouble finding water—there is an old well near here that is mostly unused, but those of us familiar with . . . who *were* familiar with all the water sources in the city knew it was there. I heard footsteps and I could have sworn that I saw someone in a cloak or a cape. But when I turned to look, there was nothing but shadows and ruin."

So why do you think you were followed? Raolin asked.

"I heard those same footsteps follow me all the way back here. The streets are quiet enough for me to know when someone else is there."

Do you think anyone else could be left? Cyrah asked Ghiselle.

"The book was very specific about the sacrifice. About where it had to take place. About who would benefit from it. I don't see how there could be any others." Ghiselle might not have known a lot about weapons, or survival, or the kinds of practical things the others did, but she did know her books and the lore. "That doesn't mean that I don't believe you, Vyleng. Who knows what it could be?"

"In any event," said Lane, "it cannot be safe to stay here for too long."

Passing the water between them, they spread out the second scroll—a star map of the skies above Faenaria, with Austium placed at its center. Constellation upon constellation, paths through the night skies, an ancient star catalogue that was, hopefully, still true. Surely Shadow did not reach that far?

"Celestial cartography," said Lane, studying the map. "Mariners have always navigated by the stars. Generally, that needs instruments and all sorts of training . . ." their voice trailed off as they traced the constellations with a worn fingertip, reading the tiny labels written precisely in silver ink. The Great Bear. The Falling Tower. The Lemon Tree. "So prosaic for something so profound."

Cyrah and Raolin bent over the map, their amber eyes drinking in every detail. *We have always hunted by the stars,* said Cyrah, *theirs is a gentle brightness. Sometimes, I think our eyes were made from star-*

dust. See here. She stretched out her right leg, pointing to the tiny label closest to her that read "Diamond Valley." *All the names are of things here, in our world, not in the heavens. We were taught, when we awakened . . .* She looked away.

We learned that this is in honor of the connection between the heavens and our world. Us, Raolin finished.

A snippet of memory uncurled in Ghiselle's mind. "That's right! I learned something similar—that star charts, the right type of star charts, can be used in conjunction with music or words or *plants* to chart a course!"

Lane hurriedly unrolled the first scroll they had looked at and then discarded. The flora of Faenaria. Diagrams of rare flowers, fertilized by iridescent bees that pushed their way through the buds then flew on to the ancient liveria trees; the bellasaria root that could bring on visions of the future; the singing lemon, named for the blooming fungi that lived on its roots and hummed at an unknown frequency.

"We are none of us navigators," said Vyleng.

"True," replied Lane "but there is only one place in Faenaria that all of these have ever existed."

"Don't say it," whispered Ghiselle.

Lane put their hand softly on her arm. Ghiselle felt the soft healing that flowed through Lane course into her. She wished it were enough.

"The Garden of Sighs," they finished.

Ghiselle's gut churned. Her throat was dry, so much so she could not get out the words: *I will never go back there.*

The ground began to rumble, akin to the opening of the Shadow Gates only days before but more subdued. They all ran toward the alcove where Aviarta was sleeping, then the world shook violently and went black.

In that small, scant moment between being awake and sleeping, Ghiselle thought she was waking to a normal day where she would breakfast with Siobahn and River, then make her way to the library. Reality flooded back to her and she remembered: that life was no more. She tried to stretch, but she could not move, could not even open her mouth. Panic bubbled up inside her, then was soothed away like pouring sand on a sparking flame.

"Shhh, don't try to move, any of you. You are safe, but only if you remain unseen."

A kind, unfamiliar hand brushed over Ghiselle's forehead. Whoever owned that voice had ensorcelled them to not move or speak. She could feel Lane and Aviarta huddled to her left, Vyleng and the rhy-owls on her right. The tumble of bricks and what was left of a wall behind them felt warm, as though sun-touched. Across from them, the observatory was now in ruins. Footfalls echoed through the streets, of what sounded like hundreds of people walking, not exactly in sync, but certainly in the same direction.

How can there be anyone left? Ghiselle wondered.

As the first of them passed her by, she realized that there weren't any left. Not like them, anyway. Those walking looked like the bird that Cillian had killed in her last breath. Like Vyleng's leg had looked as it necrotized. Ragged, leathery bags of bones, limbs at odd angles, flesh pallid or decaying, eyes unseeing of anything in this world. Cruel laughter like the bark of a rabid dog. As they walked, they faded in and out, as though they didn't have a proper form. They were becoming Shadow themselves. These were *unliving*, taken by Shadow and turned into something unrecognizable. Vyleng would have become the same, had Aviarta's touch not saved him.

"They are headed for the gates," the stranger's voice whispered. "That is why you cannot go that way."

They fell silent again as the ghastly parade passed by. *Who had they been in life?* Ghiselle wondered. It seemed like forever, but eventually the footfalls faded, although the unliving left behind a rotten stench, like fruit gone bad. Invisible bonds loosened and removed, the group looked around for the stranger who had rescued them. Ghiselle could only catch a glimpse in the corner of her eye; straight on, they seemed to melt into the shadows. A person wearing a dark hood, and long cape, voice as soft as falling rain.

"Where is Cillian?" they asked.

"How do you know Cillian?" Vyleng asked.

"My name is Nuit and Cillian is one of my spouses. Our wife waits for us in Aldis. We left here before . . . but Cillian was too far gone to travel. I told her I would come back for her. You are the only survivors. Where is she?"

Ghiselle realized that they had all just assumed that Cillian was alone, for she never spoke of spouses, nor of the child's father. Perhaps she had assumed them dead, like the rest of the city. "How can we trust you?" she asked.

"Cillian sent me word. She told me that a sacrifice was to be made to keep you all safe. She told me about each of you—the rhy-owls Raolin and Cyrah. Vyleng, and Ghiselle the historian. And Lane, who she knew would help her birth Aviarta and keep her safe."

"And the others? Did she mention—" Vyleng poked Ghiselle in the ribs to stop her from saying anything further.

It was Raolin who finally spoke. *Cillian did not survive the birth; she died as a warrior and saved us all.*

Nuit sank down, onto the rubble, shadowy no longer but solid and whole and holding their head in their hands. They were silent for a very long time.

"And the babe?" Nuit almost sounded as if they didn't want to know.

Lane leaned forward and held Aviarta out to Nuit. "Safe and healthy, and with the healer's gift."

Nuit hugged the child to their chest, then held her out before them, staring in wonder at her tiny features. They stood and looked down at the group. "I can pass the way of the unliving without harm and I can protect my child. But I cannot take all of you. We need to find another way."

You would do that? asked Raolin. *But how is it that you could survive all this?*

"My father was one of the Night People." They seemed to wait for a reaction, but there was none. Nuit rested their cheek on their sleeping child's head. "You ask if I would help you. How could I not?"

"We need to get to what was the Garden of Sighs," said Vyleng.

Ghiselle clenched her teeth. "I tell you, I will not go there again."

"We will not go without you," Lane said. "And we cannot survive here."

Would you have it all be for nothing, child? Cyrah's words were soft and sad. She turned to Nuit. *Can you get us to the garden safely?*

"I will."

It was late into the night when they reached the gate to the Garden of Sighs. Standing there, Ghiselle felt her knees buckle. Now it was Vyleng's turn to support her, putting his arm around the small of her back.

"They went willingly, you know," he said. "It could just as easily have been us."

Ghiselle nodded. Together, they stepped into what used to be the Garden of Sighs. In its time, this was a place that seemed made of dreams. A different scent for each path through the flowers; in full bloom, the perfume could drive one to tears, and to declarations of love. Pomegranates hung fat on the branches, and in late spring the blossoms fell in soft-petal rain. It was said that a person could roam here for fifty years and never know the names of all the plants, or understand their complex interactions. Growth, regrowth, cycling through the years.

Where once grew such wonders were now puddles of darkness, ponds full of weed and black water, stumps and ash and sadness. Under the full moon, it looked just like an old, ruined graveyard, full of collapsing graves and broken stones that haven't been tended to in hundreds of years. The enormous floral dial that stood in the center, its circumference carefully planted to cycle through the four seasons, had turned silver and smoky, as though it had somehow resisted the shadow that had otherwise consumed the city. While Vyleng and Lane began to unravel the scrolls again, and the rhy-owls flew about the garden checking for danger, Ghiselle sank to her knees and, finally, wept.

Nuit sat with her as she grieved. Aviarta whimpered and snuffled in her sleep. They were simple, comforting sounds. After a while, Ghiselle calmed her breathing and wiped her eyes.

"Ghiselle," began Nuit, "it is because of you that my daughter is alive. I only know what Cillian told me—that you had found a way to avert catastrophe, or at least survive it, in one of the old books of Miriana. We were all still believers in the old ways, the old values . . . I do not know any more than that, but it may help you to unburden yourself."

She looked around at the broken city, thought about those unliving shadows that had walked the streets only hours before. And, though exhausted, there was a glimmering seed of pride that they had made it this far. That they had survived, and into this, new life had come. Ghiselle would not let the stories of those who had gone die out with them.

"The texts spoke of the city awakening after a storm of shadow that would destroy not just Austium but, eventually, the whole of Faenaria. That if anyone was to survive, a sacrifice would need to be made. The city, you see, demanded it. The Shadow that woke the city made it so." She looked out at the silvered space where the majestic dial had once bloomed in riotous color and scent. What kind of monsters might grow there now?

"Go on," said Nuit.

"Lane and Vyleng, they didn't have anyone to lose. Among the twelve—one for each month of the year—Raolin and Cyrah, three of their parliament, their kin, drew. And both my partners—both!—drew. 'You might as well anchor the moon, dearest,' my Siabohn told me. 'But we have to try.' And she smiled as she said it!" Ghiselle breathed deeply, steadying herself. "They took the poison themselves, then we buried them standing up, facing the east so that they would never see the sunset—or what little light might filter through here. It means their spirits can never leave and the city will never be alone. That was the price they paid so that we, and the old ways, might live."

A movement caught the corner of Giselle's eyes. Nuit must have seen it, too, and they both stood up, on alert. After a moment, there was nothing else, it was all still. In the distance, Raolin hooted to Cyrah, both still on the wing. Vyleng and Lane pored over the scrolls, Lane pointing to the heavens and warbling like a blackbird at first light. Ghiselle wondered if the stars sang back. Vyleng still had his canteens of fresh water and sipped from them thought-fully. All the water in the gardens—the fountains, the pools, the ponds—looked as black as ink. Corrupted, no doubt.

"Twelve died willingly, Ghiselle, because of the texts you discovered. But they would have died anyway. Instead of that, five survived and one more has been born! All of you carry the history of this time with you. That means a great deal."

Ghiselle smiled up at Nuit. Perhaps there was hope among all this after all. Cyrah and Raolin landed next to them on silent wings, just as a shadowy figure detached itself from the ruined wall on the other side of the clock. A tall shadowy creature with a distended belly and the straight-backed carriage of a warrior. A slash of crimson marked what may once have been its lips.

Silently it mouthed, over and over, *Aviarta. Aviarta.*

Nuit handed the baby to Ghiselle and stood in front of her, protecting them both, pushing down the grief. The creature that was once Cillian walked forward, arms outstretched, reaching, reaching. Raolin and Cyrah swooped at it, hovering and flapping their wings in an effort to keep it back, but it was inexorable. It reached for Cyrah and she screeched as it pulled out a wing feather, which then crumbled to ash in its hand.

"Light and water, light and water," Vyleng muttered as he and Lane crept to what was once a lily pond between them and the creature. Lane continued their trilling to the stars, drawing the pale light toward their mouth. Vyleng passed his hands over the water, backwards and forwards, then up, like a puppeteer. Nuit tried casting another spell to bind it, but it had no effect.

Aviarta cried out, a caterwauling that split the night. As the creature began to run toward Ghiselle and the child, Lane blew out the captured starlight, covering it in a glittering net. Lane grabbed the end, fragile and strong as spidersilk, and pulled, pulled toward the wall of blackened, foul water that Vyleng had created. It yowled as the water enveloped it and splashed back down into the pond, rippling under the surface and twitching, until it lay still once again.

We found no one else here, Raolin said, *but I'm beginning to think that we can't see the real dangers, anyway.*

"So, what now?" Ghiselle asked, hugging Aviarta to her.

"We looked at the scrolls," said Lane, "and think that the grove of singing lemons was planted in the shape of the Lemon Tree constellation. Only the chart also shows the trail of a comet that traverses that constellation in the same pattern that the roots of the singing lemons were trained to grow. And the lemon roots—"

"Are symbiotic with the fungi," Ghiselle finished, remembering her botanical history. The cerulean mushrooms that grew at the base of the lemons were only the top of a much larger organism below. A huge net spread out in complicated patterns, lacing underground for miles and miles. Almost like a galaxy—star point, space, star point. "There must be more than the roads out of Austium that we used to know."

Cyrah ruffled her feathers as she spoke. *What is left of the lemon grove is on the far western side of the garden.*

What was once a sweet-smelling grove was now a mess of stumps and scattered foliage. The very faint smell of lemons, though, hung in the air. Raolin was the first to spot a crop of small mushrooms, shining like sapphires in the darkness. He and Cyrah swayed slowly, solemnly.

We hear its song, they said.

In low tones, unlike anything Ghiselle had ever heard before, they began to sing back. It was as though she had been falling, then was caught in a soft net; the song seemed to say she would fall no further. Though she knew, without a doubt, that their troubles were far from over, she could not help feeling buoyed as a trail of glimmering blue appeared on the ground, wending and winding as though it had all the time in the world to lead the group to where they were going.

The rhy-owls took flight, trailing ribbons of song behind them. Lane sung their starsong softly and the trail glowed brightly, while the stars twinkled fiercely. Vyleng and Ghiselle linked their arms, and Nuit walked behind them, their baby strapped safely to their chest. This city, life here, may have ended, but the survivors would anchor their moon elsewhere. They would not forget.

A CONFLUENCE OF STARS

Georgina Kamsika

Rania slept as deep as the dead. She lay unmoving, yet in her mind she was never still. Dark dreams merged with alarming memories to funnel her thoughts through endless strain. She called out names long unsaid. Faces twisted in fear that she'd not seen for half her life. She dreamed of fear and horror, and felt every moment of it. Her heart thundered in her chest. Bumps rippled along her arms.

The nightmare clutched her, recalling every one of her torments, until Rania snapped upright with a scream. She fought to lower her heartbeat, her left hand checking her throat, subconsciously tracing the thick scars that encircled it. Her skin was dry: no sticky blood, no torn flesh catching her fingertips. Nothing lurked in the shadows of the room, nothing living at all. She gasped, shivering despite the sweat coating her skin.

Rania closed her eyes. She was safe. She was home. Alone. Always alone. Aliette was long gone. It was another day in a long, empty string of them. She sagged back against the sheets, lowering her hand from her throat.

"Forty-something years old and still scared of my own shadow." Rania lit a lamp to banish any hints of gloom. Her home was modest and tidy; everything inside was old and worn, a little like her. One chair, one mug, one dish—just enough to exist without leaving too large a mark on the world. She had done enough of that already.

She made a drink, savoring the spiced tea. It was late in the day for breakfast, but she had no one to answer to. No one to clean the dust in the corners for.

A fist hammered on the door. Rania jumped, fear flooding through her once more. She'd lived here for years without a single visitor. The fist hammered again, knocking dust off nearby shelves.

Rania pulled her robe tight and tied it shut. She shuffled to the door, staring at the solid wood, wishing she could see through it. She heard movement: the clink of metal, the shifting of feet. She sighed and unlatched it before they could knock again.

Two humans filled the narrow gap. A pale young man stood in front, arms braced. He towered over her, his height almost as imposing as his heavy armor. Behind him stood a woman, a warrior, closer to Rania's age. Her tan skin was a couple of shades lighter than Rania's, dark hair shorn short and exposed skin covered in scars.

Rania was conscious of her old robe, of not having looked in a mirror, and of her unwashed hair. But these were her first guests in many years. She pulled the door wider.

"Hail, Rania Shadow Hunter, I am Folcard and this is Alen. We're Knights of the Blue Rose and—"

Rania turned her back on him, shaking her head. Knights. What did the Kingdom's guards have to do with her?

Folcard tried again, following her inside. "Rania, we have to talk. It's important."

Rania sat at the table and picked up her tea. "It's not important to me."

Alen had followed the younger man inside, her dark eyes sharp. Rania knew how it looked, her tiny bundle of clothes, a narrow bed tucked against the wall, a lack of anything personal. Everything as dusty and unloved as Rania herself. She lifted her chin, clutching her mug with both hands.

"We have a duty to protect our citizens. It's vital that you provide us with your aid and experience. We need a guide—"

Alen held up her hand. Folcard went silent, but Alen sensed he hadn't finished with his speech.

"It's hard just living after the stuff we've seen." Alen's voice was low, her inflections hinting at an accent Rania couldn't place.

"Takes some getting used to." Rania shrugged, glancing away. She was grateful Alen didn't comment on how long it seemed to have been, the years of life ingrained in this place. "Anyway, thanks for your visit. I'm sure you need to be getting on."

"It's the shadows, right? They don't feel the same anymore."

Her earlier feelings bubbled just below the surface. She hesitated for a moment before nodding; she felt vulnerable that this stranger had assessed her so easily.

"See, that's why we came to you. I've been in the Guard my whole life. I've fought in wars and defended families. But I've never been there. None of my team have."

"No one needs to go," Rania said quickly.

Folcard, clearly uncomfortable at being ignored, jumped in. "We do. Our scholars located a powerful artefact in the Shadow Barrens. We must have it to power a portal we now control. A team was dispatched several days ago. We lost contact with them when shadow activity suddenly increased."

Shadow activity suddenly increased—like their team rummaging for an artefact wasn't the reason. Rania shook her head. "I can't help you."

"The artefact is *vital* to us—"

Alen pushed his shoulder, not gently, to move him aside. He moved by her low table, looking at the stained-glass distinguished service medal, the blue ribbon faded.

Alen spoke, her voice soothing. "You're the only guide who can help. It's not about the artefact, not for me. It's about the team we sent in for it. We lost them. Ten people missing. We don't need you to fight anything. I have my team to do that. This is a rescue. Find the missing team, bring them home."

Find the missing people. Ten of them. Rania thought of her own team and how they'd gotten lost. Imagined if no one had come looking for them; she'd have died there. Been undead there. Obligation tugged at her.

"From the Shadow Barrens." Rania forced herself to say it, the name catching in her throat.

"From the Shadow Barrens," Alen confirmed. "They might be lost; they might be wounded. We won't know until we check. I want you there to guide me."

"No." Rania trembled. Her hand crept up to her throat subconsciously. She was scared and she didn't care that they could see it.

Folcard shouldered the older woman aside, placing his arms on the table. He leaned over Rania, glaring down. "You'll be safe. The Knights have handled worse than this before. We go in, look for the caravan, leave. Nothing to fear."

Rania looked past him to Alen. She didn't know why, but she trusted her. More than she trusted this young pup, anyway. "This is about the people. Not the artefact."

"Well, if we see it, we would take—"

"It's about the people," Alen spoke over Folcard. "You have my word."

Rania took a deep breath, held it. The scars jumped under her fingertips, wounds that had left their mark. Ancient. Perhaps it was time to move on. Perhaps she could help these people like she couldn't her friends.

"I'll go."

They set off at dawn, leaving the Northern Refuge behind them. It hadn't changed in the many years since Rania's last visit. It had spread a little farther into the canyon, and there were a few more buildings. Most of the foot traffic headed away from the Shadow Barrens.

Folcard was the youngest of the Knights, his armor polished to a gleam, the cloth pressed smooth. Alen rode beside him. The older woman also wore her Knight's armor, but it looked more used than ceremonial. Still, it was clearly well cared for, and that competence was all Rania needed.

The other two warriors, Vern and Nakia, were as alike as any other soldier bonded in battle. The man sat a little taller, the woman a little stockier, but together they moved as one. Years older than Folcard, they wore their experience like armor.

The last member, a vata'an named Mnementh, rode protected between them. She clearly knew the warriors but had her own responsibilities as their healer. She also occasionally received messages that updated their mission. Her long silver hair was braided back for travel, her clothes more robes than armor. Rania wasn't sure how old she was; she didn't know many vata'an these days, but Mnem moved with ageless grace. She looked innocent and vulnerable, like Aliette, so Rania kept her distance.

Vern untucked a bottle of Austiar honey wine from his saddlebag, giving Nakia a knowing grin. She laughed as she leaned to snatch it.

"They act like children, but they've saved my life many times over," Alen said from beside Rania.

Rania jumped, impressed at how silent the heavily laden woman was. "Four warriors. Is this your usual team?"

Alen frowned. "We form up as needed, and I wanted to move quickly. I've fought with Vern and Nakia for years. Mnem has saved our lives too many times to count. Folcard has been charged to rescue the other group and we're assigned to assist him. He's, well, he's new to us, but I trust in his training."

Rania was in no position to argue.

"We're following the warded Dejek Trail, then you'll be our guide toward Austium along the subterranean paths. The other party didn't make it to the city, so we'll scout the outskirts, head back to the trail. Home."

"Apart from the storms, the shadowspawn, and the unliving."

Alen patted the strap holding her sword in place. "I may not have faced shadowspawn before, but we've taken down plenty of other monsters in our time."

"Alen may look old and battered, but we've kept her safe," Vern called, his white teeth gleaming against his skin as he laughed. Vern was a little broader than Alen, and a lot uglier. Scars rippled across his huge arms; his nose had been broken in many places.

Nakia cuffed the back of his head, swearing softly. "Ignore this jester, he's too used to us saving him."

Rania couldn't help but smile. It was clear these three were comrades—no, friends. Despite their jokes, they had brains as well as muscles, and she suspected any one of them could get her safely through the Shadow Barrens. She felt safer knowing they would protect her.

"The new guy really wants to lead, huh," Vern whispered none too quietly.

Nakia eyed Folcard and his prancing mount. She twisted her mouth in silent agreement but kept her position.

"He's trained as the rest of us. He'll do," Alen rode past them, her voice gently chiding.

"What about you?" Vern twisted in his seat, his shaved head gleaming in early morning sun.

"Guide. I've travelled to Austium before." Rania didn't miss the way his eyes dipped to her throat, or Nakia's low whistle.

Vern and Nakia devolved into bickering about their weapons. Vern had his crossbow settled across his pommel, his scarred fingers lovingly tracing the finer workings. Nakia pulled her own weapon, confidently checking the blade for nicks or chips.

Witnessing their expertise reassured Rania. She'd spent so long alone, it warmed her to see their comradeship. With that warmth came feelings she didn't want to think about, so she buried them as deep as she could.

The two knights kept up their questions, asking about her experience before the Barrens, about her many years of service. They were interested in this new person in their ranks, making her speak more than she had for many years. Rania had almost forgotten how good it felt to connect with others.

The sun was well past the midpoint in the sky when she realized what they'd done. They'd distracted her so completely she'd not noticed their transition into the Shadow Barrens.

The trail crested over a small hill; the ruined landscape spread out before them. Ashen sand filled the horizon, interrupted only by traces of distant ruins. The oasis lay far ahead, barely visible, as a sandstorm threatened the eastern skies.

Rania wasn't sure how she felt. Was this place as bad as her nightmares, or had she forgotten its true horrors? She lifted her chin, encouraging her horse to trot past Alen. No matter. She was here to face her past. It was too late to change her mind.

A low wall surrounded the settlement. A smoking firepit sat by the clear water, surrounded by sparse buildings. There were a few locals, but no other travelers. It was quiet.

"Remove all your gear. Keep it with you," Rania warned.

"I would, of course, but why specifically now?" Alen slipped the saddle off her warhorse.

"However well we tie them, we'll lose some of the horses on this trip. They run or are taken or, I don't know. They don't last out here."

Mnementh edged closer, her own tack held in her arms. "She's right. The group we're looking for lost most of their mounts the first day."

Alen eyed her with real respect. It caught Rania off guard, pride blooming through her. She did what she could to hide her smile, but the pull of Alen's lips stayed with her, something she hadn't experienced in so long.

That feeling was probably why Rania opened up. They huddled around the firepit after their food, relaxing as the heat leeched up into the midnight sky. It had been a while since she'd spent this much time with anyone, never mind people who treated her like a friend.

"How'd you get the scars?" Vern motioned to her throat.

Nakia hissed at him from her position on watch, but Rania waved them off.

"It's fine. It happened a long time ago. Here in the Barrens. We've been lucky so far, but it's going to get bad. Real bad. We need to find those people and leave as fast as we can. We made that mistake twenty-something years ago. Aliette . . ." She sighed, her friend's eyes slipping closed in her memory. "It was a wyvern. Stunned a guard, bit the others. I'd dragged Aliette into cover. She was so young, barely seventeen. I distracted it so she could run. But it stung me with venom. I woke with my throat bandaged, but everyone else was dead. Aliette had tried to cure me, but the wyvern got her. It'd . . . it'd eaten—"

"I understand." Alen placed a warm hand on Rania's arm. "It's hard to lose people, but this wasn't your fault. You did the best you could."

"She's right. You did good, soldier." Vern thumped his chest, his action mirrored by Nakia behind him. Even Folcard nodded, his youthful face gleaming in the starlight.

Watching the knights interact kindled something in her chest. With the starlight and the firelight playing against each other, the knights shielding her from the Shadow Barrens, she forgot how dangerous it could be to have friends. She missed the camaraderie.

She should've been resting when Folcard replaced Nakia on watch, but sleep refused to come with the stars dancing above her. Alen looked comfortable leaning against her saddle, her long legs crossed at the ankles. Vern huddled up to Nakia's stocky form, holding up his crossbow, pointing out some detail that entranced her.

Folcard looked worried. Sweat dripped off his pale face, his movements jerky as he stalked about the perimeter. The other knights noticed, Vern nudging Nakia before he called over.

"Looks like he's not left Aldis before."

Folcard blinked rapidly, his mouth pulling down. "I've put in my time."

Nakia and Vern didn't reply; they simply exchanged a meaningful glace. Rania tried not to let it worry her. This wasn't like before. And even if Folcard did make mistakes, Alen was more than competent. It would be fine.

An inhuman scream tore the night, echoing through the huddled buildings. It continued to rise then cut off sharply. It sounded close.

Raina's whole body tensed. An attack? She wasn't ready. Her breath caught in her throat. She jumped up, poised for flight.

"Knights assemble!" Alen barked. Her voice echoed across the still water, twisting and warping until there were no words, just noises. The knights moved as one, Alen and Nakia in front, with Folcard and Vern at their flanks.

Rania kept the Knights close. She knew that an attack could come from any side, even above. She wrapped her arms around herself as another shriek ripped the air. It sounded nearer.

Alen threw down her coat to free her arms. She twitched her shoulders, adjusting the position of her sword.

The water splashed, a shape moving in the darkness. The wind caught the firepit. An eruption of sparks highlighted the creature: an immense serpent loomed motionless, its gaze fixed on Alen. It had a strong smell, like stagnant water, and its scales were dull.

It lunged to the water's edge, scales hissing against the rough sand. Alen braced in front of it, shielding the others.

Seeing the creature triggered all of Rania's worst nightmares. She ran, her trembling legs stumbling over the uneven ground.

She had but one thought: escape the threat. Behind her, the creature screeched. A knight grunted—she couldn't tell who—water splashing around their feet.

Rania slumped against a settlement building, her sides heaving. She hadn't remembered grabbing Mnementh, but the vata cowered beside her. Hiding behind the solid building gave her a feeling of safety, however false it might be. She peered over the low wall where the others still fought.

The serpent's jaws snapped shut with a crack like a hunter's trap. It snapped at Alen with bloodied teeth. She leapt to the side with a swift pirouette. The creature followed. Nakia flanked it, dealing a hard blow to its head. It roared, filling the oasis with a booming echo. It renewed its attack, scraping venomous teeth across Alen's breastplate. Folcard lined up a shot. It was clear these warriors were more than equal to the creature. His arrow flew true, sinking into the soft flesh by its eyes. It slithered backwards, baring its fangs. Ichor dripped onto its chest.

Alen varied her movements to distract the beast, making it difficult for it to attack. The moment it tensed and leapt, a crossbow bolt whistled through the air and pieced the creature's soft throat. The jump became a fumble and it let out an ear-piercing shriek. It thrashed backwards, its long tail driving it deeper into the water.

"Clear?" Alen called as she stalked toward the water's edge.

"Clear," Vern confirmed. "Won't be back here again."

Vern and Nakia glared at Rania. She couldn't blame them. Some guide she was, leaving them behind at the first sign of trouble. Guilt swallowed her. She could do better. Better than she had for Aliette, anyway.

Alen lowered her sword, gaze sweeping across the party. "Any injuries? No? Mnem, see who screamed and either heal or bury them. Nakia, go with her. Vern, you stay on watch for now."

They moved, following her orders, the vata striding forward with purpose. Folcard was the only one left still. He frowned.

"You okay?" Even Alen only gave her a tight smile.

"It's late, we need rest," Rania said, deflecting the question. She scanned the dotted buildings surrounded by stunted foliage.

"Thank you."

Rania stared at her blankly. She'd run away and left them behind. Why would Alen thank her?

"Your experience got you and Mnem away from the fight."

Experience. A generous way to explain her panic; however, Rania felt touched by her kindness. "How about you? You're the only one it actually hit." Rania pointed to the scuffed breastplate.

Alen's mouth twisted in a wry smile. "Bruised for a few days, but I'll live. Mnem can heal the worst of it before we leave."

"Maybe *you* should rest," Folcard snapped, then controlled himself. "We'll move on soon. You should take a few minutes while you can."

Alen's eyes danced with mirth. She tucked her head down. Rania didn't blame her. She didn't care who was leader as long as any threat was eliminated as efficiently as that naga.

As predicted, their warhorses had been injured. Two dead, one with wounds too mortal for Mnementh's healing arcana. It would be impossible to carry on as a mounted expedition. Vern negotiated with a local to care for their remaining horses.

Alen's voice was low but still carried. "Save your energy. We've got a long walk ahead of us."

Rania sighed as she shouldered her pack.

"I'm not here to play," Alen reassured her with a sly grin.

The land around them was shrouded with thick clouds that rendered the lifeless rocks almost impassable. The very air cracked with the need for a storm. The wind buffeted them, distorting all sounds, so they had no idea if there was anything nearby.

Rania led the tightly packed group as they hurried onwards. Alen barked out occasional orders, but otherwise the knights stayed quiet. Vern whispered to Nakia but Rania didn't try to overhear.

Many tired hours later, Rania saw the landmark she'd been looking for as the path dipped into the darkness. "Down here!" she called out.

Alen shifted her sword to lean over the edge. "Here. You're sure?"

Rania didn't blame her hesitancy. The trail diverted off down the edge of a rocky ledge, with only hacked footholds to show any kind of passage. If she hadn't followed it before, she might not have believed it either.

"This is their path. We need to follow their route." She lit a torch, then carefully stepped down the narrow tracks. It was pitch dark outside the halo of her light, but she could see an opening into the knot of tunnels known as the Sunless Path.

She kept the light still until the others had gathered together. The circle of illumination was small. A nearby stream trickled, the drip of water loud against the damp riverbed.

"This route isn't the safest, but it's direct and easy to follow. We need light at all times, and to be aware of everything. From sinkholes and quicksand to naga and wisps."

"But it's not that far to where they were," Mnementh added. "They could be injured or pinned down nearby."

Alen looked to Folcard, who peered into the gloom. She waited then clapped her gloved hands together. "Vern, take the lead, Nakia, the rear. Rania, Mnem, stay central. We need to keep a tight formation, and we need to be alert."

Folcard bristled but followed her instructions. To avoid his ego, Rania kept close behind him, ensuring the vata's safety. It was hard to look at her, to remember Aliette, but she didn't need anyone else on her conscience.

Their movements had slowed, partly due to the uneven floor, partly due to the minimal light. It was deathly quiet; the only sounds were the thin trickle of the Jornoovian river and the people around her.

"Floor ahead is solid, as far as I can see," Vern called over his shoulder.

"Good job, keep it up," Folcard turned his attention back to his flank. He always seemed confident once Alen set people in their roles. Maybe he was scared of giving orders. If that proved to be the case, Rania trusted Alen would push past his fears.

"Looking good back here," Nakia confirmed from her position.

"I always look good from the back," Vern exclaimed before Alen shushed him. Vern stowed his jokes and took point. He moved with deft grace, picking out a safe path and directing those behind him.

They'd been walking for hours when a sound echoed in the distance. A shifting sigh, the bounce of pebbles. The group froze. Nothing. Alen motioned to Vern. He lifted his crossbow, letting it precede him as he stepped around a rock pillar. Rania and the others followed.

The earthquake happened quickly. A sharp jolt that caused Rania to stumble. Mnementh fell to her knees with a cry. Rania offered a hand as a few stronger shakes shook the whole cavern system. Alen grabbed her outstretched hand and steadied her. Dust drifted down from above. Small pebbles and larger rocks bounced down. Vern cried out, cupping a hand to his head. Nakia pushed through and grabbed him.

"Keep your positions," Folcard barked.

Nakia ignored him, pressed a hand to the bleeding wound on Vern's scalp. Rania pulled Mnementh to her feet with a jerk, keeping her gaze on their rear. The vata trembled as she ducked to avoid more debris.

"Report!" Alen called out as the larger trembles faded away.

"Vern's down!" Nakia sounded worried.

"Vern's fine, it'll heal." Vern rubbed the blood off his brow with the back of his hand.

"Rania?" Alen leaned closer.

She became aware of her breathing, roaring in and out as if she'd run down the riverbed instead of standing still. She waved a hand in assent, angry at herself, and at Alen's concern.

Rubble lay strewn across their path. A new breeze whistled down the narrow tunnel. Pools of water stained the muddy banks.

Mnementh cast something—Rania wasn't sure what—and light bloomed around them. Shadows lurched away from them, shifting and moving in time with her. Rania hated it. Every movement was a beast coming for them, every shadow a lethal threat. She had to fight to keep her breathing steady. Alen stopped by her and clasped her shoulder. Rania straightened at her touch.

"No movement," Vern said as his partner retook her position.

"We're close," Mnementh murmured. "We should see signs of them soon."

Alen raised her sword, moving to Vern's side. "Let's move."

Rubble laid strewn across the path, with dust and pebbles rattling down. They took each bend with care, stopping to check the integrity of the ceilings. One wide tunnel was blocked entirely by rubble, causing Rania to re-think their route. The new path led them deeper underground. They passed signs of a struggle, some discarded bags, old dried blood, but no evidence of anyone still living.

"Looks like no one was seriously hurt," Alen said, her voice low.

Rania wasn't so optimistic. Blood smeared the walls, and the remains of food packets floated in the stagnant puddles. She checked every damp hole and every shadowed corner. Sweat slicked her skin despite the coolness of the caves. There was no doubt in her mind that this party had met a similar fate to her friends. Alen, noticing her nervousness, adjusted her stride to walk beside her.

Alen was kind to her in that way, Rania noticed. The swords-woman never made her feel damaged or delicate, just someone worthy of spending time and effort on. She was so busy staring at Alen that she almost missed it. She froze, murmured, "Look."

Alen shifted into high alert. She braced her arm in defense and moved to stand beside Vern. Her light revealed a scene of destruction worse than anything Rania had imagined.

The party had made a last stand. Their packs were piled into a barricade, blocking them in against the rock wall. The cloth had been ripped open, scattering their belongings across the dry river-bed. Everything was spattered deep red. Blood pooled on the rock floor, with a flurry of footprints skittering in all directions.

They hadn't got far.

There was nowhere to go, nowhere to hide. Rania trembled. She could run from this, but she'd be alone again. However dangerous this looked, she was safer surrounded by the knights.

Vern squeezed past the barrier, Alen at his back. Their lights highlighted the devastation beyond. Rania ducked her head. No one could have survived that much blood loss. They had to be dead.

"Mnem, check them," Alen called, but she sounded resigned.

But Folcard pushed past before the vata could move. He raised his light, examining the corpses. He counted them out loud, sounding frustrated when one was missing.

"Find the last person," he said. "They can't have gone far."

The other knights fanned out, slowly widening their search. They moved through the cave system, keeping silent—even Vern wouldn't joke about this.

Rania stayed still, watching Folcard. At first, she thought he was examining the bodies to see how they died, or perhaps performing some kind of funeral rite.

He was searching the bodies. The relic. It had always been about the relic.

Cold anger burned in her stomach, rising up through her chest. Each corpse was bloodied and broken, limbs bent at all angles, flesh torn, bones exposed. How many people had died for one artefact? How many would Folcard risk of his own party? One of them? All of them?

"There!"

A shout interrupted her before she could vent her fury.

The knights spun to face the noise. Vern gestured toward an almost-blocked tunnel. They moved carefully, pausing to check every dark corner. Alen hesitated, then nodded toward the shadowed opening. The rubble shifted, small rocks tumbling down the slope. Rania glimpsed something moving.

Nakia pivoted, her sword raised before Alen lifted her own to block it. The swordswoman snarled, furious, but Alen ignored her. She leaned forward, aiming her light into the tunnel. She stayed like that for a long moment before beckoning behind her.

Rania looked to Mnementh. Rania's legs were stiff, knees frozen, feet glued to the floor. The vata looked over her shoulder, a query on her face. Rania forced herself to join her.

Alen had crouched before some rubble. A woman, not long into adulthood, lay still, half-buried. Rania caught the older woman's eyes. Alen shook her head slightly, just once. Rania moved out of Mnementh's way as the vata tried, futilely, to heal her.

The corpse was filthy and covered in wounds, her lower body crushed. One hand lay clenched at her chest.

Folcard edged closer. "Do you see the artefact?" he asked. Mnementh brushed some of the matted hair off the woman's face, shaking her head. Folcard pursed his lips, glaring at the body in frustration. He pulled the curled hand away from her chest and loosened her fingers. A disc glowed faintly in the dim light.

"Perfect!" Folcard snatched it, peering at it as he wandered away.

It was hard, harder than Rania could bear, to see another group fail. She had come to help them and she'd failed at that, too. Anguish clawed at her throat, knowing the struggles they went through only to die and risk rising again, corrupted. She wouldn't let anything happen to this party. She must succeed now where she had failed her friends.

"We have the relic. We should check for supplies, then leave."

"No." Rania stood up, brushing the dust from her knees. "We need to burn her body."

Folcard shook his head. "We don't have time for this. We'll pray for them back in Aldis."

"It has nothing to do with respect," Rania snapped, silencing him with her anger, "and everything to do with the corruption of this place. This poor woman died recently, perhaps today. She might rise again as an undead."

Folcard opened his mouth to argue, but Alen pushed him aside. She wasn't gentle.

"You heard her. Let's light a pyre then leave."

Rania appreciated her support, relieved that she didn't have to waste energy arguing. She and Mnementh scoured the makeshift camp for kindling while the others dealt with the body. Heat and light filled the caverns, yellow flames flickering up toward the low roof.

The bright light should have made her feel safe, but the shadows drew closer. Rania could sense it, the darkness lapping at their feet like waves. She strained to listen. Nothing but the crackle of fire and the drip of water. Then, faintly, at the edge of her hearing, the soft slide of feet. A shuffling step. A splash in a puddle.

"Something's coming."

Folcard looked up from the relic, glaring at her. "I said we'd get moving, you're the one who wanted to wait."

"Alen!" Rania gave up on the knight's leader. She pointed into the deepest shadows. There wasn't anything to see, not yet, but terror clutched at her.

Alen drew her sword, moving into position. Rania grabbed Mnementh, huddling behind the others. Alen pivoted, tracking their progress across the cavern.

The heat from the pyre made Rania sweat, the smoke stinging her eyes. Silhouettes from Rania's worst nightmares crept out of the tunnels. Humanoid shapes, long sunk into rot and decay, slumped forward. It was hard to see how many there were—the flickering light only highlighted a moving mass. Like moths to a flame, the undead lurched out of the tunnels: rotten faces with hollow mouths that gaped as they moaned, they swarmed out of the darkness, limbs flailing, stumbling into and over each other in their desperation.

A crossbow bolt sailed overhead, Vern instantly racking up another; his whole body was an extension of his weapon. The same was true of the swordswomen, moving to intercept the shambling creatures. They danced and pivoted in unison, slashing back the attackers. An undead screeched, body falling at Alen's feet, but still more clambered out of the dark.

Rania didn't know why she'd agreed to come. She might've been lonely, but she'd been *safe*. Why had she chosen to confront her nightmares? Because she thought she could help these people? Because she had to atone for her friends?

"Move out, retreat to the stairs."

Alen's voice rang out above the chaos. Folcard lowered his bow, his face damp with sweat. It was clear that he was lost. He stuttered something incomprehensible, completely out of control of the situation.

"Retreating!" Rania panic-shouted, tucking Mnementh's arm under hers as she stumbled along the slippery riverbed. Vern ran alongside her, his crossbow never still. The undead were mostly behind, but Vern clipped any near their path.

Nakia grunted from pain. Rania didn't want to stop, didn't want to care, but she couldn't leave anyone behind. She had enough nightmares—she didn't need more guilt every time she tried to sleep.

She was terrified, but her anger burned stronger. Anger at being sent out for a relic, at the monsters attacking them; but mostly focused inward, for putting herself in this position. She chose to be here. She had to help.

She dug deep into herself, clawing past the years of pain and torment. Deep down, hidden and almost forgotten, she found her spirit. She controlled her breathing until her blood beat through her neck, arms, eyes. Focusing on that feeling, she pulled on that light, tension building until she called forth a shining sphere almost twenty feet across. It pulsed through her, throbbing waves of heat and light. The undead screeched, an infernal noise as they burst into flames. She held her light until they were nothing but ash.

Nakia limped out of the smoky shadow, her face pale, one arm hanging loosely at her side. Alen appeared at her side. Her sword dripped with a dark ichor. Alen caught her gaze, smiling gently.

"We're okay. They've gone. We've got a clear spot for a moment."

Rania relaxed, sagging slightly against the other woman. It had been some time since she'd last used that skill. She'd long worried that the darkness had touched her soul. It seemed it hadn't.

"I never expected anything like this," Mnementh murmured.

"Neither did Folcard." Nakia glared at the Knights' leader, resentment and pain warring on her face.

Folcard turned his back, his fingers clutching at the relic in his pouch. Just as Rania feared, that was all he cared about. Alen moved to block Nakia's line of sight, her glare cutting between them. Nakia held her anger a moment longer before slumping back.

"We have to get back to the stairs, but the route may be blocked after those quakes." Rania said quickly. "We drove them off, but they'll soon be drawn back."

"*You* drove them off." Alen smiled her thanks. "How are we for supplies? Bolts? Water?"

Mnementh shook her head. "A little water. Most of our packs got left behind due to our fast retreat."

Alen forced back a grimace. "Okay, so it's a quick march back to the oasis. We left a cache there."

"I'm our scout, I'll find the fastest route out of here," Rania said.

"I'll go with you, I can keep it well lit," Mnementh summoned light, pushing the shadows back.

Rania led them past the fallen boulders, sucking quicksand and fresh ruptures. She moved as quickly as she dared with their wounded. The tunnels blurred around her as she stepped over a new crack in the ground. She had one focus: the distant stairs dug into the rock walls that she could just make out. Her breath burned her throat she pushed toward them.

She had to drop Mnementh's hand to haul some debris from the steps. Folcard lowered his bow to help. He favored one leg, the other bruised and bloodied. She dug into the dirt, her short nails cracking as she heaved the loose rocks to one side. Rania scurried up as soon as the rubble was clear. Her feelings warred within her—the desperate need to escape the darkness, the fear of what might be above, and, finally, her desire to help, to scout ahead, to find a clear path for her friends.

Rania fell to her knees on the sand as the others followed. She counted them: four, five, six. All safe.

"I thought for sure someone was going to die." Vern rubbed the fresh damage on his armor.

"Death isn't the end to this nightmare," Rania said, waving a tired hand. "They were all people once." Adrenaline and exhaustion numbed everything, but the pain of knowing she could have recognized a rotting face in those caverns, that each one of them had lived a life before they were lost, drove her on. She hadn't been able to save them. She only hoped she could save her new friends.

"Rania is right, which is why we have to move." Alen held out a hand, pulling Rania to her feet.

Time ran differently in the Shadow Barrens. Rania had no idea how long they'd spent underground, but the storm that had threatened them was now in full swing. The oasis was a day's march at best, but the storm was a problem. Dense clouds covered the horizon, their color shifting and changing like a bruise. They swirled rapidly, the howling winds dragging darkness with them.

A bloodied Alen took the lead, leaving Vern at their rear. Nakia and Folcard supported each other, limping along with the uninjured vata healing what she could. Rania walked a pace behind Alen, calling out directions to pass the worst hazards.

The dark storm clouds made it hard to navigate, but Rania could tell they were barely half a day from the oasis. They'd made it. Battered, injured, a little wiser, but she'd guided them through.

An enraged shriek stopped her in her tracks. The clouds shifted, displaced by something huge. A distant, glistening shape filled the skies.

Her muscles went rigid, the terrified patter of her heart drowning out the storm, voices, the world. The shadow rolled over as the giant shape broke through the clouds with two flaps of its enormous wings. Another shriek tore the air. Pale eyes sharp with malice focused in on her, on them, as it swooped toward them.

The whipping wind pulled her from her panic. She scrambled for cover, voice already hoarse from trying to direct the others over the howl of the storm. The stirred-up sand and the lack of light made it impossible to see. She staggered toward a tall outcropping, sinking against the rough stone. Her body shook with the stress, her hands clenched tight as the others limped over to her.

Behind them, the shape in the sky dipped closer. The ground shook as it landed, too close. Alen rolled to one side, but the others were knocked to the ground.

"Wyvern!" someone yelled. Someone else screamed.

Rania couldn't think or move. A huge body, snake-like tail, massive wings. It was the object of her nightmares, more horrifying than she remembered.

The beast reared back, its wings extended. Rising on legs wider than a tree trunk, its sword-sharp claws ripped into the dirt inches from her friends.

Her friends. Rania couldn't let this happen again. She dived forward to pull Alen under cover. She was no longer fearful—there were too many things to concentrate on. Four friends still in danger. An escape route. A giant wyvern.

Folcard had pulled Nakia away from the beating wings. They were both bloodied and bruised, barely able to support themselves. There'd be no help there. Vern had placed himself in front of the vata, his crossbow a joke compared to the size of the beast.

"Mnem, run!" Rania screamed.

Mnementh hadn't moved, swaying as she stared up at the monster. She looked so tiny, so young. Just like Aliette.

Rania surged forward, twisting away from Alen to grab the young woman. The wyvern tensed at her movement. Rania didn't care. She reached for Mnementh. The wyvern's tail whipped through the air; its sharp tip glistened. It swung down, toward the vata. Vern pushed Mnementh out of the way. The point buried itself in his side. Vern screamed, stumbled a step or two, then collapsed. The vata lay in the dirt next to a giant clawed foot. Out of range for rescue, but unharmed.

"Poison, we need to save him." Rania flinched at the memory of the sting. It had debilitated her in seconds; she was unconscious in minutes. Vern didn't have long.

"We need to save them all." Alen dragged herself up with a grunt. Rania couldn't see a wound, but with everything they'd been through, she wasn't surprised the other woman was in pain.

Alen lifted her sword, roaring to grab the monster's attention. It turned away from Vern's prone body as it poised itself to leap. Alen leapt first, her sword flashing in a short, sparing cut. The wyvern deflected her blade and slashed its massive claws at her face. She barely parried the blow, stumbling backwards.

Rania edged around the fight, moving toward the others. She couldn't just stand back and watch. She dipped toward Folcard, ignoring the twinge of pain as she dropped to his side. The wyvern's rough scales had torn at his exposed flesh, leaving him bloodied.

"Okay?"

"We'll live," Folcard muttered as he bandaged a wound on Nakia's leg.

"Only if that dies," Nakia muttered. "Stop using this as an excuse to touch me and go kill it, Folcard."

He opened his mouth to argue before Nakia slapped his shoulder, a smile on her face. He flushed. Rania lifted Nakia's sword and left him grabbing his bow.

Alen lunged underneath the wyvern, slashing at its exposed belly. She cut through the scales, but it wasn't deep enough. The wyvern roared with fury, hopping backwards to defend itself.

Rania had lived in fear so long, it was hard to believe what she was seeing. But it was true. The wyvern might be a terror in the skies, but on the ground, they had an advantage. They could kill it.

"We're faster than it! Keep moving."

Alen raced around the side of the beast. It turned to follow her, ungainly stamping movements shaking the ground. Rania used the creature's blind spot to dart in and rip her sword through one of its thin, membranous wings.

An infernal shriek reverberated. The beast tried to fold its wings, screaming again when the wounded wing didn't move. It took its fury out on Alen, talons raking across her metal armor. The desperate blow knocked Alen onto her back, sword held up to defend her face.

Rage built inside Rania. *Not again.* Her blade shimmered as she ducked and rolled underneath the damaged wing. She stopped by a giant taloned foot, dwarfed by the monster. Rania slashed upwards, toward the shallow wound in the creature's scaled hide. She threw her whole shoulder into it, driving the blade deep into its stomach. The wyvern reared back, a screech echoing across the barrens. Alen slashed her sword across its exposed throat.

The wyvern curled up, falling backwards with a loud grunt. The weight of it ripped at the sword, tearing at Rania's arms. She let go as the beast crumpled. It shuddered, legs extended, fangs bared. There was an arrow buried deep in its eye.

Nakia whooped, slapping Folcard hard on the back. Mnementh picked her way past the dying creature to squat beside Vern, checking his wounds.

"We did it." Rania put distance between herself and the wyvern's corpse. She let out a shaky breath and slumped to the ground, unable to stop herself from trembling. This time it wasn't out of fear, or guilt, or pain. Relief brought tears to her eyes, wetness streaming down her cheeks as she smiled, overcome with victory. They had done it. She had conquered her nightmare.

Vern's voice was weak but clear. "I knew you would."

Rania laughed, eyes shining, the wind drying her cheeks. He was safe enough to make a joke after Mnementh had cured him, just as Aliette had done for her. Or really, not like that at all. No one had died this time. As she watched her friends pick themselves up and put themselves back together, she knew this wasn't the past; this was now. This was a new beginning. She wept for memories finally resting in their graves, but more than that, for the relief of the lives of her new friends.

Hot winds swirled around the canyon as Rania sank back into the bed. The priests had finally finished worrying over their wounds.

Folcard and Nakia sat by the fire outside the inn as Vern roasted some animal he'd caught. Mnementh lay curled up on the nearest bedroll, exhausted after healing their most serious wounds.

Mnementh managed a small smile. "We did okay, didn't we?"

Rania leaned close, hugging her with one arm. "We did more than okay." She glanced to Alen, sprawled out next to her. In sleep, she looked younger. Still tough, still tired, but at once both fierce and peaceful.

Without her, without all of them, Rania would be dead. Mnementh, Vern, all of them. Around them, life in the refuge continued, the low laughter reassuring her. She listened as Vern opened some honey wine, wondering if she should join them.

Perhaps after a nap. She patted the bed, a little harder than her own, with lumps and dust and rough sheets. Still, it was the first time in many, many years that Rania was no longer afraid to dream.

A QUEST FOR HOPE

Rhiannon Louve

Tiren adjusted the pack on her shoulders as she reached the outer gate. She could only leave during the full moon, so of course she'd had to trick her loved ones into believing she wouldn't leave this month. She hadn't wanted them to try and stop her.

And of course, Yussa hadn't been fooled. There he was, lounging against the massive gate post, eyeing her as she approached. Councilor Isabis had yet to arrive, it seemed. The moon wasn't quite full yet.

Well, there was nothing for it. She braced herself for the worst and walked over to him.

Tiren had always thought that Yussa was beautiful—tall and lithe, with fine features and graceful limbs. Right now, he was as pale as the moon herself, almost ghostly in comparison to Tiren's eternal moon-dark midnight. Yussa could, today, be mistaken for a vata'an, a symbol of her people's arcane diminishment, just like her vata'sha self. But in Yussa's case, the appearance would last only a few days. For most of each month, he could be seen for only what he was: hope incarnate. He was a young, vibrant vatazin, his parents' and his community's pride and joy.

Tiren knew that her family loved her, and that vata'an and vata'sha enjoyed the same rights and privileges as all other citizens of Mount Oritaun, but . . . growing up with a friend like Yussa, Tiren had always felt the difference between them. She knew everyone around her was happier to see him than to see her—even during the dark of the moon, when the pair matched perfectly in coloring.

It didn't matter. People knew. Yussa was the future they wanted. Tiren was the future they feared. Other young vata'an and vata'sha didn't like to talk about that feeling—that subtle sense of being less, being eternally disappointing no matter what they accomplished—but Tiren knew she wasn't alone in feeling it. Everyone tried to pretend it made no difference, but children could tell. Deep down, they could always tell.

The world of Mount Oritaun was crumbling, slowly decaying, and when vatazin parents could not breed vatazin children, it reminded everyone of their community's approaching doom.

"Hey," Tiren greeted Yussa. "Come to see me off?"

"You're really going, then." He pushed off the gate post and strolled over, stood opposite her. He didn't uncross his arms.

How long had he been this much taller than her?

It reminded her that they were both adults now, just barely. The thought was still surreal.

"I'm really going," she said.

"This is stupid," Yussa told her for the ninety-seventh time.

"Everyone keeps telling me that," she said. "But I'm still going. I'm ready."

"I can't come with you." To Tiren's surprise, Yussa's voice shook. She glanced sharply at him. Saw real pain in his eyes, and a slight sheen of tears. She never would have expected him to show this kind of emotion.

"Of course you can't!" Without meaning to, Tiren lay a hand on his arm. When had his arms grown so huge and solid? Just touching him made her feel safer, made the whole world feel more real. Suddenly shy, she withdrew her hand. "Vatazin wither out there. I'd feel as if I were killing you every day."

"Is this about Frelle?" he asked. "I mean, I don't want to sound arrogant, but . . ."

"Ew. No. It's not because you're marrying someone else, dimwit." That had hit Tiren harder than she would ever admit—even though she'd always known he didn't see her that way, that she'd never seen *him* that way, either. But his engagement had only steeled her resolve. "You know how long I've dreamed of doing this."

"Dreamed," he said. "Now you're serious. It's different."

"We're not children anymore," Tiren said. "It's supposed to be different."

Somewhat to her relief, Councilor Isabis arrived then, the little rhy-bat flapping up to land on Tiren's head, as she often did since Tiren had begun pestering her for this favor.

Ready, youngster? The bat's voice in her mind was somehow tiny and large, adorable and dignified, all at once.

"I can do this," Tiren said, for both their benefit. "I'm ready."

She suspected that the rhy-bat councilor said something to Yussa then. He dropped his arms and sighed, nodding. "Come back safe," he said to Tiren. "I won't forgive you if you don't."

"I will." She forced a smile through misty eyes. "I'll be back before you know it, with everything we need to restore Mount Oritaun to its former glory."

Yussa snorted at that, but he stepped aside. The guards opened the smaller side gate for the rhy-bat Councilor of External Affairs, as they had every month for many a year now, and Tiren stepped outside with her.

Tiren had seen the Barrens before. It had taken her months to convince Isabis to let her do this, and the later stages of the convincing process had involved joining the councilor's monthly forays, to prove she could handle herself in the harsh conditions. The first day and a half of Tiren's expedition, therefore, was much like the last two had been: dry and forbidding, treacherous and uncomfortable, but nothing Tiren and the good councilor couldn't handle.

They avoided most dangers altogether by knowing the Barrens well enough to see signs of trouble before walking into it. This time out, they encountered nothing they were unable to avoid—aside from a few mindless unliving creatures, which Tiren easily laid to rest by herself.

She took this as a good sign.

But then it was time for the rhy-bat to return to Mount Oritaun—before the moon began to wane and the mountain faded back out of reality.

Last chance to back out, the rhy-bat teased.

"You know I won't do that," Tiren replied.

The little bat nodded from the gnarled limb of a stunted and nearly leafless tree. The dry, wind-warped branches rattled as Isabis clambered about between them.

I know, the rhy-bat said, *and I don't want you to. You're officially here as an agent of the External Affairs Commission, charged with a fact-finding mission I have asserted is vital to long-term community security. If you make me look bad, it could undermine my authority for years to come.*

Tiren swallowed hard. She hadn't thought about things in quite those terms. "I won't let you down," she said.

Yes, well, I won't force you to go, Isabis replied. *This expedition was your idea. We can wait until you find a few more volunteers, or . . .*

"No." Tiren was adamant. "Now is the time. I can do this." She'd started to literally dream about it, almost every night. If she waited any longer, she thought it might drive her mad.

All right, youngster. Did Isabis sound almost proud of her? *Selene guide you. I look forward to your report when you come home—even if it's next full moon.*

"Selene guide you, too, Councilor." Tiren vowed internally to prove the councilor right for trusting her. "To the next moon and beyond."

And with that, the little rhy-bat flew away, back toward the enchanted mountain fortress they both called home. A chill ran through Tiren, but she shook it off. She'd see Mount Oritaun again. She was doing the right thing for her people. Even if she hadn't been born vatazin like Yussa, Tiren could become a symbol of hope, too. She was certain of it.

That night, the shadow storm hit.

Tiren saw it coming, and far off. A moonlit night might as well be daylight to a vata'sha, and Tiren was well on her guard for such things. She scrambled up a high dune to gauge the storm front's speed and trajectory. As Isabis had taught her, Tiren used arcane sight and ignored the natural wind—wind could lie when a shadow storm raged.

This one was huge and seemed to be aimed right for her, but Tiren still had some time before it arrived. She picked up speed and changed directions, toward a jumble of rock and dead brambles that her map called a "defunct oasis." It might not offer water anymore, but the rocks would bolster her tent against the unnatural buffeting of a shadow storm's winds.

Tiren reached the rocks before the storm, but barely. What mid-sized stones she could find, to hold her shelter down, she had to gather and place at wrenchingly high speed, all while reeling from mind-searing gales of corruption, even at the storm's outer edges.

Tiren was trembling from exhaustion by the time she crawled inside her sturdy tent, at which point she was forced to catch and destroy two skeletal snakes and a skeletal rat that had scuttled in ahead of her. She whispered a prayer for the poor creatures' souls and dumped them out a flap—which the wind made quite difficult to re-seal.

And then came the waiting.

And waiting.

The shadow storm lasted a grueling *four days*.

Tiren handled the first of them well. She ate and drank sparingly, did stretching exercises every few hours—as best she could in the little, cramped space—and sang songs and recited poems to keep her spirits up, despite the audible and spiritual howling all around her.

She did not, however, sleep well that night, waking constantly to every sound in case more small, unliving creatures—or nightmares of the same—were crawling all over her.

Only in the wee hours did her other dream return to her—the dream that had brought her out here in the first place, that had begun calling to her each night: she dreamed of becoming hope for others.

Once that dream arrived, the little skeleton creatures of her nightmares sighed with relief and were laid to rest at the mere sight of her. And Tiren finally slept.

The second day was harder, especially knowing that the full moon would pass before nightfall. Today, Mount Oritaun would fade from the world until the next full moon.

Even when it reappeared, it wouldn't be in the same place.

Tiren was stuck out here. She'd chosen her fate. She would survive or not, but she could not take back the decision. It was harder to believe she'd done the right thing, pinned down as she was in this tiny canvas shelter. Tiren wept in the late evening, and found herself apologizing aloud to her family, to Yussa, and to her other friends, for not having appreciated them as they deserved until now, when so far away.

The second night, Tiren's nightmares were of her loved ones. All of them hated her for having left. She made it home to them, battered and bruised, chastened by failure, only to have them reject her and throw her back out into the storm.

But Tiren had known what she was signing up for when she ventured out alone into the Shadow Barrens. She knew better than to let the foulness of the storm take hold in her heart. Once again, her dream of becoming hope steadied her, and she found her resolve. She rallied on the third day, using arcane meditation to pull her spirit back into balance, despite the harshness of her conditions.

She'd brought two small books with her as well: one, a notebook for recording observations made during her travels; the other, her favorite book of essays, the gathered thoughts of Mount Oritaun's wisest historical figures. After scrawling a few musings in the notebook, Tiren re-read each of these essays, taking new insight from their words, as she often did.

Her nightmares were fewer that night. She almost believed the storm had passed, but the winds refused to die. In the late morning, they surged back higher and stronger than ever, as if the storm had unnaturally turned on itself (as shadow storms could certainly do), just to blast her with one last cyclone of despair.

Tiren ultimately spent that fourth, miserable, pinned-down day wasting pages of her notebook on bad poetry, just to keep herself sane. Several of the latter scrawlings descended into quite disturbing imagery, which Tiren wasn't sure she shouldn't tear out and burn.

By the time she deemed it safe to emerge from her shelter, digging herself up through the sand that had half-buried it, Tiren was out of water and nearly out of food. She thought she'd come so well prepared, but it hadn't occurred to her that a storm of such fury could continue raging for so many days at a stretch.

Consulting her map, Tiren oriented herself toward the nearest water source. If all went well, she would reach it before collapsing of thirst.

But Tiren's fortunes remained foul. A band of walking dead had followed in the wake of the shadow storm, dogging her steps the entire way to the watering hole.

To avoid fighting all of them at once, by herself, Tiren was forced to keep moving day and night for two days, with only the barest snatches of rest. She arrived at the water source before collapsing, only just, but decency forced her, before actually approaching the water, to make sure she didn't lead monsters into a shelter where other exhausted people might be gathering. She stopped where a small, rocky canyon offered a tactical bottleneck to lay her unliving stalkers to rest.

Tiren's swordplay and arcana were up to the task, even in her diminished physical and emotional state—animated corpses were not terribly challenging opponents, so long as they approached one or two at a time. Finally, after dispatching her pursuers, Tiren arrived at the watering hole in sorry condition for dealing with the naga that lay in wait there to ambush thirsty travelers.

So much for keeping monsters away from the water.

After *that* fight, a wounded, poisoned, and discouraged Tiren settled in beside the moderately foul-tasting covered well and a half-crumbling stone shelter, to rest and heal.

She'd thought she'd been so prepared. She'd been so certain she was *meant* to undertake this journey, so *sure* she could be the one to halt her people's slide into destruction and despair.

Everyone had told Tiren she was arrogant and foolish. Everyone had told her she was a silly little girl, likely to die out here. Everyone had said that if one simple explorer could solve Mount Oritaun's problems, of course the solution would have been discovered and implemented generations ago.

Everyone had been right.

Tiren hwas useless, and already was teetering on the edge of her own doom.

Though the naga's venom had left her trembling and feverish—and caused her to twice vomit up what water she'd consumed—Tiren nevertheless forced herself to build a fire from the scattered dry brush and fallen branches around the outer edges of the watering hole's meager vegetation.

If she didn't burn the corpse of the naga who'd tried to slay her, it would rise at night and attack her again—and vile, corrupted creatures always rose as more powerful unliving monsters than ordinary creatures did. A naga might not come back as a mere walker.

Luckily, the wood of the local, gnarled trees was hard like stone and burned hot as a kiln, or Tiren could never have gotten the pyre high enough to purify her enemy to its bones.

Once the pyre was lit, Tiren meditated for hours to heal herself, first guiding her body to break down what remained of the naga's poison, and then aiding her wounds in their mending. All of this was hungry work, however, and Tiren hadn't eaten for two days.

As soon as her wounds were closed enough that she wouldn't cause new bleeding by moving around, Tiren forced herself to hunt up some manner of supper. That night she dined on a tasteless, stringy gourd from a nearby plant and a bitter-fleshed roasted viper. She thanked both the plant and the snake for the life they gave her, and even said a little prayer over the still-burning naga, in hopes that its soul would be purified in the world beyond.

By the flickering pyre-light, a much-chastened Tiren resolved to stay at the watering hole until the new moon, at which time she would employ visionary magics to discover where her home had reappeared, and plan her route to return to Mount Oritaun as quickly as possible.

It would be embarrassing, yes, and disappointing to the few who'd believed in her, but if she came back alive at all, it wouldn't be a total loss. If Tiren returned hale and whole, she could even try again at a later date, with better provisions, the wisdom of experience, and maybe even manage to entice a few volunteers to join her.

She wouldn't disappoint Councilor Isabis too much, at least.

That was what Tiren tried to tell herself as she licked her various wounds, both physical and spiritual, in the aftermath of her disastrous first week in the Shadow Barrens. It wasn't easy to see this failure in so positive a light. She did take careful notes of what few observations she had made. She decided not to burn her terrible poetry, in case its insight into her emotions during the shadow storm could be of use to Councilor Isabis upon her unceremonious return.

At night, Tiren found that her dreams of hope had themselves become nightmares. They seemed to scream at her with an urgency she couldn't meet. Instead of becoming a symbol of hope, Tiren now curled in on herself, to hide from the heartbreak of embodying new despair.

The dreams tried nightly to drag her away from the well, back out into the wind-swept Barrens, but Tiren refused them. This time she would be responsible and practical. This time she would stay put. She had to wait at the well until the new moon.

Her people did need her. She *had* come out here for a reason. But Tiren wasn't strong enough to meet that need, to serve that reason. For all her talent with arcana and the sword, when it came down to fulfilling what she'd arrogantly believed to be her calling, Tiren had turned out to be nothing but a fool.

She wasn't anyone's hope. She was just a stubborn girl who'd thought too highly of herself.

And belief in herself became harder still with the new moon. Scrying was difficult for Tiren—it was an arcane ability she'd struggled to learn. It took her three days of trial and error to determine where Mount Oritaun had reappeared, and when she finally located its new surroundings on her map, Tiren realized there was no possible way she could make it home before the next full moon.

It lay on the opposite edge of the Barrens, with only one route past reliable water, and that route would double the distance of the trek. It was impossible in the time she had.

She would have to survive out here for another month. Longer, if the mountain didn't choose to reappear in a location she could reach in the two weeks or less she would have to get to it.

Tiren had known all along that this would be a complication of the coming-home process, but that had seemed so distant when she left. She hadn't thought she'd be returning for years, or more.

She hadn't thought that the Shadow Barrens would defeat her utterly in her very first week.

She felt so stupid.

Tiren knew, too, that she now faced one of the biggest dangers of the Shadow Barrens: one's own negative thoughts. Negative thoughts were natural, of course—part of being alive, certainly nothing to be ashamed of—and yet, even if they were both innocent and unavoidable, they were nevertheless a point of vulnerability, a crack in one's spiritual armor through which Shadow could slip in and take hold.

Tiren had always been such a hopeful person—optimistic to the point, some told her, of madness. She'd assumed she'd be immune to such things. Now that she was out here, however, facing dull, mundane, exhausting trial after trial, Tiren couldn't tell how many of her hopeless musings were her own thoughts, worn down inexorably by circumstances, and how many were the whisperings of Shadow all around her, chipping away at her soul's defenses, deliberately weakening the core of faith and will that made her who she was.

Tiren made note of this in her notebook. It wasn't a new insight, but it felt different to experience it for herself than to read of it in others' accounts. She hoped her own perspective on the phenomenon might prove useful to someone, someday.

She hoped she didn't die out here.

With her route home closed for the time being, Tiren considered her options. She could wait at the watering hole for another month, but food was already scarce. If she stayed any longer, she'd make things difficult for the local wildlife—who already suffered enough—and for whatever other desperate traveler next stumbled into this meager excuse for an oasis.

Also, despite her meditation, Tiren's nightmares were growing worse. She was needed, so very needed—she was the last hope left in the world and she was worthless, utterly worthless. Tiren shivered just remembering them. She feared even trying to sleep again, which was hardly a recipe for long-term health or sanity.

She needed to leave the Barrens. That had, of course, been the plan all along, but in the rush to take shelter from the shadow storm, followed by the forced march to refill her water stores, Tiren hadn't had the luxury for things like directing her route toward the edge.

Now she studied the paths available to her. Any would take a good long while to get her to what should—if Mount Oritaun's arcanely acquired data was correct—be healthy, normal wilderness. The map had been reliable so far. Tiren would have been dead without it. She had to trust it now.

One route looked clearly shorter and less dry than the others. It would take her south, and might—if she were very lucky and very fast—even find her past the edge of the Barrens before the next full moon. Maybe. Certainly before the next new moon, assuming she survived the trek.

But Tiren hated that route, and she couldn't explain why. Instead, a longer course, with somewhat sparser water-sources, drew her attention. This one led northwest, toward Jarzon, and eventually met up with the northern portion of the Dejek Trail, where Tiren might encounter other travelers.

Perhaps that was why the route appealed to her. Perhaps she was lonely. She'd certainly never spent so much time alone in her life.

But it felt like more than that.

It felt like the same pull that had dragged her away from Mount Oritaun in the first place. The call to become a symbol of hope? That's what she'd thought it was, but now she wasn't sure. Without finalizing her decision, Tiren forced herself to meditate in hope that tonight she could sleep. Perhaps the morning—however thin and dark and eerie, as they tended to be in the Shadow Barrens— would bring better insight.

That night, a voice called to her in her dreams.

Please! it cried. Pain and desperation suffused its tone. *Hurry! You are my last hope.*

Tiren woke long before the dull, greenish Shadow Barrens dawn, packed up her pack, and broke her fast on the last of another flavorless gourd. She closed and barred the protective stone cover on the bitter little well and was an hour's walk from it before she realized she'd gone northwest without thinking.

She supposed that meant she'd chosen her route.

Tiren didn't entirely trust the decision, but . . . something inside her felt lighter to be moving again. And the thought of turning back all but turned her stomach.

She hoped this wasn't just another foolish, stubborn impulse.

She hoped her luck held a little better this time.

Tiren pushed hard her first day back on the trail. She had about four days of rations prepared, and the next water source on her map was not a reliable one. If she couldn't fill her canteens there, it would be five days total to the next trustworthy well. She couldn't afford to dally.

Even once she finally stopped to sleep, Tiren found herself restless, eager for tomorrow. She meditated to avoid the Barrens' ubiquitous nightmares, and seemed to largely succeed at her task, but nevertheless woke early to a dream of a long, lonely howl.

You're my last hope. The words from the previous night's dream rang through her mind, and she found she couldn't bear the thought of going back to sleep. She packed up early and forged ahead once more, driven by an urgency she couldn't explain, but that she knew in retrospect had been with her all along, growing ever stronger.

She'd heard tales of those who succumbed to Shadow, of being lured away from their homes, out to the Barrens to die or be corrupted beyond redemption. Faced with the growing possibility that her very life's calling had been inspired by something other than her soul's true path, Tiren forced herself, as she walked, to consider the possibility that she herself was falling prey to such enchantment.

Alone in the Barrens, after everything had already gone so wrong, Tiren found herself unable to trust her own judgment on much of anything. The world was harsher than she'd ever guessed, and she was smaller and weaker in face of it than she would ever have believed mere weeks ago.

She didn't *think* this was Shadow, driving her. Beyond that, she couldn't say. She only knew that she had to keep moving.

She was running out of time.

The first well wasn't dry. Tiren stopped there long enough to refill her supplies, and to dine on another of the stringy, bland gourds that seemed to be the most reliable food source out here. She'd also learned to roast and eat a few species of local beetles and grasshoppers, which were actually tastier than the gourds.

Almost as soon as she'd eaten, however, Tiren found herself back on her feet and moving. She just couldn't seem to keep still any-more. For the next two days, she grabbed only quick naps after meals—waking always to the same, desperate dreams—and spent the rest of her time on the move.

About a quarter mile from the next well, for reasons she didn't entirely understand, and despite the bouncing, jangling weight of the pack on her back, Tiren broke into a jog.

You're my last hope. She remembered the words from her dream. Did it mean anything? She wasn't sure. She only knew it continued to resound in her head.

Well, she'd wanted to be a symbol of hope . . .

Tiren topped a rise in the increasingly rocky terrain and looked down into a small, dry canyon. A tiny round shelter had been built over what her map marked as the most reliable well for leagues, aside from those regularly maintained on the Dejek Trail.

The shelter itself, however, was not what caught her eye; a flock of six harpies leapt and cavorted mere yards from the structure. They surrounded a gaunt and bleeding wolf.

The harpies spoke no language Tiren could understand, but she could hear them cackling cruelly as they jabbed at the wolf with pointed sticks, or darted forward to slash it with their claws while its back was turned. A filthy rope served as a leash for the wild-eyed creature, tied so viciously tight that the wolf's neck fur had rubbed raw in places. Each time it tried to fight back against its attackers, another harpy yanked the leash, sending the tormented wolf choking and coughing.

Every time the creature yelped in pain, Tiren remembered the desperate, lonely howling in her dreams. Wolves didn't belong in the Shadow Barrens. Either this beast had been brought here against its will, or—

No. There was something about those golden, canine eyes . . . This was no ordinary wolf.

Tiren dropped her pack. Within two heartbeats, she had her short swords in hand. She paused only long enough to center herself for the channeling of her oldest and greatest arcane ability: to enhance her own strength and speed.

Then she charged.

The harpies heard her coming. Two broke away from their tor-turing circle, wheeling to meet Tiren's blades. But Tiren had fought harpies before. She spun and leapt, disabling a wing on her way past the first and an arm on the second.

"Get away from that wolf!" she cried. "I will give no quarter to those who stay to fight me!"

Whether they understood her or not, she did have the harpies' attention. Only one stayed back to hold the wolf's leash. The others abandoned their torture game and turned to surround Tiren instead. Not even the wounded harpies fled at her warn-ing.

Tiren felt strangely unafraid. "Then let's fight!" she snarled as they closed ranks around her. She twisted around, leaping, kick-ing, and slashing with the fury of a thousand sandstorms.

The wolf, on the end of its filthy, bloody leash, wobbled on its feet and collapsed. Tiren couldn't assess the creature's condition, she was too busy fighting five opponents. She did glimpse—between traded blows of claw, boot, and blade on all sides—that the harpy with the leash looked anxious to join the battle. She seemed to be calling for someone to take the leash in her stead. She certainly wasn't paying much attention to her prisoner.

Well, at least Tiren had bought the wolf some reprieve. Grinning fiercely, she redoubled her efforts, blocking a claw with her left blade even while she spun and kicked with her right foot. The kick was a feint, but it lured in two harpies at once. While in each other's way, Tiren exploited an opening in the stance of a third harpy, distracted by the collision. This one hissed and leapt back, bleeding, but there were still four more to harry her. Tiren had to end this quickly. Even with her boosted strength and speed, she couldn't defend against so many opponents for long.

Two of the harpies coordinated just right: to block one, Tiren couldn't dodge the other. She instead deflected the first onto her leather cuisse, but the blow landed hard, bruising her to the bone. That sacrifice allowed her to dodge the second strike, but a third harpy interfered in her counterattack. A disabling slash became little more than a smack with the flat of her sword.

It was a bad convergence, and the battle's momentum shifted. The harpies were laughing again, and all three of the wounded bird-hags rallied to support their allies. Their renewed confidence could prove deadly for Tiren, especially if it outlasted her arcane enhancements.

Tiren bellowed in a wordless rage. She tumbled acrobatically, getting to a better position between them, but the harpies' wings let them fly right over her. They re-surrounded her faster than she could finish off even one.

Another well-timed claw strike made it past Tiren's guard, finding the soft flesh beneath her leather armor and ripping open a gash in her right side.

Perhaps she should have been afraid after all.

Perhaps she'd been stupid yet again.

Then: a scream.

It came from behind Tiren, where the wolf lay. She couldn't turn to look, but the sound was a harpy's. Instantly, her opponents' eyes told her that everything had changed.

Pain jangled Tiren's senses, but she didn't let the opportunity pass. She made a counterstrike here, exploited an easy dodge there, and finally twisted herself around toward the fallen canine.

The leash was slack and unattended. The harpy who'd dropped it lay bleeding, arms raised in surrender. The wolf had rallied, eyes clear, claws shimmering arcanely. The tormented creature pressed them to the former-tormentor's throat.

Another harpy broke away from Tiren to try and rush the wolf, but before drawing near her feathers burst into flame. The other harpies screamed, staring at the flames as their companion flailed around, trying to extinguish them. Tiren took this as an invitation to disable a wing on the last remaining uninjured combatant. Another harpy burst into flames near the first.

The harpies fled. The battle was over.

Panting, Tiren turned to watch them flee, swords still at the ready. A trickle of either blood or sweat dripped down her belly.

The harpies never looked back. They disappeared over the surrounding rocky hills. Tiren didn't think they'd return.

Someone requested psychic contact. Tiren granted entry.

It was the rhy-wolf. She turned toward him. Even bleeding and bedraggled as he was, he seemed beautiful to her—a creature so noble he might as well have been a unicorn or a griffin. Tiren had never seen a live wolf before, and yet, somehow, the very sight of him felt more like home than she'd felt . . . since long before leaving Mount Oritaun.

You're real. The wolf's words trembled, shimmering through Tiren's mind like music notes, whole symphonies of emotion. *I thought I'd dreamed you.*

My dreams were nothing so clear, Tiren replied, *but perhaps I'm finally beginning to understand them.*

I knew you'd come, the wolf said. *I almost gave up, so many times. The third time they caught me, I was too exhausted to even shape arcana.* His voice faltered, then rallied. *But I knew. Hope was on the way.*

At his phrasing, Tiren sank to her knees and burst into tears. The wolf stepped toward her, and, without thinking, she wrapped her arms around him. Even after everything he'd been through, his fur still felt soft and luxurious. He leaned into her embrace, resting his cheek against hers.

I am Sky, the wolf said.

Tiren, she replied. *I think I may have come here to find you.*

Of course, Sky said with confidence. *That's how it works.*

Sky's injuries were extensive, but none severe, and Tiren could heal herself. The harpies did not return to bother them, and the well was surprisingly deep and clear. The rhy-wolf and the vata'sha spent a few days in the little, round shelter, recuperating and getting to know one another.

On the third day, Sky was ready to travel.

"I'd planned to head north, toward Jarzon," Tiren said, "but I don't feel drawn to that route like I did before. Would Jarzon even be safe for people like us?"

Sky snorted. *It is not safe there, no,* he said. *Fleeing Jarzoni humans is how I ended up in the Shadow Barrens in the first place. I was on my way to Wyss, where I have been told people like me are welcome and accepted.*

Tiren nodded. "Then let's go to Wyss. It's as good a place to start my quest as any."

So, Sky asked, *you still plan to seek a new hope for your people? Even after all you've been through?*

Tiren shrugged. "I seek to bring hope," she said, "in general. I took on too much at once before, and almost lost hope myself. But it turns out that bringing hope back to even one person was enough to remind me who I am." She stroked Sky's fur, and he nuzzled her hand. "So, from now on," Tiren said, "I just want to bring hope wherever I go, to whomever I meet. I'm sure I can find people like who need some in Wyss."

Sky licked the tip of her nose. *And the people waiting for you at home?*

Tiren laughed. "Oh, they're very good at scrying there. I'm sure they'll know I'm all right." Sobering, she added, "I won't stop looking for whatever it is they need. I'll go back when I find it."

I have a good nose, Sky teased, gently. *You'll be much better at finding things, now that I'm here.*

WHISPERS IN SHADOW & BONE

Michael Matheson

"I think there's something wrong with the map," Atla says to Korre from the other side of the cart's bench as they make their way through the Lake of Broken Glass, Ino's ghost hovering nearby, making considerably less noise than her companion. But Korre can still smell the charged ozone of the dead woman, can still feel the crackle of her like lightning in the distance. Korre hasn't seen anything since she was ten, not since she woke up one morning stone-blind. Then spent the better part of the four decades that followed building her life as a huntress in spite of it.

Atla sighs in frustration, and the map rustles in the younger woman's grip as she does her best to navigate. Following directions is . . . not Atla's strong suit. Barely a year into her training as a huntress' apprentice, a lot of things still aren't her forte. But she'll learn. And Korre won't hold this particular difficulty against her—the Shadow Barrens are tricky enough to navigate at the best of times, even for those not making a lengthy detour through the region's biggest salt pan to avoid still worse dangers.

Korre smiles to herself, the reins resting light in her hands as her horse leads them on, Gallus seeing where they're going well enough for all three of them—and navigating better, too. The scent of his sweat and the straining harness leather washes over the huntress. The strain on the dray horse is worsening as the heat of the day intensifies—they'll need to rest him soon; get him out of the sun, even if it's just under the wagon's shadow, before he overheats. Probably before they're out of the Lake.

The cart sways hard as Gallus veers them left, then right, trotting in slow arcs around immense, staggered crystalline towers. The salt tang of them acrid-sharp this close to the tree trunk-wide spikes, mingling with the musk of overheated horse fit to make Korre gag. Gallus is oblivious to her pain as he nickers happily at even these brief respites from the oppressive heat while they pass under the occasional shade of razor-edged spires. The crystals rise what must be dozens of feet high from how long it takes the cart to pass out of tracts of shadow reaching out for them like grasping fingers; Korre counts off the seconds to measure the height of the formations, wary lest anything large enough to skewer them sound ready to topple.

The silt of the salt pan crunches steadily under the oversized wagon's wheels as they trundle along the cracked earth. But solid ground is good. Better than hitting the mud patches: great gouts of poisonous muck deep enough to swallow a body whole.

She turns toward Atla's voice. "I don't think the map's the issue. Sounded like it was drawn recently enough, anyway. Unless you've been bilked yet again by another handsome saleswoman . . .?"

The old huntress doesn't need to see Atla's blush to know it's there. The young adept is still coming slowly out of her shell after so many tragedies, not the least of them Ino's death at her hands before she learned to control her fire. She has less fear now, a developing willingness to trust, and a fledgling belief that maybe her fire can do more than just kill. But Korre hopes her apprentice will remember to keep at least some part of herself hard. She won't last long as a huntress otherwise.

There's a soft shuffling of cloth as Atla adjusts her hood for the sixth time this hour (by Korre's count), the sun burning down blazing hot. Atla may be Jarzoni, but she respects the sun for its killing heat. Even Korre's much higher tolerance for heat has its limits, so she too has been making sure to keep well covered—no point risking sunstroke. The old scars on her face and neck and hands, at least those not under well-oiled leather armor, still itch where the sun touches her skin. What winds there are gust full and stifling against her face, drying her sweat almost as fast as she sheds it.

"Wish we could have just traveled through a shadowgate," mutters Atla, the rustling of the map growing noisome as she struggles to refold it. Korre hears Ino sigh, and the map's rustling fades into the crisp sound of paper easily folded, the ghost taking over. Atla harrumphs loudly, followed by the quick crinkle of paper being snatched away and the slap of leather as the map is stuffed into Atla's pack amid the clink of glass vials, coins, and other sundries.

"Yes, that would have gone well . . ." says Korre. "Because even *if* we could access some of the most dangerous artifacts in Aldea and use one without releasing yet more darkfiends into the world, the chance of corrupting ourselves in the process is *entirely* worth a shortcut."

The smooth cotton of Atla's sleeves whisper against the rougher material of her cloak as she folds her arms. "How is that any different from traipsing through corrupted cities full of marauding darkfiends, chasing someone foolish enough to wander into the Barrens?"

"What's not to love about a rescue mission? If Efrida didn't think her sister was still alive out here she wouldn't have sent us after her."

"Kanauld's six weeks overdue. I think you mean *recovery* mission."

Korre shrugs. "She could still be alive. All those years spent as a royal courier—all that confidence, all those narrow escapes . . . It would have stood her in good stead when she left the Queen's service to follow her own passions."

"Confident *and* foolhardy. Great. Do none of these people ever think about the idiots like us who have to go save them from themselves?" There's a wet *sploot* as Atla noisily spits a mouthful of salty grit over the side of the wagon. "So much easier just chasing down frauds, cheats, and murderers."

"Less fulfilling though."

Atla's hood swishes as she shakes her head. "What kind of loremaster thinks they're going to survive a trip to *Ebonwatch*?"

"Why do you think you're with me on this trip?" asks the huntress with a sly smile. "You're my fire insurance."

"That joke just keeps getting funnier every time I hear it . . ." The bench creaks as Atla shifts, the young fire user trailing off as she listens to Ino. The ghost so quiet even Korre can't catch her words. "No," Atla snaps in response, "it is *not* funny."

Korre laughs, and reaches out an elbow until she butts Atla's shoulder. "Besides, at some point you have to stop training and head out and face the real dangers of the world. Come on, when's the last time we had a bounty this challenging? It'll be fun!"

Korre can practically hear Atla's thousand-yard stare. "Kill me now."

Long miles later, Korre cracks her back as she rises from the bench, her muscles gone tight from sitting so long. They've stopped to rest Gallus under the shade of a spire. Judging by its cool shadow, this one juts at least several times as high as the wagon. Once Korre unties his harness, she feels Gallus' equine bulk brush past as he wanders off to seek shelter in the shade. Nearby, her apprentice talks up a storm amid the clang of cookware, conferring with Ino about the coming meal. The food in Aldis is inordinately better than what the adept grew up with in Jarzon. Nothing like a country of ascetics and religious fanatics to ruin the simple joy of food. Korre taught Atla a few of her family recipes, but Atla's taken keenly to cooking in the year since becoming Korre's apprentice, stocking their wagon well enough to feed a group several times their size. In *that*, at least, Korre can say her apprentice excels.

The huntress lets her two charges, living and dead, talk as she listens to the wind. Whatever's been trailing them hasn't exactly been trying to hide its presence and, as she strains to hear, she catches the familiar, steady crunch of gravel echoing faintly across the salt pan. To the best of Korre's knowledge, nothing makes its home on the Lake of Broken Glass—no prey out here to lure predators. And though the stench of shadow infests everything here, it can't hide the stink of this rot. It's a rot not just of body but of spirit. Ghouls— likely those who died trying to cross the pan—coming slowly, not whole enough for running or lacking the strength. Matters little either way. Mindless ghouls would be faster to deal with, but cunning ones would make better training for her apprentice.

She cocks an ear back Atla's way and hears her apprentice still digging through their stores, distracted by culinary possibilities. Korre shakes her head.

"Atla," she calls sweetly, pointing a thumb over her shoulder in the direction of the stench. "Deal with the ghouls, would you?"

Pans and pots clatter to the ground amid Atla's startled whispers of, "Shit. Shit." The undead roaring in baleful cries now that they've caught sight of the stalled wagon. Korre feels the rush of her apprentice charging past, Atla's smell changing from clean sweat to the burning skin that announces the fire she's calling to wake. Layered over it, the charged ozone of Ino's presence crackling around them both. Atla's fire is better controlled with the ghost calming her mind and guiding her flames. A form of willing possession Korre doesn't wholly understand, but it works.

"I'll make lunch," Korre calls over her shoulder. She whistles a jaunty tune as the rush of Atla's spirit fire supercharges the already heated air. Before the undead start screaming.

Several hours later, the air cooling toward night and the rhythms of the cart returned to the now-familiar sway of open, rocky passes and stunted scrub grass beneath them, Atla's still silent.

"What's the matter?" asks Korre innocently. "You didn't like lunch?"

"How long did you know they were there?" asks Atla, every word bitten off through a clenched jaw.

"Oh . . . a few miles?" says Korre. Ino's chuckle floats out from somewhere beside the apprentice, and the huntress can hear Atla grinding her teeth. "Give it time," Korre says, smiling. "Takes more than a year to get this good."

Gallus pulls the cart up short and Atla's quiet awe lets Korre know that they've reached the ruined Citadel of Ebonwatch. Night has long since fallen and the wind howls frigid. The huntress doesn't need to share Atla's view to feel how cursed this place is. Or how immense. The chill gusts cascade over flattened structures and what stone remains of shorn towers and immense domed vaults, playing a mournful tune as it whistles through gaps and hollows.

The huntress can only imagine the sight from the tales she was told as a girl, begging her mothers for stories of the world's nightmares. Back when she dreamed of one day marching out to cleanse the darkness, wherever it sheltered. Looking to follow in the footsteps of a loved, long-lost parent who had disappeared on her own quest to rid Aldea of the shadows.

Those long-ago tales rest fresh and fearsome now. She summons a child's vision of a citadel once bright as the blazing sun, now mired in glowering purple from corrupted shas crystals; bold flourishes and frescoes adorned its walls in the days when it was still a consecrated temple of Anwaren, before it fell to the covetous desire of a Sorcerer King. Before the fiends he summoned felled him in turn. Before Feyna Drass, empress of legend, wrested control of that terrible darkness for herself. Until she, too, fell, taking the whole of Faenaria with her.

The Ebonwatch of Korre's memory a child's dream of heroic deeds and fairy tale nightmares to be slain.

But some nightmares are all too real.

"Yeah . . ." says Atla, pulling the huntress from the memories of her mothers' stories. "We're definitely not finding Kanauld alive."

Korre's knees strain on the incline of the hill leading up to the citadel, cool bellows' worth of air shivering across the uncovered patches of her skin. At each step, she tests her footing against the possibility of loose rock and scree before committing her full weight. The careful pattern and pace of the climb is second nature after long decades of hard hunting.

The cart rests at the bottom of the hill covered under a camouflaging tarp, Gallus not willing to head any closer to the cursed ruins. Ino is a steady presence drifting with the two living women as they all make their way up the hill in near-perfect silence. Even Atla's footfalls are a whisper compared to what they were a year ago. Korre allows herself a small smile at her apprentice's progress.

But that pride fades fast under the weight of the Corruption that steals her breath as the hill's incline flattens at its crest. The thickness of that miasma an unmistakable demarcation even from the rest of the Barrens. And Korre knows they've finally reached the edge of Ebonwatch.

At first, she thinks it's just a quirk of the wind atop the height. Everything a jumble of sound, nothing ringing right off the stone and metal and glass. Only the edge of soft words instead, just out of hearing. Like a stone dropped down a well—the faintest of echoes clattering through her skull. She stretches out a hand to touch the crumbled wall of the citadel, as much to steady herself as to verify that the walls stand where they should. Solid metal there under the pads of her fingers: cold, jagged, *wrong*.

The huntress shudders, her skin screaming to be away from the touch of these walls. Away from whatever makes its home in the sheer, shattered maze of this place. Whatever was called and never left.

But, amplified by the touch of the metal under her hand, she can make out voices:

"Leave her. She won't survive. But you can," says Korre's first mother from beyond the grave.

"*What has your apprentice ever done for you but be a burden?*" asks her second mother, equally dead.

"*You could be safe. Warm. Protected. Loved,*" says her third mother, the one long vanished into Kern, spying in service of the Crown. Long mourned by wives and daughters alike.

"*We could* fix *you,*" says the voice of the healer who first told her she would never see again.

Korre pulls away from the wall with a start. Rage drowning out the whispers in the wind.

She is *not* broken.

She has spent *years* unlearning the damage done by that one, hateful word. *Decades* fighting the pity of those she apprenticed under. Hunters and huntresses who never thought her good enough to train for more than a year at a stretch. All of them expecting her to fall to unseen claw, fang, or blade.

But she's outlived all of them. Masters and monsters both.

She places a hand on her apprentice's shoulder to warn Atla of what's there, but falls silent as she feels Atla trembling beneath her touch. Whatever the voices are telling her has set Atla quaking with her own roil of emotion. She can feel heat building on the air around them as Atla's fire flares to life. As her apprentice starts to lose control.

"*Whisperers,*" Korre says just loud enough for Atla to catch. "Rifling through your head like thieves. They think they know you because they can feel your pain. But they don't *know* you. They don't know what you survived. Don't know how strong you are. You do not. Let. Them. Win." Atla doesn't reply, her breathing growing heavy and rapid. Korre directs her next few words to the spot where the ghost's presence crackles on the air, hovering somewhere beside her former lover. "Ino. Take her back to the cart and keep her there. I'll go find the loremaster."

Atla grasps Korre's arm, a drowning woman clutching shore.

"No. I'll come." Atla lets out a long, slow exhalation. "I'll come . . ." she repeats, more for herself than for Korre.

The huntress nods and pats her apprentice's hand, feeling the tightness of that desperate grip against her skin.

Together, they rise.

As they make their way through the labyrinth of Ebonwatch's ruin, the feel of being watched prickles Korre's skin like razors. Old bones crunch underfoot, the pathways littered with them. Those relics enough to tell what happens if things here turn their full attention to a party.

For half an hour they move through frigid halls unmolested. The sense of creeping dread broken only when they enter a chamber whose shifting echoes tell Korre its ceiling still stands, though the room itself is a dead end. She hears Atla draw in a sharp breath as they cross the threshold. Korre stops, her hand on the hilt of her sword.

"What did Efrida say Kanauld's necklace looked like?" whispers Atla. "The one she said Kanauld never took off?"

"White jade in a silver circlet, strung on a leather thong," answers Korre, already knowing why her apprentice asks. From the unmistakable rattle of bone and soft shush of cloth in the corner across from them, it's clear the chamber is not empty. The hiss of spirit whistling through exposed jaw and the jangle of metal on bone are an added, cruel confirmation that they've found the woman they sought. What's left of her. Korre offers a silent prayer for the dead, and draws her blade.

"I hate being right," mutters Atla as the heat of her flame—even the smallest flare of it—warms the air beside Korre. "If she's risen as undead, at least she didn't die corrupted."

"That will be little comfort for her sister."

"Better that than not knowing."

"We'll see if Efrida agrees," says Korre as the collection of bones begin clacking toward them, the skeleton having finally sensed them.

"Quick and quiet," instructs Korre. There's shuffling as Atla shifts her stance and grunts an accord, then Korre darts toward the heart of the rattling.

She aims her sword for the clink of metal on bone and slices free the necklace, hooking the thong on the length of her blade to carry it toward herself, out of the reach of Atla's fire, just as a burst of heat sets her leaping back to avoid being singed. Atla is as good as her word: no roar on the air, only the rushing whoosh of bones burning down to ash in a flash fire so hot Korre can barely breathe.

When it's done, the huntress can hear Atla stirring charcoal about as her apprentice toes what's left of the skeleton. Ino's presence crackles free from Atla's form—Korre can hear the ghost offer her own, longer prayer for the dead. Sometimes the huntress wonders if the symmetry of the already-dead asking for grace for the newly fallen holds more weight than terrestrial prayers.

"You got the necklace?" asks Atla.

"I did," says Korre as she re-sheathes her blade. The huntress runs a thumb over the curve of the metal and stone, thinking how best to break it to Efrida that her sister is well and truly dead. Then pockets the necklace to keep it safe until she can return it to their client. "Are the rest of her things here?"

"Her bag," says Atla, voice muffled as she turns away. "Whatever killed her didn't take any of her provisions or tools. The journal's here, too." The sound of flipping pages echoes strangely in the room. Korre reaches out to trace the walls, finding them curved. "Efrida will be happy to know that survived, at least," Atla adds more quietly, before gathering Kanauld's things.

Korre leaves her to it, turning her face toward the cold air pouring in from the halls beyond the room's threshold. There's something different there now: new sounds. Ino's ozone grows stronger as she comes to listen beside the huntress, both straining to hear what's coming. Then she catches it, claws scrabbling over stone, the chewy scrape of chitin over debris. Voices, closing in.

"Grab what you can," Korre whispers urgently. "We need to leave. *Now.*"

Korre stays small and low, keeping one shoulder to the broken wall beside her and the cold blast of the open air above. Atla's footfalls are a second behind her own, skulking silently past the citadel's returning inhabitants on the other side of the stone barrier. Korre doesn't need to see their slatted chitinous flesh or the burning coals of their eyes to recognize Soldier darkfiends returning from a hunt. The pungent odor of blood and offal in their wake tells her all she needs to know. It's not a stench she'd ever hoped to encounter again.

She stifles the gag building in her throat as she leads Atla and Ino along the walls by feel, using the mental map she made on the way in to trace an alternate route back to the breach through which they entered the citadel.

A click of claws on the stone directly above them, accompanied by a rattling snuffle, sets the three of them stilling as one. Above her, she can hear first one Soldier chittering in their direction. Then another. And another. Guttural exchanges passing back and forth between them in a language Korre doesn't understand. The stench of the creatures is overwhelming this close to their infernal flesh.

The odds are not in their favor.

Korre draws her blade anyway, slipping it from its sheath in a silent exhale of well-oiled metal. Behind her, Atla builds her fire, the smell of burning sage and charring flesh overlaid with Ino's ozone. The huntress readies herself, angling her blade's honed edge to better cut on the rise as she prepares to vault toward the nearest creature she can sense. Her heartbeat narrowing to a single, slow hammer. Every muscle tensed to spring.

A chorus of shouts and answering cries erupt from farther off in the citadel, and the fiends above them retreat, their claws clicking staccato rhythms as they scuttle off in the direction the women had been heading.

Korre lets out the breath she'd been holding. She slumps against the wall with her skull to the stone, letting the cold of it clear her head. The air behind her loses its superheated charge as Atla winds down the flare of her arcana and Ino's crackling presence slips free of the adept once again.

The huntress almost jumps as Ino's disembodied voice whispers next to her right ear, "Men. Many men. A convoy."

"She's right," says Atla, the swift swish of her clothes giving away her imprudent glance over the lip of the broken wall. "Looks like several dozen, finely attired. Tall, balding man at their head."

"Sorcerers. Corrupted. Power on the air," says Ino.

"Should we be concerned or relieved that the darkfiends didn't kill them on sight?" says Atla.

"Concerned, definitely," says Korre, trying to think of an alternate route around the massive audience chamber she remembers lying directly in their path. Comparing what she knows of the route with the stories her mothers' told her of Ebonwatch's history. "Shit," she concludes. "No way around. Not with this many fiends to slip past."

"Well, we can't go through . . ."

"Oh?" asks Korre, smiling wickedly. "Why not?"

"I hate this plan," says Atla as Korre follows the shattered stone barrier until she feels the familiar cracks of the wall bordering the circular audience chamber. The loud commotion from the massive room on the other side of the intervening stone masks the sound of their approach.

"You hate every plan that doesn't involve burning things to the ground."

"Because that's what I'm *good at*," whispers the adept.

Korre opens her mouth to reply, cut off instead by the thunderous clap of a pair of massive, leathery hands. Everything in the chamber falls dead silent.

Then, from somewhere in the center of the room, the sound of a man clearing his throat fills the air, accompanied by the velvet swish of trailing robes being swept along the ground. A male voice rings out. Strong, middle-aged, speaking in the clear, measured meter of a learned adept.

"Hail, unclean spirits of pride and wrath, servants of the Frozen Star and the Black Horn, mightiest of the exarchs' agents." The sorcerer's voice dips near the floor and his clothes muffle his words as he bows and rises once more. "I, most unworthy servant of the Lord of Austium, come bearing entreaty. My infernal master seeks an alliance with your most august selves to our *surely* mutual benefit."

"Your lord sends fustian *mortals* to beg alliance?" answers a booming basso voice from a raised position somewhere at the back of the chamber. It's *almost* human, but there's something subtly wrong about it, as if other words linger on the air beneath what's spoken—as if issued from many throats at once. Korre can hear the scythe of a smile in those words. Can almost hear the sharpness of those inhuman teeth.

The huntress swears violently under her breath. A Servitor. Of *course* there's a Servitor in Ebonwatch. As if Watchers, Whisperers, and Soldiers weren't bad enough . . .

"To *offer* alliance," spits the sorcerer, his voice bristling with offense. Then he pauses to recover himself, and his next words are honeyed as he remembers where he's standing. Korre can hear the forced calm in his voice—can hear the sweep of his sleeves against his robes, imagining him beseeching, hands upraised in mollifying gesture. "Our lord seeks the finding and fall of Mount Oritaun, for the bastion eludes him. Your power and cunning would be invaluable in his quest. My own lord wields vast knowledge, and powers of his own. United, with your power augmenting his, none could hide from his dread sights."

"I am hearing only what *your* lord gains by this treaty. What does he offer"—asks the Servitor, its voice angling away momentarily, followed by the wet sounds of a long swig and a swallow, before the fiend grunts in appreciation—"for this . . . *alliance*? What does your lord think I do not already possess?"

"Is power not its own reward?" asks the sorcerer, voice gone sly. "Or if raw, unfettered power is not to your *particular* taste, my lord is certain he can find a way to keep you bound to this plane. Does not such an offer merit—"

The Servitor sighs, cutting off the sorcerer. "*Enough.* I grow bored with your 'entreaties.'"

"But . . . dread lord . . .? The prospect of remaining in Aldea as you please . . . Surely . . ." says the emissary, at a loss.

"*But . . . dread lord . . .*" mocks the Servitor in a falsetto tone, before breaking into cold laughter, the other darkfiends joining in until the whole hall rocks with it. Below the hooting of inhuman voices, Korre picks up the uneasy shuffling of a few decidedly human feet, their steps an unsteady counterpoint to the mirth that shakes what remains of Ebonwatch's walls. "I come and go as I wish. It matters little to me how brief be my jaunts in this realm, for I always return. Do you have *any* idea how many have come here before you? All seeking to collar us like rabid dogs." Korre picks up the sounds of immense folds of rough, leathery skin rubbing against each other as the Servitor shakes its enormous head. "Your lord presumes to offer *me* power? *I*, who was ancient before he ever stepped forth from shadow to walk this world? No, little emissary, we will *not* ally with your own 'dread lord.' And I would bid you tell him so. Or would so do were you returning to Austium. But I grow famished after so much talk . . ."

"You would not *dare*!" demands the emissary, before the rest of his words are cut off by a meaty thunk, and all else that slips past his throat are wet gurgles.

"Of course I would," laughs the Servitor. Then to its followers, it booms, "Indulge yourselves!" The Austium delegation can only manage the briefest of startled cries to frantically call up power to defend themselves before the fiends fall on the sorcerers.

"*Now!*" hisses Korre, sprinting forward. She keeps one hand to the encircling wall of the audience hall, then slips through the break in the crumbling stone as soon as she reaches it, trusting Atla and Ino to follow swiftly behind. Sword already drawn, she cuts down what men and smaller darkfiends cross her path as she races around the edges of the immense chamber, the hall echoing with a swirling maelstrom of chaos as men and things that are not men scream and die and kill. The stench of blood and ichor fill the air, and warm gore splashes across Korre's skin as she runs. Arcana fires free through the chamber—too much of it and too volatile in too little space. The huntress is singed near a dozen times by fell energies as her sword dances on the air before her. None of it slowing her down.

"Have I mentioned how much I hate this plan?" Atla yells after

Korre as they emerge miraculously unscathed from the audience chamber into the passage on the far side.

"Less talking, more running!" the huntress throws back. Only Whisperers and Watchers in their path now, the Soldiers occupied elsewhere, or they'd never have made it this far.

"Get down!" yells Atla as a massive white-hot heat flares to life behind Korre. The huntress flings herself to the ground as Atla's stream of liquid fire rushes above her. Somewhere ahead of their path, darkfiends squeal as they crackle and wither.

Atla and Ino pick the huntress up as they race forward, Korre too out of breath and too queasy from Atla's oft-used fire-vomiting trick to be more than passingly indignant at the assumption she can't get up on her own.

Then there is only running, and wind in her ears as the screaming grows distant behind them. The keening of the dying and the hungry receding far too slowly for Korre's taste.

Stone gives way to uneven, rock-strewn ground and the hill dips under their feet, and still they run. Only stopping to rapidly clamber into the cart, ready it as quick as they're able, and set a terrified Gallus clopping as rapidly as he can manage away from the horrors of Ebonwatch.

"So, what do we do if they decide they want to come after us?" asks Atla, voice wavering from exhaustion. The sun is already beating down mercilessly, though it is not yet at its zenith. Korre has driven them on all night, not willing to stop until they're as far from Ebonwatch as Gallus can take them. Though the horse is none too keen on quitting, his pace has slowed considerably since they made their escape. They'll have to break their journey soon.

"I don't know," says Korre, "they seemed to be eating pretty well when we left." The huntress raises her face to the sky to let the sun warm it. The cold from last night has seeped into her bones. After being in the presence of a Servitor, she's not sure she'll ever be entirely warm again.

"But is that *enough* food for an entire horde of fiends?"

"I think the question you should be asking is whether it's worth coming after just *two* women. Doesn't make much sense to spread a meal that far among that many mouths."

"True. And some of them had far more than one . . ."

"I'm not sure I needed to know that detail?"

"I had to see it; you have to imagine it." Atla pauses, her breathing quieter, and Korre waits for what her apprentice has to ask next. "What do we tell Efrida about what happened to her sister?"

"The truth."

"That she died horribly in a barren hellscape, surrounded by fiends after chasing mysteries that no one cares about?"

"*No*," says the huntress with infinite patience. "That Kanauld resisted the Corruption. That she died doing important work, helping others understand mysteries the world has lost. That she died doing something she loved."

"We're not mentioning the burning-her-down-to-ash part though, right?"

"Nope," says Korre. When Atla doesn't venture any other questions, Korre leans back in her seat, letting Gallus take over the navigation, and asks: "Do you want to talk about what the Whisperers said to you?"

"No," says Atla too quickly.

"Is that a 'No, we're never doing that,' or a 'No, not right now'?"

Atla doesn't answer for a beat. "I'll let you know when I figure that out."

Korre just nods. Lets the silence trail a moment. Then turns her face toward Atla. "You did good last night. You're getting better."

"Like, full-fledged-huntress good?"

"Oh shit, no," laughs Korre. Atla joins in. Korre can feel the warmth of Ino's smile as well, though the ghost remains as spare as ever in adding her voice to the conversation. "You'll get there though."

Korre hears the creak of the seat as Atla mutters something unintelligible, and leans back against the covered wagon. A long rustling of fabric tells Korre her apprentice is settling her hood down over her face to go to sleep.

Korre lets her drift off. She's earned it. The huntress is content to sit with Ino's charged presence beside her, ever vigilant. And when Atla's ready, they'll talk about what the Whisperers told her. They'll *both* talk about what the Whisperers tried to promise them. Korre's not entirely certain what the Whisperers offered Atla. Her apprentice has her own demons to face, but the huntress knows about some of them—the ones Atla whispers about in the night-mares from which she still screams herself awake. And Korre can guess at more.

She's not sure exactly how alike their histories are, but she knows Atla still thinks she's broken, in so many ways—despite all the healing she's done under the huntress' wing.

Just like Korre used to.

Maybe, just maybe, with time, she can convince Atla she's not broken. Because neither of them are.

It's a truth it took Korre a long time to believe. But she's done enough living to know it in her bones. Has for a long time. And one day, maybe Atla will, too.

For now, she lets Atla sleep. They have a long road ahead of them.

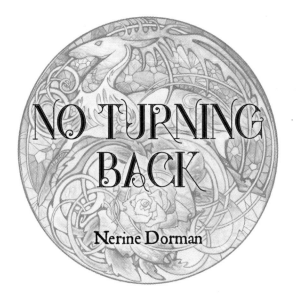

NO TURNING BACK

Nerine Dorman

"What are you doing, girl?"

Selyn nearly dropped the stone she'd been about to toss at the bottle she'd set up as a target, and turned around to face her boss. She hadn't expected him to bother looking for her here, down behind the inn's stables. As far as she knew, no one knew she was here. It was a small measure of privacy that she'd sought after weeks on the road south.

Zeiros stood with his arms folded across his chest. "You making a mess again?"

She glanced at the bottle, the lone survivor of the half-dozen she'd scavenged from the rubbish for her target practice. "Amusing myself. What, you have a problem with this?"

Zeiros rolled his eyes, making his frog-like features appear more comical. He squinted at her. "Good girls shouldn't be throwing stones. We need to go. Now. And go out the back. Don't let anyone see you."

"But I thought we were—" She stopped herself. Back-talking the man wasn't a good idea, but she couldn't help it. Why was he so adamant about leaving all of a sudden? They'd barely arrived, and were only due to set out once the last of their expedition members arrived over the next day or two.

"Mistress Rahalla will have to join us on another trip. Get the mules ready. *Now*." Despite the absurdity of this short, slightly rotund man ordering her as if he were a knight, his tone brooked no argument. She sighed, dropped her stone, and trudged back to where the animals were kept. So much for a relaxing evening.

You shouldn't have to put up with his nonsense, Larc commented. The three-legged rhy-dog sat with his ears pricked, like a small gray statue on a hay bale near the door. He was barely visible in the dim lantern light at the entrance.

"Last I checked, I'm being paid to put up with whatever nonsense he deems fit to offer me."

It's not too late for you to turn back.

"This argument again." Selyn sighed in the gloom of the stables as she made her way over to Zeiros' two mules. They were old beasts, and by all rights should have been put out to pasture years ago, but their minds were still bright. They nuzzled her. The bay with the blaze down his forehead she'd named Cider, because he liked to nip, and the sweet, flax-maned chestnut was Honey. Zeiros thought her overly sentimental for naming them, but these were her charges, and it felt right to give them names.

This is the last chance you'll get to change your mind about this journey, Larc said.

"Why are you so adamant about me not going?" She paused, reaching for the halter, and met the dog's gaze.

I'd rather not see you get hurt. It's dangerous out there. He bent his head and chewed at his left paw.

"I knew the risks when I signed on." She shrugged, swallowing a small weevil of trepidation. Selyn had known Larc all of three weeks, ever since she found him ghosting them on the road to the Northern Refuge. So far, his instincts had proven correct when he'd warned her about a party of bandits ahead on the road, information she'd passed to Zeiros. And there'd been other occasions, like when he alerted her to an adder hidden under a log when she'd been out collecting wood.

The risks may be more than you're ready to face.

"You don't need to come with." She finished putting the halter on one mule then started with the other.

A large gray horse she hadn't noticed before peered at her from the stall across the way. Its eyes were bright with intelligence. It observed her.

"Oh, hi," Selyn said. A rhy-horse? Here? She didn't recall seeing any knights or even the Sovereign's Finest in the common room.

I'd listen to the little one, if I were you, the horse replied. Warm notes of concern rippled in its thoughts. *I've heard some less-than-wonderful things about that employer of yours.*

A shiver of unexpected emotion passed over her skin. Her first rhy-horse. Speaking to her.

"Thank you for your concern." She inclined her head to the horse. "But with all due respect, I'm well aware of the dangers I face. And my employer has been good to me so far." So many horror-filled tales. Yet Zeiros assured her that he was an old hand at exploring the Shadow Barrens. That alone made her feel somewhat better about this venture. If only she could feel the same confidence now, on the cusp of her journey.

The rhy-horse snorted. *No one's ever prepared for what they find out there.*

"True," she said. "But it's my decision to make." Thing was, this was the second greatest decision she'd made for herself—agreeing to accompany the explorer on his journey. The first had happened that morning when she'd realized she wasn't ready to be cloistered away like other young Jarzoni women who displayed even the barest scrap of magic. A sleepless night of prayer had not brought any illumination other than to go—one of the most difficult and heart-wrenching choices Selyn had ever made.

Now that she was mistress of her own fate, she supposed she'd become stubborn. Not even a rhy-horse would sway her from her path.

I told you, Larc told the rhy-horse. *She's a hard-headed one. "Just one trip," she tells me, then we're off to Aldis. But you know how it is.*

The horse shook his head, as though ridding himself of troublesome flies, then regarded Selyn calmly. *Good thing you have this brave pup coming with you then.*

"We look out for each other."

Aye, and that's about all we can do, when all's said and done. This is no place for someone like you, lass.

"I'm not planning on making a career of exploring the Shadow Barrens."

"Girl!" Zeiros called from outside. "Are you done yet?"

Larc became a gray blur that slipped between the feed barrels. Like any rhydan in this region, he was wary of Jarzoni and wouldn't show himself again until they were well on their way and he was certain only Selyn was around.

"Oh damn." Selyn hurried with the rest of the tack, fumbling in the gloom. As if to mock her, the mules were, well . . . as mules were wont to be. Cider and Honey tested even her patience. Honestly, she couldn't blame them. She wasn't all that keen to leave the relative comfort of the inn, either.

They were on the trail within the hour, Zeiros at the head of a party of twelve—six scarred mercenaries and four fellow explorers. The latter were paying a small fortune to take advantage of Zeiros' experience on this expedition. Selyn did her best to ignore Zeiros' clients. They were all the same to her: wealthy, privileged, and completely oblivious to what was going on around them. Cutter Faine was a retired Aldin sea captain who thought no one noticed that he often enjoyed the contents of his small silver hip-flask. Jerza Potter, most recently from Elsport, complained bitterly about everything, and had most likely nagged her late husband to death—what she was doing on this expedition was a mystery to Selyn, and she was not about to inquire. The other two party members were taciturn, middle-aged Jarzoni men who spoke little and kept to themselves. Zeiros only ever called Hedden and Caro "sir," or referred to them as "the grim ones" when he discussed them with his employees. All Selyn knew was that these two were from Leogarth, and she did her best to avoid them as much as possible—just in case they asked her any personal questions. Not that her family would go so far as to send someone to fetch her back, but she didn't want to take any chances.

And she didn't blame Larc for his reticence, either. If anyone would feel uncomfortable with Larc's "corrupting nature," it would be these two.

And here she was, leading two recalcitrant mules along the Dejek Trail, at the rear of a mad venture into corrupted lands. Mouth dry, she peered longingly over her shoulder as the lights of the last sanctuary were swallowed in the twilight gloom. Perhaps it was a mercy that she couldn't see her surroundings. They traveled with no light and in complete silence, and she had to trust that Zeiros knew the way—as he claimed. If they strayed from their route they'd be lost. Or eaten. Any number of awful things might happen. Her hands grew clammy where she held onto the mules' leads. The animals shook their heads often, as if trying to jerk out of her control.

"It's all right," she reassured them, though she didn't feel any such confidence herself.

Every once in a while, she cast out for Larc's presence, gratified that he returned her thoughts. It made her feel a little less alone knowing that her friend shadowed them.

There is nothing untoward, he sent her. *At least not nearby.*

As if that meant that trouble might not be sniffing after them.

I'll warn you if anything comes too close, he added.

Selyn pulled her coat closer to her body. Her skin felt as if a thousand tiny insects were crawling all over her. Corruption, too. It was one thing to face the walking dead, or even a wyvern; it was quite another for a more insidious evil to affect her—one that her friend couldn't warn her about.

Was this really worth the spoils retrieved from the tomb of an apparently illustrious Faenari ancestor, as Zeiros claimed?

Onward they trudged, stopping only once, near dawn, for a small drink of water and a bite to eat. Though calling it dawn might appear an exaggeration, for the near-impenetrable cloud of shadow that shrouded their world cast everything in a peculiar greenish light so that what stars shone were reduced to misty ghosts. Their trail snaked through broken country with weathered, rocky ridges often contorted into strange shapes. The air itself held a faint musty flavor that furred the back of her tongue, and even the small gulps of stale water she took from her ration did little to dispel the taste.

Perhaps what struck her most about the landscape was the sense of watchful silence. No insects. No birds. Nothing. Just an omnipresent heaviness in the air, as if some disaster might befall them without warning. The adventurers huddled in a knot, and only Zeiros appeared unaffected by his surroundings. He stuffed a pipe with weed and puffed happily until it was time for them to shoulder their packs and continue on their journey.

Daytime brought little relief from the gloom, and they continued until they arrived at a circular encampment protected by a rough drystone wall. Zeiros assured them the well water here was sweet. Cider and Honey were sweating and twitching when Selyn hobbled them, their eyes rolling at the slightest disturbance, be it the unclasping of someone's pack or the dry, crunching footfalls as one of the mercenaries went off to relieve himself.

"I'm so sorry," she told them as she brushed them down. "I wish I could make things better for you."

They calmed somewhat by the time she gave them their feed in a bag, but she still felt awful on their behalf. Poor dumb brutes. Unlike her, they had no choice about being here.

Zeiros insisted that they make no fire out here, that they conserve what fuel they carried with them for when they reached the Sunless Path. The mere thought of the insipient subterranean journey made Selyn shiver as she handed out the dry rations. Zeiros had supplied quantities of traveler's cakes wrapped in waxed paper.

Hardly fine fare, but better than nothing at all.

Selyn waited until the explorers had arranged themselves around the unlit hearth, with Cutter Faire plying everyone with sips from one of his ubiquitous canteens. When she reckoned no one would notice her, she summoned what courage she possessed to slip away from the campsite. She wouldn't have to go far. Larc had tucked himself into a nook between two nearby boulders.

One grizzled mercenary standing watch by the exit nodded to her as she mouthed about needing to take care of nature, and she couldn't help but glance back to see whether Zeiros was watching.

Thank goodness no. He was nodding to something Cutter was saying, his face scrunched up in mirth while he lifted a canteen for another sip. Selyn darted around the rocks and trotted over to Larc's hiding spot. The rhy-dog bounded out of his shelter and danced around her in greeting as she crouched.

"I am so glad you're well," she said, enduring his rough tongue licking her face.

And I you. He pulled back his teeth in a canine grin, tail swiping the air furiously.

She checked his paws and his coat, but he was whole. Then she set down half of her travel ration for him. "You need this."

Larc cocked his head at her. *Are you sure? I can do with less.*

"I'm sure," she said, even while her stomach grumbled a little.

He tapped the parcel with his front paw. *No, you take half. I am sure I will find something along the way.*

"You know better than to eat anything that might live here," she admonished. "Besides, I'm sure I can sneak something out of the packs later if I'm truly famished."

This seemed to mollify him somewhat, and he gobbled down the offering so fast she knew she'd done the right thing. Larc had already been on the thin side when she'd first encountered him. This land would punish him terribly still, and he needed more care than he was willing to admit.

She'd brought him a tin mug of water, which he lapped up greedily. If only Zeiros hadn't shown such antipathy toward the rhy-dog the first time she'd encountered him. Then he needn't hide. He'd be safer with the party.

Satisfied that he was cared for as best she could, she watched him settle back in his spot, and then turned and made her way back to the campsite. Selyn was barely around the cluster of boulders that obscured Larc's hiding spot from view when she collided with a body coming the other way. All breath was knocked from her and she staggered back only to have Zeiros grab her arms.

"What are you doing out here, girl?"

"I went—"

He shook her so hard she nipped her tongue. "Don't tell me that ratty little dog is following us!" he roared.

It felt as if all the blood had drained from Selyn's head and body, pooling somewhere beneath her feet. *Oh, mercy, if he'd seen Larc . . .*

"I went to relieve myself, sir," she said, willing herself to meet his gaze.

"Then why did you take that mug with you?" He looked to the mug in her left hand.

"It's my time, sir. I needed a little water—"

"Enough!" Zeiros punctuated the word with another hard shake. "I don't want to hear about it. And if I find that you've got that stinking little cur following us, Gaden is an expert marksman. Unlike me, he won't miss."

Selyn squeezed her eyes and shook her head, more to avoid having to maintain eye contact with the furious man than anything else. "No sir," she mumbled.

"Now get you back to the mules! I can't afford any stragglers. This isn't a picnic at the seaside."

Selyn ducked just in time to avoid a vicious, back-handed swipe, and though she didn't turn to look back, she was certain the man glared at her until she'd made it all the way back to the campsite.

Fear trilled through her. Was it the all-pervading danger of their journey that had eaten into the man's soul, to turn his face into such a rictus of anger? Selyn hurried to her pack and busied herself with its contents while she willed her pulse to slow. She was certain that everyone in the camp must've seen this little interchange between her and her employer; her cheeks were aflame with the shame.

Zeiros was a lot like Father. Quick to anger.

Though *he'd* never tried to strike her.

Are you all right? Larc asked.

Selyn exhaled a deep breath she'd held a lot longer than was comfortable. *Okay.*

He's not a good person.

I know. You've told me that a hundred times before.

The dog remained silent, though she was aware of how he held his awareness close to hers. Comfort and love flowed between their connection, and her vision grew unaccountably blurred. What was she doing out here so far from home? Even though home had become as untenable as traversing this wasteland.

No tears. She wouldn't give any of these awful people the satisfaction of seeing that Zeiros had gotten under her skin. There was work to be done, and if she could prove her mettle on this expedition, surely crossing the marshes would be as simple as breaking old crocks with well-aimed stones. What she'd give now for target practice, to hear the satisfying shattering of old pottery or glass. A child's game, really, but it grounded her, gave her certainty.

After she checked the mules' hobbles one last time, she rolled herself in a blanket and used her pack as a pillow. The mercenaries would take turns keeping watch—not that falling asleep with these men on sentry duty her made her feel at all safe—and she had to take advantage of every scrap of rest she could glean. The Light alone knew where they'd end up.

Selyn's dreams clutched at her with ragged talons as she tossed and turned on her makeshift bed. Ofttimes she found herself walking from one windowless chamber to another, seeking for that one aperture to the outside world, only to find herself in yet another sealed-off chamber. All the while, shadows whispered on the edge of her hearing, using words in a language she could almost understand if she tried hard enough.

Yet every time she paused, a hand on a doorknob or pressed against the paneling of a heavy wooden door, another voice would shout her name—distant yet bright—and she'd push on through. Eventually she woke at the change of the last watch, and couldn't get back to sleep again, no matter how hard she tried.

Every small sound reached her, be it the sleepy snuffling of the mules or the muttering of one of their clients, twitching in uneasy rest. This was not a good land, and if she considered the weight of the many weeks that still lay ahead of them, Selyn feared the dismay that crawled across her heart.

There was nothing for it. She rose long before Zeiros and the others, and tried to distract herself by currying the mules. At least Cider and Honey appreciated her efforts, relaxing visibly under her ministrations. They were lucky in that they didn't know where they were going, and a nasty, crawly concern made her wonder if Zeiros ever intended to bring the animals back once they reached their destination. It would be so like him to cast them aside if they became inconvenient or had served their purpose.

Despite there being no discernible difference between night and dawn, their party was back on the trail at a time that Zeiros determined. One foot before the other, her pack's straps cutting into her shoulder, Selyn walked. The routine was mind-numbing. Whoever had spoken of adventure in glowing terms had obviously left out the sheer day-to-day drudgery of travel. Gloomy morning bled into noon that barely qualified as twilight, before darkness once again shrouded the broken landscape. What made this worse was that every once in a while, a strange, piercing cry would break the silence, sometimes answered by an equally spine-tingling call. Whether they were resting or walking, the entire party would grow very still. Waiting. Watching. But nothing ever came. It was reassuring that the mercenaries kept watch at night, even though Selyn had her doubts that their weapons would do much good should a wyvern—or something worse—come for them.

Selyn's only consolation was Larc, her determined shadow. She didn't see him every day but was sure to leave portions of her meals behind for him, and water when she had any to spare. The times that she did see the rhy-dog, his ribs had grown prominent, his coat ragged. They spoke little but didn't need to. She likened their connection to how it was when she walked down a dark passage, fingers of one hand trailing lightly against the wall, to touch something solid. A bond that could remind her that there was more to this world than noxious dust, stale sweat, and dry rations that got stuck in her throat when she tried to swallow.

Perhaps a week into the journey, they left the Dejek Trail and followed a faint track that veered off in a southeasterly direction. The lands here were even more broken, their route dipping between eroded ridges and numerous gullies and treacherous patches of scree.

Larc's warning came shortly after Zeiros deemed they were about an hour's march from their intended destination—at last an entrance to the Sunless Path.

You're not alone, Larc said, and passed on an impression of a large, slithery being following them along the ridge that ran parallel to their trail. The fear that he tried to stop from spilling over their shared link made her mouth go dry.

Next to her, Cider put his ears back and snorted. Whether this was because he picked up on the warning from Larc or due to detecting their stalker, she wasn't sure. But what to do?

Zeiros had employed her thanks to her knack with animals. "I'm tired of having issues with the pack beasts," was his reasoning, which suited her. At least he welcomed her ability, and she'd been able to put it to good use.

But now . . .

She eyed the ridge but didn't see anything untoward. Granted, the twilight murk made it difficult to tell if any *thing* was up there. A sickly, nacreous mist was folding down the fissures, boiled off into nothingness, and all she wanted to do was hurry along.

Well, she could use the mules as her excuse. Selyn picked up her pace and began overtaking the two Jarzoni men who trudged just ahead of her. One turned and shot her a filthy glare, for the mules' hooves plumed up dust. Sure, Zeiros would be angry that she'd come forward with "those dirty beasts," as he called the luckless pack mules, but this was a life-or-death situation as she read it.

"Master Zeiros," she called. "A word, please."

He held up his hand to call a halt then turned to her, his round face rumpled in displeasure. "This had better be good." He strode toward her.

"Apologies, sir, but this can't wait," she said quietly.

Zeiros regarded her, his wide nostrils twitching—a sure sign of anger.

"The mules are uneasy, sir." This she said so only he could hear, though she could see the raw-boned Jerza Potter peering at them intently. Light, if that woman overheard what was being said, her jaw would flap enough to set fire to the entire party within a minute.

"What do I care? It's your job to keep them in line."

"Sir, with all due respect, there's . . ." How could she say this without sounding completely paranoid? "There's a . . . *thing* . . . tailing us. On that ridge above."

"Oh." He pressed his lips into a thin line. "This is unfortunate. I was assured . . ." Zeiros turned away from her and clapped his hands twice. "Come, come, people. We need to catch a hurry-up." He strode back to the front of their line and started walking again.

Jerza cast an inquiring glance Selyn's way, but she pretended not to notice and instead waited for the two Jarzoni to walk ahead of her while she took her place at the end of their party again. She couldn't help but shiver, and was half-tempted to quest out with her senses to see if she could verify what Larc had communicated to her.

Don't, the rhy-dog warned.

But—

Just keep going. Hurry. This is not your fight. Run. Live.

To her gratification, Zeiros quickened their pace to the point where they all verged on trotting. Putting one foot before the other consumed her full attention, for the ground was uneven. More than once the mules yanked her arms, nearly jerking her off her feet as they picked their way between boulders and over loose slithers of shale. Every moment she expected death to leap off the ridge and land upon them, for surely the mules would be the best target—being the largest and possibly biggest meals, that is.

Once or twice, their clients turned to glare at her, as if it were somehow Selyn's fault that they were rushing at near-breakneck speed, but she was too occupied with not twisting an ankle to worry overmuch about their discomfort.

Are you keeping up? she sent Larc, worried now that they were leaving him in the dust.

No response came, not even the slightest acknowledgement. This chilled Selyn. What was the rhy-dog doing? Surely he didn't intend to face their pursuer on his own?

Sick at heart, her vision blurring from tears she daren't let anyone else see, she pressed on. It would be so like Larc to do something foolhardy. Hadn't he regaled her about the time he'd faced down a corrupted boar? That was, after all, how he'd lost his hindleg, when the beast had gored him.

Just when Selyn feared she'd fall behind, Zeiros called a halt.

"It's here somewhere," he muttered, pacing a short length along the road while he studied the rock wall to their left. To Selyn's eyes, the surface looked exactly the same as the rest—flat and unremarkable. They were wasting time. What was going on?

Twitchy mercenaries stood with crossbows at the ready. They didn't have to be told that danger was afoot. Everyone turned and gasped as a small spray of pebbles rattled down the sheer cliff to their right. They were trapped here, the trail having dropped for a half-mile into a gully, following what must've once been an ancient watercourse.

Yet nothing leapt at them, except Selyn swore she heard high-pitched barking. Just what was the rhy-dog doing? Fear and concern were at war in her belly, but she was well aware that there was precious little she could do. Especially against a monster that dwelled in the Shadow Barrens.

Run. Live.

"Come on, come on," she murmured, but Zeiros seemed unconcerned for his party's growing agitation.

The two Jarzoni men had drawn their swords, and even the retired sea captain looked shifty, his hand on the pommel of the ornate dagger he kept sheathed at his side.

A terrible, metallic shriek sounded from above—the kind of sound that made Selyn's blood curdle.

"Ah-hah!" Zeiros crowed as he pushed his palm flat against a section of rock that to Selyn's eye looked exactly like the rest. A faint humming, right at the edge of her hearing, and Cider jerked back his head with a strangled squeal.

"It's all right," she said, and made soothing noises, but both animals were tugging, trying to move back. It took all of her strength and wit to keep them from bolting.

"Are you coming?" Zeiros yelled at her. "Or do you want whatever that is out there to eat you?"

Fighting to keep her hold on the mules, she glimpsed the man standing at the slot of a tunnel that had materialized out of the rock. That hadn't been there before.

"Quickly now."

Come, please, Selyn said to the mules over link, sending them all the love and reassurance she could. *It's going to be safer through there than out here. Please.*

For a heartbeat, she thought Cider would bolt. Both animals had their ears back, but then she pushed with her ability and the animals acquiesced, stepping smartly into the shadowed tunnel.

Selyn found herself inside a small chamber that had clearly been shaped—the walls were smooth, the roof itself curving into a gentle arch. The passage was wide enough for two to walk abreast, and sloped gradually down.

Like the rest of their party, Selyn stared about her in wonder. Outside, another shriek sounded, and Selyn jerked.

"What was that?" Jerza asked.

"Wyvern," Zeiros answered, but he looked unconcerned as he dusted off his cloak. "Even if it could see the entrance, the monster wouldn't fit through all that easily."

All that easily didn't sound all that promising. By the Light, Selyn prayed Larc was all right.

"What is this place?" the Jerza pressed.

"It's one of the routes to the Sunless Path. This goes about a quarter of a mile down. A shortcut, if you will."

"Well, that's a relief," the woman said. "Considering what I paid for your services, you're proving your worth as a guide."

His smile was very white in the dim interior. "Naturally, madam, for I am the best."

Ugh. Selyn was glad no one saw her pull her expression into a moue of distaste. If the man could get any more smarmy, she'd vomit. But she had to give him this much: he was smooth. Which was half the reason she'd most likely agreed to his terms in the first place. So far, their only sticking point had been the rhy-dog. Zeiros' hatred of all rhydan rivaled even that of a Jarzoni priest.

Thinking of Larc now hurt with all the pain of a rusty blade dug deep into her belly. A medium-sized rhy-dog was no match for a wyvern. She'd heard enough stories about the fearsome monsters to know that even a squad of knights would be hard pressed to deal with such a menace. She could only hope that Larc was canny enough to remain out of the creature's clutches. Only time would tell, but the not knowing would leave her sick at heart.

"Light guide you, Larc," she whispered.

Carrying lanterns powered with shas crystals, they descended along the throat that led into the depths. Their light did little to dispel the darkness, only pushing it out of the way until it swallowed up the world behind them. Boot soles and hooves scuffed and clopped on the smooth stone floor, and from time to time the mules slipped. No one spoke, and every so often Zeiros would pause and they would all end up straining to hear any tell-tale sounds of pursuit.

Perhaps the silence, punctuated only by the creak of harness and the shuffle of feet, was worse. Selyn expected there would be sounds beyond what was familiar—maybe a slithery naga slinking in the darkness, or worse. Currently, she couldn't think of worse.

Presently their tunnel spat them out into a wider thoroughfare. Zeiros explained that this was one of the main tributaries of the Sunless Path, a lesser-explored portion that would bring them to areas that had not been completely stripped by looters and treasure-seekers.

"The village where we shall rest lies ahead," he said. "There is a water source there that we may use, and the space is defensible. I haven't seen a corrupted spider here in at least two years." This last statement made him cackle.

Jerza snapped, "I am not amused."

Neither was Selyn. She wasn't overly fond of creatures that possessed more than two sets of legs. There was something alien about spiders, a calculatedness that chilled her, that suggested if they were large enough, they'd have no qualms about adding people to their diet.

The route they followed now was broader—an ancient subterranean watercourse that had been reduced to a dry channel with a sandy bottom. The mules' hooves crunched against the substrate, and the beasts seemed happier that they were no longer sliding down slick stone floors. They were still uneasy about the enclosed space, but then again, so was she. It didn't take a great leap of imagination to feel the weight of the stone pressing downward. How far below the surface were they?

Ahead of her, the two Jarzoni men muttered to each other, while the retired sea captain seemed chipper enough, often striding forward to consult with Zeiros or falling back to confer with Jerza. Their mercenary escort remained on edge, the men's hands often sliding to their sword pommels.

It was impossible to gauge the passage of time here, but even when they rested for a few hours, Selyn went to sleep exhausted and woke feeling as if an entire herd of mules had stampeded over her. It wasn't even the awful dreams that had her in their clutches the moment she closed her eyes; it was the constant dull, thudding headache, as if she'd been drinking the night before. Her skin prickled uncomfortably, and she was certain it was more than the accumulated dirt and sweat.

On the second "day" in the tunnel, as she went around a corner to relieve herself—within shouting distance of the nearest guard—Larc made contact with her.

I am well, he sent, though the tone of his greeting communicated a profound sense of exhaustion.

Selyn rose, releasing a small cry of relief, and pulled up her hose and straightened her skirts. She peered out into the darkness beyond the tiny light of her lantern but could see nothing.

Where are you? she asked. *How did you—*

It will take more than a wyvern to finish me. The rhy-dog's smugness made her smile. *There are advantages to being small and fast, even if you only have three legs. All beasts have three and a spare. That's what a wise old rhy-cat once told me.*

Larc remained in the darkness, despite Selyn's need to see him. She shared his fear that the mercenaries would feather him with crossbow bolts the moment they clapped eyes on him.

"Girl!" Zeiros called. "What are you doing out there?"

I must go, she told the rhy-dog. *But I will leave food out here for you later.*

Thank you.

That evening, if she could call it that, they came to a ruined village that had sunk beneath the ground at some point during the distant past. Or maybe it had always been here. She supposed it no longer mattered, for its past denizens were long gone—the only living things they found here were masses of tiny bats that clung like overripe fruit to the ceiling. When disturbed, these little creatures filled the air with their chittering and whirring wings. A crack split rock above them, and she supposed this was where the bats gained egress to the outside world, for they constantly came and went from here in a manic swarm. Tiny red eyes made pinpricks in the darkness when the lanterns shone where they huddled in inky masses.

Selyn brushed her awareness against theirs, but recoiled instantly from the crackle-fizz of corruption that infected them. What had she expected? Anything that lived out here eventually became corrupted. She would too if she stayed here much longer. Money be damned. Selyn grimaced and busied herself caring for the mules. They were on edge—more so than usual. The last thing she needed now was for Larc to say, "I told you so."

Do you feel anything? she queried Larc.

This place . . . He sent a mental shudder. *The sooner we move on, the better.*

Later, she left him a small meal and a measure of water. She'd retrieve the mug before they left. Zeiros had been rationing their water. He said if they carried on drinking the way they were, they'd not have enough to get back, and there were no guarantees of finding drinkable water now that they were on this stretch. Someone had been using more than what they were allocated. The man had looked meaningfully at Selyn, as if this were somehow her fault, yet she couldn't bring herself to feel guilty over the small amount she'd stolen for Larc. She'd simply been drinking less herself.

There was muttering among the clients, but what could be done? As it was, her tongue cleaved to her palate most of the time, and her skin felt too tight. Signs of dehydration, she supposed. When they returned to Northern Refuge, she'd soak in those hot springs for half a day. The mere thought of that piping hot water easing the strain from her muscles made her nearly delirious with want.

Anything to feel the sun on her face.

They bedded down in one of the ruined homes—the first time she'd had walls surrounding her in many nights. Selyn should have felt safer, except now she felt boxed in with all the people lying down right by her. Two of the guards watched by the door—they'd barricaded the only other exit with a pile of debris.

Yet if something bad were to happen, surely there'd have been more chance of that occurring while they'd been sleeping out in the tunnel? Unable to shake her concern, she rose and took a lantern so she could go check on the mules, which had been stabled in the house next door. The guard, whom she knew merely as Tom, nodded at her as she passed him. Not a bad sort, really. Not that she'd tried to get to know him beyond "pass the kettle" or "I'm going to go take care of my necessities just around the corner."

Cider and Honey huddled next to each other, as far from the door as they could get. Honey trembled and rolled her eyes when Selyn whispered at them to be calm, that nothing would go wrong. Lies, really, because their journey thus far had been charmed, even though they'd narrowly escaped the naga. Was tonight the night? Or day?

When we get you out of here, I've friends who will help you across the Veran Marshes, Larc said, then gave a rather canine sneeze from within the makeshift stable.

"Oh!" Selyn gave a small cry and turned to where the rhy-dog was seated next to the mules' harnesses.

Dismay bloomed in her as she made sense of his conditions in the low light. Every rib stood out in sharp relief, and a poorly healed gash along his left flank could only have been made by a large claw. One ear was torn clean through, but his eyes were still bright. Tears blurred her vision as she knelt down to embrace the dog.

Larc groaned in her arms. *I really don't like to be hugged.*

She let go and studied him, her heart thumping wildly. "You should have come to me with that sooner," she whispered.

You've enough to worry yourself with, he answered. *Besides, I've been looking after myself for a decade already. What's one little scratch compared to what I've already endured?*

"That's not a little scratch."

He huffed. *I'm fine. What's more important is that you warn your people that there's a horde of walking dead shuffling along the passage. They'll be here within an hour.*

"What?" It felt as if an abyss suddenly yawned beneath her.

Do I need to explain to you what's coming? It's time this boss of yours gave up this expedition as a bad job.

"No, no, you don't need to explain further." She scrambled to her feet, backing toward the door. Walking dead. That was the last thing she'd ever wanted to see. "How many?"

At least a hundred that I could count.

Once outside the dwelling, she paused in the gap between the houses, listening, except it was nearly impossible to hear anything over the thudding of her pulse and her own ragged breathing. Was that a moan that she heard, or simply an errant breeze that reached them through a crack in the tunnel roof?

And how in all the gods' names was she going to tell Zeiros *how* she knew about the oncoming threat? She'd have to betray that she'd known Larc had been tailing them all this time.

It doesn't matter, Larc sent to her. *It's not like he succeeded in killing me the first time he tried. And he can hardly be angry with you for doing your best to stay alive.*

Selyn sucked in a deep breath and steeled herself as she stepped back over the threshold. Zeiros had bundled himself up at the farthest corner, no more than a lump beneath his blanket. She crouched down next to her snoring employer and shook his shoulder lightly.

"Boss?"

"Ngghhh." He twisted around, his face contorted. Then his eyes snapped open and he scowled at her. "What?"

She lowered her voice so only he could hear. "There's . . . there's a horde of walking dead converging on us."

He sat up so quickly he nearly headbutted her. "What?"

"I've . . . my rhy-dog friend has followed us all this time. He says they are less than an hour from here."

Zeiros struck so fast she couldn't escape him. He grabbed her by her tunic. "What? I thought I told you that the dog was to stay away from us or I'd kill it."

"He's my *friend*." She squared her shoulders.

"I don't give a damn about whether he's your bleeding friend." Zeiros lurched to his feet but didn't relinquish his grip. He shook her so hard it felt as if her teeth rattled. "You disobedient wretch!" The man gave another shake then let go. She staggered back a few paces and fetched up against the wall.

"This complicates things," he muttered, then yelled, "All right! Everyone up! Pack your things. We go. Now!"

Mumbled complaints followed.

"What is the meaning of this?" Cutter rumbled as he sat up. "We've barely bedded down."

"And if you'd rather not be rent limb from limb by the ravening undead, I suggest you get your bones back on their feet and start getting ready," Zeiros snarled. He turned to Selyn. "From which direction are these things coming?"

"From where we were supposed to go," Selyn answered.

"Oh, for the love of all that's unholy!" he cried. Zeiros stood for a few heartbeats, clenching and unclenching his hands, his gaze distant while he clearly considered his options. He straightened and clapped his hands together. "There's nothing for it, we'll have to take a detour. It's a longer route, but it will be easier to defend against pursuit."

He started yelling orders at the mercenaries. Selyn took that as her cue to harness up the mules and take care of the packing. By the time she returned to where Cider and Honey were stabled, Larc had made himself scarce again, though when she quested out with her thoughts he sent back a reassuring nudge. He was there. Keeping watch.

Once they were ready, they set out, their fellows' expressions tense, because in order to reach the detour Zeiros wished them to follow they had to travel part of the way toward the oncoming horde.

"We should turn around," one of the Jarzoni men said to his friend. "I fancy our chances better if we return to the Northern Refuge."

They glanced over their shoulders at Selyn.

The other fell in step next to her. "You carry the bulk of our supplies, and with only the three of us, we'd go through less of it than with the rest. What do you say, girl?"

That's not such a bad idea, Larc chipped in.

"So, you'd abandon the others," Selyn said, as much for the men as for Larc. She might not like Zeiros, Cutter, and the rest, but she still wouldn't wish a death sentence on them.

"By the gods, I can hear them!" Jerza cried out ahead.

The closer of the two Jarzoni men grabbed the mules' leads from Selyn's hands, which caused the normally placid Honey to let out a high-pitched bray that drew their entire party up short.

"Hey, what—" the nearest mercenary cried as he spun around, only to have the other Jarzoni man draw his sword and thrust it through the surprised man's gut.

Selyn fought to get the leads from the Jarzoni man's hands, but he was bigger than her and shoved her hard so that she fell against the tunnel wall. Her breath was driven from her, and she smacked the back of her head and the world started to spin.

She tried to gather herself as the moaning of the oncoming horde became audible—a terrible rasping, gasping storm of awfulness that triggered a fresh wash of fear. By the time she'd recovered, Cider had clattered off back the way they'd come, the two Jarzoni men and three guards were bleeding out on the ground, and she only just managed to grab Honey's lead before she, too, followed her companion.

There simply wasn't time to do more than pelt after Zeiros, who was swearing enough for an entire ship full of pirates. Her breath rasped in her throat as she stumbled along, fearing with every corner they rounded that they'd run into the walking dead.

They found the narrow opening sooner than expected and hurried in, two of the mercenaries taking the rear to hold off possible pursuit. Honey barely fit without the pack, so they wasted precious time redistributing what the mule carried. The moans of the undead and the awful thunks of swords striking flesh lent fresh urgency to her work while Honey kept lashing out with her hooves.

"Behave, please," Selyn pleaded.

"Hurry up, girl, or we're leaving you behind!" Zeiros shouted.

Cutter and Jerza had already gone ahead with the mercenary captain, Gaden.

"Do you want to carry your own supplies?" Selyn snapped.

That seemed to shut him up, but he didn't raise a finger to help her.

Rock walls pressed down from both sides and the air was thick. Each breath felt as if she was drawing a foul syrup into her lungs. And Larc was somewhere back in the main tunnel, with a ravening horde of walking dead between them. If he'd survived the wyvern, surely he'd be canny enough to keep out of the clutches of the dead? She could only hope.

They started moving again, and not a moment too soon. The sounds of the mercenaries keeping the walking dead off their tail faded into the distance as they wormed their way through a series of passages so narrow she could reach out to either side and touch smooth stone. Someone had shaped this honeycombed network of tunnels, and she didn't want to think too hard about who or even *what*.

How did Zeiros even know about this route? The man instinctively knew exactly which branch to follow. And how were they ever going to work their way back to a safe haven again? If something happened to Zeiros, there was no way she'd be able to retrace her steps.

These dark thoughts chased themselves end over end while they fled. Should she see the bright side that they now had fewer mouths to feed?

After what felt like an eternity, their tunnel coughed them out into a chamber so tall their lamps couldn't illuminate the ceiling. Pale walls of stone shot through with green-blue veins vanished into an inky pool, and on either side of the oblong space stood a set of double doors.

"We don't have forever," Zeiros said, somewhat unnecessarily.

"Is this the place?" Cutter asked, side-eyeing a manky pile of bones and rags dumped in one corner. Were those round objects human skulls?

"Indeed. I have been here but twice, and each time we've struggled at that point." He gestured toward the ornately carved door to their left. "I've kept the other door closed, but we will be able to open it from the inside."

"I should hope so," Jerza remarked. "I'm not looking forward to having to wade through the undead back in those mole tunnels."

"Which is why young madam and Gaden will be packing a barrier a little farther in." Zeiros' smile told her that this was an order, not a suggestion.

"Of course, sir," she said, swallowing back the need to lay on the sarcasm. "As soon as I've hobbled our mule. We wouldn't want our only remaining beast of burden to wander off now, would we?" Not that Honey would have far to go here.

To her surprise, Gaden came to help her with the mule. Gray at the temples, and despite a long-healed scar down his left cheek, he wasn't an unpleasant-looking sort. A hard-on-his-luck kinda person, like she was. Not that she'd gone out of her way to befriend him.

Once they were done, they left Zeiros, Cutter, and Jerza poring over the locking mechanism while they returned up the detour.

"How far do you think we need to go?" she asked Gaden.

He'd gone on ahead, drawn sword in one hand and their only lantern in the other. "Just a few twists and turns, I suppose. I saw a pile of loose rocks as we came down that will make our life easier."

Now that it was the two of them, alone, a sense of awkwardness descended on Selyn. Or perhaps she was simply starved for decent conversation. Anything to distract her from the very real fact that they were blocking off the only route that Larc would have to follow them. He'd be stuck with the walking dead. Maybe she could persuade Gaden to leave a small gap for the rhy-dog.

A past quake had created a fault in the tunnel, a slowly shifting section where rock was being displaced. Given time, the tunnel would be truncated here, with one section sliding behind a curtain of solid stone, cutting this route off from the rest of the network.

"Maybe the undead won't even follow us this far," she said while they moved rocks.

He grunted. "I wouldn't count on that. Those things have been sent after us by someone. They won't stop until they sniff us out. And sniff us out they will. We're only buying time."

"Dare I ask who or what?" Selyn sought out a likely rock and lugged it to where Gaden was working. He took it from her with thanks.

"A sorcerer, perhaps? Austium's not too far from here. The Sunless Path passes right by it."

"I did not want to know that."

"Well, now you do." He flashed her a grim smile.

"Have you worked long for Zeiros?" she asked.

"Nah. Me and my boys signed on about a week before you did."

"Oh." She had assumed that the men had been serving Zeiros for far longer. "So this is your first time down here as well?"

"Second. Went with another explorer about twenty years ago. Didn't come this far, but it's not unfamiliar territory. Now go bring me some of those smaller stones. Need to pack them first before we try some of the bigger uns."

They ran out of things to talk about soon enough; besides, they needed all their strength for the job at hand. Each stone weighed twice as heavy on her heart.

Larc, where are you? Selyn didn't expect an answer, but when her query was returned with a tired, *Wait,* she couldn't help but smile.

"Gaden? Can I ask a favor?"

He paused, and mopped a brow with his wrist. "What is it?

"You know that rhy-dog?"

"The one the boss keeps wanting us to shoot on sight?"

"He's the one who warned us about the walking dead . . . and the wyvern earlier. He's here, now. We need to let him through."

Gaden frowned. "Boss's orders . . ."

"We wouldn't be alive now if it weren't for Larc. Please, Gaden. All I ask is that you let him through. You can pretend like you didn't see him. *Please.*" That last word came out tattered at the edges.

He sighed. "Very well. It can't hurt us any more than we're already hurt."

They waited, the silence eating at her until the faint tick-ticking of the rhy-dog's claws on the stone spoke of his arrival. At her prompting, Gaden reached over the gap and lifted Larc through.

"You're indestructible," she said, kneeling down so she could face Larc.

He rewarded her with lick to the face, from which she recoiled with a laugh. *Not indestructible. Just cunning. Now you can finish your wall. I lost those undead about two hours ago, but they'll get here eventually.*

The work went quickly after that, the rhy-dog's eyes glinting in the lantern light as he watched them.

There's something I need to tell you, Larc said as they made their way back. *I've not been entirely truthful with you.*

What? She faltered in her walking.

I was sent to follow you. By my friends in the Sovereign's Finest from Aldis

Why?

Your employer is a sorcerer. He's been taking parties down here to open an old, forbidden tomb so he can sacrifice them as part of a ritual to unlock a door that will allow him access to a great artefact.

She nearly laughed out loud. *What? Zeiros? He can barely tie his bootlaces. Him a sorcerer? Have you taken leave of your senses?*

No. But now you know why I didn't want you to come.

You could have told me sooner.

Would you have believed me?

She almost didn't believe him now, except she'd seen so much that this last fact wasn't entirely outside the realms of possibility. *No.*

Regret flowed across their link, as well as love. The rhy-dog pitied her, and cared for her. Deeply. And he spoke the truth. As much as she didn't want to believe him, he spoke the truth.

"What now?" she murmured.

We try to stay alive. Until help comes.

Help?

You honestly didn't think I'd come down here without backup, did you?

And the wyvern? She slowed down, hating that Gaden was taking the light with him, but if she returned to that chamber, it would surely not end well for her.

Yes. My friends helped. Though it meant we nearly lost your trail in the process. We needed your party to reach the chamber so we could take action against not only the sorcerer but also neutralize the potential for the artefact to ever be empowered. We've been searching for it for years, and this is our first solid lead.

Selyn sank to her haunches as Gaden vanished around the corner. By her estimation, he'd be exiting into the chamber within a few more feet. She couldn't follow.

"What now?" she whispered.

We wait.

"What about the others?"

They're as good as dead.

"We can't let that happen." Even if Zeiros was a sorcerer, he was one of the most ridiculous, awful, and horrible people she'd ever encountered. If she had the element of surprise, surely she could best him physically.

You can't possibly be thinking of going up against him.

"Let me decide." Though fear had her in its jaws, she rose, feeling her way along with moist palms against smooth stone. "I can sit here in the dark, waiting for him to come find me before your 'help' arrives, or I can at least try to do something."

You'll be safer here. We can find somewhere to hide.

"Until he comes to find me once he's done with the others. Which he will. We both know that."

The rhy-dog didn't disagree with her.

Her mouth dry, she inched her way toward the exit. A weird, nacreous light flickered as she snuck closer, and a voice declaimed strange words that she didn't understand, although the meanings couldn't be good at all, for all the small hairs stood up on her arms and nape as she moved to peek into the chamber.

He didn't exactly wait to get started, Larc commented.

He was willing to sacrifice me and Gaden in case the undead swarmed him before he finished, she replied, not sure if she should be grateful.

If he hadn't, you'd be dead now.

Or worse.

Because there was worse.

Three bodies were sprawled on the ground, a coruscating blue-green haze flowing in a maelstrom above them, the light turning the scarlet of their spilled blood black. Standing by them, facing the door he wished to open, was Zeiros. From this angle, she had a good view of the bald patch on the back of his head. She prayed he didn't glance over his shoulder. Gaden had clearly tried to rush him, judging by the way he still clutched the sword, but he'd been struck down before even reaching Zeiros. An honest-to-the-Light sorcerer.

Either he's arrogant in his power or he thinks I'll be too afraid to do anything, she told Larc as she withdrew into the shadows.

He's arrogant and *dangerous.*

He's got his back to me, but I've got really *good aim.* The stone her questing fingers found was roughly the size of a chicken's egg and fit her palm perfectly. Her hand shook, but she steadied herself with a deep breath, feeling how the moisture from her skin slicked the stone. It was smooth, as if it had tumbled in a stream for eons. It would flow, tumbling one last time from her grasp as she let go. There would be no turning back. And that revolting man's head was bigger than a glass bottle.

Selyn took aim and threw. At this range, there was no way she could miss. There was no going back from here, but forward . . .forward, she could do.

WANING MOON

Caias Ward

In another time, the world outside Mount Oritaun would be green and vital. Faenaria was a land of color and fragrance and wisdom, a luxurious jewel among nations. Now, in this time, it was the Shadow Barrens, the light of Faenaria torn and dimmed in the Shadow Wars that made the Faenarians flee to other realms and be known as nothing more than Roamers. It nearly destroyed the Children of Selene. In the Barrens moved Mount Oritaun, tied to Selene's grace as she turned in the sky, a phantom until the moon stood again full, fading again to another place to avoid the perils of shadow. While the moon moves the mount, in the Hiathaeum we move, to power the Shadow Storm Ward to drive off the storms that would corrupt us and grind the mount to dust. By Selene, may we have wisdom and light.

Har'shea's feet and arms and body moved to the tale in her head, which she had set to the music in the Hiathaeum. It was not the names of the positions in the middle circle, but it was how she best kept her rhythm and flow after several centuries, in the Hiathaeum ballroom. There, what was once natural cave is now carved and crafted through centuries of work she had watched from the beginning. Stalactites stabbed downward from the ceiling, carved into chandeliers and lit with natural crystals spraying light throughout. Murals of the Faenari past stood between giant mint-green pillars carved from the chamber walls, the paint rising up to the ceiling. In the middle of the vast vault was a distortion of light and power; a more careful look showed it was a giant shas crystal, a pillar from floor to ceiling barely distorting the light. She remembered when they brought the crystal here over three centuries ago.

She danced in the middle of three circles, a sea of ribbons and veils swirling. The dancers of the middle circle, violet-hued vatazin, twisted and sprawled and rolled, cloth gossamer and opaque ebbing and flowing as they twisted off of backs and thighs and hands. Inward, toward the shas crystal pillar, the circle of dancers—a mix of vatazin and vata—spun with tornado-grace, whirling on pointe and heel and knee. Outward, in the widest circle, the vata and vatazin dancers jumped, upward, reaching to the moon, coming down on first one foot and then the other. They shuffled to the right, then left. They twisted in mid-spring and pounded the floor with resounding force masked by what music swarmed the chamber. Musicians played at a stage, a frantic conductor tempering the music as needed, dancers moving with and against each other, closer and farther away.

To the unaware, it would appear a passionate spectacle, and the performance of a lifetime. To the vatazin who danced the spirit dance, the Children of Selene who made the Eternal Dance of creation take physical form, it was an arcane ritual. Here, their magic flowed from them to the shas crystal. Here, that magic powered the Shadow Storm Ward, one of many means of keeping Mount Oritaun safe. Day to night, night to day, the spirit dancers gave all their magic through dance, hours at time. Har'shea was on her fifth hour for today, her second hour in a row, her body wrapped in yards of red cloth that waved and snapped and folded in on itself as she moved. Dancers swapped in and out, exhausted and bruised.

Har'shea spun, rolled on her back over the dancer who knelt to act as a platform, and snapped out her twisted cloth ribbon. It went too far, cracking at another dancer's face. The dancer pulled his head back, unharmed but out of position for a moment. The circles shuddered as everyone adjusted to Har'shea's misplaced movement. A pulse rode up the shas crystal, as though someone had stuck their finger into a stream of water and diverted it. Dancers pulled back as the stream of magic splashed them, wasted effort and steps of movement not going to maintain the ward. Soon, the crystal was clear, the circles moving as they should.

Har'shea raised her arms, making an X with her forearms. A vatazin raced into position, Har'shea pulling him into place as she broke from the middle circle. She made herself small as she passed the outer circle and stepped to the wall. The other dancers went to pat her on the shoulder, touch her arm, and let her know that it was okay.

It was not okay, and she spun and writhed away from them, the yards of ribbon falling off her aging body. All she wore now was the barest slip of short pants and a top. She slipped into her sandals and scooped up her walking-robe. It fell on her body like a death shroud by the time she left the music and rhythm behind.

Har'shea did not stay near the Hiathaeum much of late. She preferred to walk the world she knew, to see what she danced for each day. Mount Oritaun had grown emptier as centuries passed following the end of the Shadow Wars, but the solitude calmed her mind. She watched as vata passed her on her way home. More and more, the vata'an and vata'sha, "true vata" and "dark vata," moon-skinned and night-skinned, were the children born in Mount Oritaun rather than vatazin, even from vatazin parents. They were no less loved, though, their static skin of light and dark the measure of the failing magic of the vatazin and the shape of things to come.

As always, she stopped at a market. It was sparse and quiet in what was known as the Goiaenium. Arcana gave the appearance of a healthy sky, sunrises and sunsets rather than a giant cavern in a mountain. Now, it was the gloaming before the rise of the waning moon, though that false waning moonlight would show very few people. Her skin, like all the vatazin, was in sync with the moon phases. She was violet now, her skin going from violet to indigo to ebony as the moon waned; then, as the moon waxed glorious, she would change again, from ebony to indigo to violet, then to the color of moonlight as the moon rode full in the sky.

In the ages before, it had taken all her grace to make it through the press of crowds that filled the shops and stalls even at this time of night. Now, she held her arms wide, spinning in her sandals, touching no one in the cavern. Even if her arms were yards and yards long, as long as the dancing-cloth with which she miscalculated today, she would touch no one. The lone occupants of this particular area were a family of traders closing up shop and a hunched, folded-over vatazin woman bundled in robes. She had a home, Har'shea knew. The woman did not go there, for her husband was a permanent patient in the Heartward, trapped in his own mind by the horrors of what he saw while spying on the forces of Shadow.

Har'shea walked from the traders, where she had purchased a variety of foodstuffs, to the woman. Her name was Caelida and she was a crafter of light, a maker of intricate lanterns illustrating scenes of mirth. Now, she sat in different places, and people would give her food, which she would take without expression. Har'shea sat with her and ate as she did, spiced bars of mushroom soaking in a broth.

"Caelida," Har'shea said, "is there anything I can do to help you?"

Caelida ate, not looking to Har'shea.

Ages before, Har'shea shaped hearts, to touch the mind and bring hope to others. Now, though, each day she reached her hand to hold Caelida's; each day she fought the urge to shape this woman's heart. Har'shea's magic was not for shaping hearts, or calming beasts, or shielding the mind—not now—but for powering the Shadow Storm Ward. She wanted to say as much to Caelida, how she could not tire herself, that all of her magic went to holding the storm at bay.

Caelida ate, not looking to Har'shea.

Har'shea left after wishing Caelida good night. She made her way to the Hearthwalk, the colors of the "sky" for a moment cheery. She soon escaped the colors, into farther tunnels sparsely lit and peopled. Finally, she reached her home, nothing much more than a stout door built into the wall, leading to caves. In another time, a large family had lived here, neighbors on both sides, the walkways bright. Now, few came here, and fewer still lived here, which suited her fine.

"Is Taman here?" Har'shea said to the austere and dim room beyond the empty foyer, feeling another presence without bothering to look.

"Your protégé let me in," Narus Molvan said from a chair at a table in the kitchen. "They are in the studio. I saw your stumble."

Narus was of indeterminate age, common among most vatazin by appearance alone. Her long hair was pulled back tightly, her clothing severe and functional. She was younger than Har'shea by centuries; Har'shea had taught her the middle circle, and then the outer and inner when Narus was barely an adult. Har'shea had developed many of the steps of the Shadow Storm Ward, the way to channel the arcana of the spirit dancers to keep the storm at bay. She had documented her body's movement and the channeling of power, sheets of choreography, a libram of grace transformed to magic.

"You were there?" Har'shea said as she walked into the kitchen. It had a table and chairs, a cupboard, and a cookstove long-unused. Whatever flat surfaces were carved from the stone for use in meal-making and meal-sharing were bare even of dust. The only light in the kitchen was a small glow-globe set on the table, in a stand that may have one time been a box for spices, long empty. Har'shea did not sit, instead standing in the edge of the brightest light of the glow-globe.

"I didn't want to put you on the spot," Narus nodded. "I figured I would meet you here, but you took the very long way home. Taman came soon after I arrived; I think they were moon-struck by my reputation as a Hiathaeum dancer. They tripped over the doorway, flat as it is."

Narus laughed at her own words. Har'shea smirked, but not to reassure Narus.

"You have given so much of yourself," Narus said. "Each day, you give your magic to quell the storm. Then you give your time to train other spirit dancers. You live in this cave rather than in the Sky Quarter, where there are actually people and light."

"And I know what you are going to say," Har'shea said.

"You overextended on a Rippling Wave today," Narus said. "You threw off another dancer."

"And you have made mistakes," Har'shea said.

"I have," Narus said. "And I learned from them, and I am in my prime. I took a break for research, and only came back when the wards weakened and they needed me. I have danced for over one hundred and sixteen years. You have danced since the beginning. This was not your first stumble, or misstep, just the first one in which others beside me noticed. And those stumbles and missteps are becoming more and more common."

"And?"

"It may be time to contemplate an end, my friend."

"Leave my house."

"You have a protégé," Narus said, "and they are skilled—"

"They are not ready."

"When will they be? When you trip on a Fluttering Pass? When you are in Fifth Stance and twist your knee? When you die in that circle, and not before?"

"Leave, now."

Narus stood carefully, deliberately. She walked to the door, turning to half-face Har'shea. "You have a legacy," she said, adjusting her coat, dawdling on the buttons. "What you make of it is up to you. Do you want to be the one who turned dance into a ward against the shadow storm, or the crone who let her pride break the circle?"

Har'shea walked from the kitchen to the foyer door, pulling it open roughly. Narus stepped through, and Har'shea slammed it. She hadn't even put down her bundle of food, still cradling it in the crook of her arm. She exhaled and walked back to the kitchen to put it down, placing her palms flat on the table and letting her shoulders sink in her stretch. Her head touched the table, her body oozing down and folding and refusing to stand for a while. She kept her eyes closed, not looking at the room, the food.

The future.

Taman.

Har'shea slid upward and walked around the table, leaving the kitchen. Her walking-robe fell to the side as she traveled down a hallway, listening for footfalls and thumps. It was much brighter here, glow-globes gathered and piled and hung haphazardly. The room was nearly forty by forty feet, the stone floor of the rest of the home transitioning to tightly wedged and placed plant boards, springy and sturdy. The room was filled with strange furniture designed not for sitting but for vaulting, rolling over, and springing from place to place.

A vata'an did just that, their milky skin stark even in the brightness. They moved with a languorous ease so counter to their youth, their pulled-back hair barely shifting except to drop as their head hung during a move. The cloth ribbon wrapped around them as part of the dance of middle circle did not flow and wave and snap but slouched as they twisted over an angled bench the height of a knee. Much of it was wrapped around their arms, a poor substitute for the twists and weaves of it through the limbs of the other dancers.

"What are you doing?" Har'shea grumbled, walking over to a table and lifting up a thin strip of wood.

"I'm breaking down the Roll to Light," Taman said. They were the color of fresh snow and moonlight, barely covered by a pair of short pants. Their skin glistened with the sweat of exertion and youth. They vibrated with nerves. "My examination is coming up."

"You don't need to 'break it down,'" Har'shea said. "You need to be able to do the moves, fully and as you feel them. You shouldn't even be here. You should be at the ballroom, watching the dance."

"I was helping at the Heartward," Taman said. "Soothing those who were shadow-struck"—referring to those who had seen too many horrors in their fight with darkfiends.

"Soothing?" Har'shea asked. "How soothing?"

"The Heart Shape," Taman said. "Least I can do to—"

Har'shea rapped the floor next to Taman's feet. They jumped, skittering away.

"You fool! Your magic is for the Shadow Storm Ward! It is to hold back the shadow, not to get some patient in a ward to mumble less!" Har'shea paced, taking up space as Taman shrank at their mentor's ire.

"I don't say this to you to be cruel," Har'shea softened her voice. "I say this to you because to take upon this duty is to live a mundane life. No arcana. No reading the minds of others, no lifting their spirits or swaying them, no use of your magics. All that we have, all that flows in us, must power the Shadow Storm Ward. Rewrap yourself and First Stance, please."

Taman stepped to First Stance next to one of the low tables: feet spread, leaning onto the right, ready to push off. They took the time to rewrap themself with the fabric; it would, in the dance, unfurl itself and then come back to the dancer.

"Begin."

Taman sprung left, placing a foot on the low table. In the dance, this would be someone's thigh they would push off of and land. Taman rose up and shuddered as Har'shea caught them across the back with the switch, Taman colliding with it rather than the switch hitting them.

"What are you doing, Taman?"

"First Stance to Climb the Pass," Taman said.

"Too slow, wrong position" Har'shea hissed. "Reset."

Taman reset to First Stance. First Stance to Climb the Pass. Climb the Pass to Slide with Shadow. Slide with Shadow to Lateral Reach to Ribbons Fall to another Climb the Pass to . . .

And every move, every step, every position not precise or

accurate or passionate enough, the switch was swung. It wasn't swung as punishment but in such a way that if Taman were not in the perfect position at the absolute right moment it would strike them somewhere. Strike it did, red cloth torn, white flesh marred. Always, the reset to First Stance, sweat mixing with blood, cloth soaked, positioning tables and steps slippery.

Snap. Reset. *Snap.* Reset. *Snap.* Reset.

Snap. Reset, again and again and again.

"Enough," Har'shea said.

"I need to practice," Taman said.

"Rest," Har'shea said. "Practice at the Hiathaeum next week. The practice chamber on the outside edge. You are off until then."

"I need to practice—"

"You will rest," she said. "You will take the week off, you will recover. Spend time with friends. Sleep. Anything but dance."

Taman fumed, throwing the swathes of their fabric wrap off and changing into other clothing. They didn't bother to wipe down, blood seeping through their undershirt. They threw on a smock and pants, pacing about and speaking into the air.

"But no magic," Taman growled. "And no dancing. Think about how I have to be ready to dance, what I have been training to do since I was a young child. Think about what I can actually do while you continue to stumble . . ."

Taman's mouth shrunk and their words trailed as Har'shea closed her eyes.

"You heard Narus and me speaking?" Har'shea said.

Taman nodded.

"And you think I am punishing you because you are going to take my place?"

Taman said nothing.

Har'shea waited in the silence, a full minute, before speaking.

"I'm not punishing you," she said. "I'm making sure you are ready. The shadow storms which rip around Mount Oritaun will tear our home apart without the actions of dozens of dancers. I wouldn't have taken you as a personal student unless I thought you could live this life as I do. But I may have been wrong."

"I will be ready," Taman protested.

"You aren't," Har'shea said. "You move too carefully. You take no risk when you dance. Every move is paper-perfect . . . but we do not dance on paper. We dance on boards, and stone, and on our feet. How many times did I strike you because you were not exactly where you needed to be, because you were worrying about where you should be?"

"I . . . I don't know."

"Enough that I know you are not risking anything," Har'shea said. "And that means the magic will not flow from you."

Taman slipped on shoes, eyes sunk to the floor. They didn't bother looking up, didn't bother to say goodbye. They left in a clumsy slouch, feet dragging, shoulders hanging, devoid of grace; all of Taman's grace was left on the practice floor, droplets of sweat and blood, a few yards of red cloth.

Har'shea sat on one of the low tables, her hands on her thighs, breathing in short huffs and feeling very old.

"It's the *taenil*," Har'shea said to Caelida, "which brings out the nutty flavor of this particular mushroom broth. Not as warm as I would like, but I wanted to bring some to you."

Caelida sat on a bench near one of the entrances to the Goiae-nium, sipping at the broth Har'shea had given her. She was silent, as always, while Har'shea talked and drank. Mostly, it was about the world which Was, Before the Shadow. Still, some of her own problems crept into the conversation.

"But they have so much talent and they don't understand it," Har'shea said as she sipped. "They . . . are me. Me, if only I had danced when I was twenty-three and not over two hundred years old. Me, only if I had not been dancing for hundreds of years. This week of dancing took so much out of me. I made so many mistakes. Few others knew, but I did. Taman is me, if only they took the necessary risks. And I don't know if they are ready to take my place."

Caelida put the cup down in her lap, empty. Har'shea sighed and took it, wiping it clean.

"I wish you got as much out of this as I did," Har'shea said. "Is there anything I can do to help you?"

Caelida said nothing, hunched and folded in her robes. Har'shea nodded. She knew she couldn't shape Caelida's heart, only feed her body, so she said goodbye. She needed to get to the Hiathaeum. She needed to make sure Taman was ready to . . .

Ready to take her place.

Every step through the mountain felt like the creaking of doors and the rubbing of floorboards. In her mind, her shoulders ground in their sockets, her knees buckled. She spun in circles in thought and her ankle shattered, and she choked herself on her own dance cloth. She climbed steps and imagined her tendons tearing. She opened doors and phantom memories of shooting, stabbing pain raced through her wrists. Her back throbbed and her shins screamed in her mind's eye. She had none of these pains at this moment, but they were all fears or memories of this past week, where she danced less and less and rested more and more.

Already in the practice chamber, Taman and others danced the middle circle's role in the Shadow Storm Ward. Da'ana, one of the vata'sha students looking to dance the Shadow Storm Ward, matched up with Taman often, the nature of the passing in the circle bringing them together as they unfurled their yards of cloth and twisted over each other. Others spun and turned and launched off each other: Orlen and Bashar, vata'an boys; She'mok, Launen, and Welso, their skin indigo like all the vatazin at this phase of the moon. There were others Har'shea did not know, in the circle and to the sides of the room. They must be Narus' students, she thought, or students of the other dancers; they were all so young.

Gennom, a vatazin boy, held a switch in the middle of the circle. He was not the best dancer, but he was strong-hearted and focused and picked up positioning well. He placed the switch with a snap in locations as the dancers moved in time with a cluttered assemblage of musicians to one side. Drummers and throat singers and zither-players played familiar tones as the circle expanded and contracted, ribbons flying in the air, dancers meeting and separating. Wherever the switch was, the dancers were not, Gennom's memory of the choreography matching the dancers.

She watched Taman, his grace and power . . . off? She watched the circle, she watched Gennom. She listened to the music. She shook her head, her hands balling up and squeezing tight. She went over her own little paragraph in her head, counting the steps; she used the story as a check for the ward, to see if it ended at the right time from what would be Taman's First Stance.

Seconds off. Har'shea finished her story in her head several seconds before Taman reached the point they were supposed to reach. Everyone was following Taman's lead and their pace, rather than the music or Gennom's positioning of the switch.

"No!" she said, "this is wrong! You are off! Taman does not set the pace! You!" she pointed at the musicians, "too slow!"

Har'shea burst through the circle and pulled the switch from Gennom's hand. He cowered as she stepped in the way. The other dancers scattered until she swung the switch and cut the air.

"First Stance," she said flatly, "off of Taman's position."

The young dancers trembled as they took their places—Taman first, then the others. Har'shea motioned to the musicians to play. The music rose. The dancers moved. The switch found Taman. No matter how perfect they thought they were, how precise their placement, how accurate their movement, the switch was snapped at them. White skin ran red, marked thighs and heels and shoulders and arms. The music did not stop, and neither did the placement of the switch; Har'shea knew the moves exactly, and the music was just so, so Taman was *wrong*.

"Stop, stop," Har'shea called off the musicians. She dropped the switch, rubbing her forehead, trying to find the words. "I'm sorry I failed you," she said, shaking her hands by her face. "I do not have the means or the words to make you take the risks you must take. I cannot make you commit. I can no longer teach you."

"But . . ." Taman trailed off.

"I am sure someone else will take you on as a student," Har'shea said. "Narus or Jolynu or Frevan. With my recommendation. But—" she paused, sighing "—I failed you. I'm sorry. I'm going home."

Har'shea walked away from the students, feeling the creak of old bones and tired flesh and exhausted soul.

Taman took two steps before sitting on the floor, ripping the cloth wraps off their body, burying their face in them and howling.

It was a week of staying in for Har'shea, whose body and heart and soul ached. She did little more than stretch and sleep. Her skin went ebony in time, as the waning moon does to all vatazin. Narus came to her home several times, pounding on the door, pleading with her, then going away dejected at the silence. Sometimes morning, sometimes evening, sometimes midday, the same result. It was the time deep in the night that finally provoked a response, Har'shea opening the door at knifepoint.

Gennom nearly fainted, stumbling back before catching himself.

"What foolishness is happening?" she hissed at him, clutching a dressing robe against herself.

"They're going to cripple themself!"

"Who?" Har'shea said.

"Taman . . ." Gennom didn't dare look up.

"What do you mean?"

"Solier is using a blade instead of a switch," Gennom said.

Har'shea curled her lip in a snarl, racing to dress in the dark.

"He was going on and on this week about how he has to risk it all to prove he can do it," Gennom said. "He is going to have—"

"I know what he is doing," Har'shea snarled. "Find my shoes!"

It was a secluded cave off the Goiaenium, a place the students made into a refuge from brutal training and stress. It was something the teachers knew about but ignored, giving students their own space and not even tracking where it would show up. In this incarnation of escape, the lights were colorful and bright, the hoarding of glow-globes flooding the chamber with brilliance. Garish cloth hung and swung from the ceiling. Here, they relaxed and paired and tripled off, and more, and drank strange brews— anything but danced.

Tonight, as Har'shea and Gennom shoved through a gathered crowd of students, a group readied to dance. It was the circle, the middle circle, everyone set to prepare for Taman's First Stance. In the middle of the circle stood Solier, holding not a switch but a rapier, his careful hand in the steel lace of the guard. To the side, musicians sat on furniture crammed and stacked to the stone walls, readying both heirloom and improvised instruments. The noise of stretching and tuning stopped when they realized who had arrived.

"So this is what my students do when I am asleep?" Har'shea said, nose to nose with Taman. "Risk their limbs, their lives?"

"I am not your student anymore!" Taman screamed.

"Some still are though," Har'shea said, motioning to the others, "and those that aren't, their teachers will certainly doubt if it was the right choice to take them on."

"You didn't doubt, though," Taman said. "Or did you, because you are here?"

"I don't know if you are ready," Har'shea said, "or if you will ever be, or if I am the right teacher for you even after all this time."

"I need to know," Taman said. "I need to know if I am good enough. And I can't do that with a switch striking me. It's all been too easy for me, these years. It comes to me like breathing. You said it yourself. 'Paper-perfect,' but no risk. Now, I'm risking it all. My legs, my arms . . . my body. If I am not in the right position, if I am too fast or too slow, Solier's blade will show us. And you will know if I am ready to take your place. If you will feel that the circle will stay unbroken if I am there instead of you."

Taman wiped their eyes. If it was from the lingering of sweat or tears . . . Har'shea knew too well.

"Reset to First Stance," Har'shea said.

Taman stepped to First Stance cautiously, rewrapping themself in cloth. Har'shea waved to the other students in the studio, beckoning them to take their positions in the middle circle. Each found their spot as needed to represent the never-ending dance, unbroken for centuries; each took a position to accommodate Taman starting in First Stance. Ribbons unfurled, dancers kneeled or leaned or twisted, all a frozen moment of the Shadow Storm Ward.

Solier took his place in the middle of the circle; Har'shea stopped him. Understanding, he handed her the rapier and stepped back into the onlookers. Har'shea stepped through the circle to the center, comfortable with the sword in her left hand. She looked to the dancers, to the watchers, then to the musicians, nodding for them to play.

A beat played on a barrel, a makeshift table. The zither strings sang out. A voice vibrated from deep in the throat of a young vatazin boy, pitch upon pitch soaking into cloth or bouncing off stone. It became not one but a half-dozen rumbles of rocks and splashes of water from an underground stream, joined by steps and stomps of the other dancers, snaps of cloth wrapping and unwrapping from them. First Stance to Climb the Pass. Climb the Pass to Slide with Shadow. Slide with Shadow to Lateral Reach to Ribbons Fall to another Climb the Pass to . . .

Through all this, Taman moved. They weren't paper-perfect now but threw themself forward and back like they were shaking free their soul. They fell and sprang off the other dancers, swapped spots and slid under legs and rolled over backs. They twisted and turned and recovered their cloth wrapping, as though it were a fight with the shadows that ripped around Mount Oritaun. Taman smiled, almost laughed, folding himself and growing large to the music; to the beat, which shook the floor and furniture and vata. And always, always, Har'shea's blade swiped and snapped just the barest distance away from where Taman should be. If Taman was too fast, or too slow, or out of position, the blade would find them and let them know they were not ready.

In the Hiathaeum, Har'shea danced. She snapped the cloth wrap, wove it among others, and reclaimed it. She pitched and leaned and sprung and turned, her skin a few days from its darkest ebony. The throat singers shook the hall with their voices, the strings and drums and wind instruments keeping measure for the three circle, the conductor keeping time. Many dancers spread along the walls, a sea of ebony interspaced with the jet of the vata'sha and the moonlight of the vata'an, to where there was no space to see the murals on the walls.

Har'shea raised her arms into an X.

Taman, uncut, unscarred, stepped forward. They found a spot to pass through the outer circle. They found a place next to Har'shea and pivoted, Har'shea stepping to where they were a moment before. It was a change in dancer like any other, except for the briefest brush of fingertips, the barest smile, the tiniest tear for both. Har'shea slid out from the middle circle to the outer, and then to the crowd. They applauded as Har'shea grabbed her walking robe and slipped into her shoes. They touched her, smiled at her, cheered for her last dance.

She turned and pointed to Taman and their first dance, their waxing moon.

The audience turned to Taman; Har'shea took the distraction as opportunity to leave. She had important tasks to attend to, like stopping at the market for food and then seeing if she could shape Caelida's heart and hold back the shadow, even for a little while.

FAITH & DEEDS

Rhiannon Louve

Tersha always felt a bit useless on palace duty. As a Rose Knight, she felt she should be doing more for Aldis than wandering around a beautiful, peaceful building that was, in her opinion, already adequately defended by the members of the Aldin Guard. But a certain number of Rose Knights were always assigned to palace duty, and this season that number included Tersha.

She'd learned tricks, both on her own and from various mentors, to keep herself alert regardless of the tedium of her assignment, which she used today as she paced her designated route through the halls. Rose Knights were responsible for patrolling much wider palace sections than the regular guards working those same chambers and halls, which made it much easier for Tersha to retain interest in her duties, but it also meant that it could take a full hour or more for her to complete one circuit of her patrol route.

She'd been assigned to this route for two months now, however, and though it was only predawn, the first half of her first circuit of the day, Tersha was already growing dangerously bored.

Then the palace alarm was raised. Tersha's first response was gratitude for the diversion. When she learned the alarm was due to something as ostensibly harmless as a simple theft, her second response was to decide that she didn't have to feel guilty for her first response. However, she took her responsibilities seriously, and hurried toward a section of palace not far outside her regular route.

Upon arrival, Tersha again reassessed her relative level of entertainment at the state of alarm, considering that perhaps she should feel guilty for her response after all. The scene into which she arrived was the tucked-away, camouflaged, near-secret chamber commonly known as the "Sovereign's Workshop," a well-appointed underground craftsroom built into a natural cavern beneath the Noble Assembly.

Not every sovereign used the Sovereign's Workshop for much of anything—Queen Jaellin, for example, was not known to frequent the place—but Varti the Builder had designed the little chamber for constructing models of her architectural projects, and King Lartik, after her, had used it for his experimentations with old kingdom artifacts. After those two alone, the name had stuck, and other sovereigns or their close loved ones had made use of it in the centuries since.

Considering some of the things that had been designed or experimented upon in this workshop, it wasn't a place one wanted something stolen from.

Tersha was the first Rose Knight on the scene. As soon as she arrived, the guard officer in command trotted up to her respectfully. Tersha was younger and less experienced, and was always a bit embarrassed by the general deference shown to Rose Knights everywhere she went.

"What's the situation, Gelem?" Tersha tried to offset her perceived status by memorizing the names of all the regular Aldin

Guard she encountered on her route, and treating them as equals. She wasn't sure it accomplished much, but at least they seemed flattered by it.

"We have guard in direct pursuit of the intruder," Gelem replied, "and two Rose Knights in other parts of the palace moving to intercept."

If that was the case, then what was Tersha's role here? "What's been stolen?"

"That's just it," Gelem replied. "We don't know yet. It's small enough to carry in one hand, and Reld over there saw a flash of what she thought was a leather case. Or wood. Brown, anyway. But it's still dark out, and a lot of the lamps haven't yet been lit. We've got guard looking for witnesses along the route, to see if we can get anything more useful, but . . ."

He didn't have to explain. Tersha wasn't much of a seer, but her greatest visionary skill was object-reading. "Do we know where it was taken from?" she asked.

Gelem nodded. "This way."

He brought her to an open compartment, large enough to house a helmet perhaps, or a boot. Nothing larger.

"A nearby noble was able to reach her Majesty psychically," Gelem said before Tersha could suggest it, "but she only confirmed that she never comes down here. She didn't know the compartment existed."

Nothing else for it then. With second sight, Tersha could see that the compartment had been long-imbued with arcana, perhaps to conceal itself, or to preserve its contents from the passage of time. Perhaps both, though as she examined the exterior design, she wasn't sure if it would have needed additional concealment, so flawlessly were its mechanisms and edges incorporated into the lines of the molding.

She ran her fingers along its surfaces, both interior and exterior, but nothing came to her of its own accord. Tersha sighed. Of course it wouldn't be that easy.

"I'll see if I can get an image," she told Gelem. He nodded stepped back, to give her space to work.

Taking a deep breath for focus, Tersha summoned arcane energies into her body, channeling them into her fingertips, her eyes and ears and other sensory organs, and into the nebulous cloud around her head that was how she visualized her own mind. Once this arcane pool was established, Tersha reached out to the compartment floor beyond her fingertips, drawing it and its surrounding walls into her field. Next, she pushed her pool backward through time, which was a process she herself didn't fully understand, despite a lifelong natural talent for it.

If she succeeded, her arcane flow would encounter sensations, memories, or strong emotions that had previously come in contact with whatever object she'd chosen to read.

Tersha felt as if she'd established a proper connection with the compartment interior, felt her arcana flowing exactly as it should, but . . . the attempt still failed. She sensed nothing, as far back as she could go. The thief, who supposedly had been here mere minutes ago, didn't register to her reading, perhaps due to arcane shielding of some kind. Further back than minutes there was just . . . darkness. And silence.

Tersha kept pushing, kept reaching, but nothing ever came. Finally, she found herself sagging against the wall, nearly out of breath.

Just as she ceased, she noticed a lingering scent in the air.

"Do you smell that?" she asked.

Gelem frowned and shook his head. "I only smell dust."

Tersha realized that she, too, had smelled only dust—prior to the start of her arcana. "Then I did get something, but it's not much. The thief smells like roses." The description felt off somehow. Tersha frowned, considering it further. The scent still lingered in her mind. "No, not roses. It's different. Not something I've smelled before. More cloying, and less . . . friendly."

She shook her head, feeling dizzy. Had the scent been on the thief or inside the compartment? Or both? No, now she was overthinking things. It was on the thief, she was sure.

She still didn't know what had been stolen.

"I don't think this chamber has been opened in generations," she said to Gelem, going on to explain the disappointing details of her reading. "I can't imagine how anyone even knew there was something here to steal, much less could figure out what it was."

Gelem frowned. "So, we still don't know what we're looking for, or how dangerous it might be."

Apologetically, Tersha nodded. "We just have to hope the other team catches the thief."

Some minutes later, after a short rest and another failed attempt at reading the burgled compartment, Tersha heard her immediate commander speaking within her mind.

Hirell has tracked our thief to a nearby residence. We're moving to surround it. Tersha, we need you on site to identify the object when it's recovered. Clear directions to the location followed.

I'm not the best person for this, Tersha replied over the psychic link. *I haven't gotten a thing from the compartment yet.*

You're the closest object reader available. Just do your best. You'll also have seniority among the Rose Knights on scene, so be prepared to take charge when you arrive.

The contact cut off, and Tersha could only accept her assigned fate. She relayed her information to Gelem, and jogged out along the route she'd been given.

The fight in the thief's lair was over before Tersha even got there. As soon as the literally underground hideout was appropriately surrounded, the Rose Knights on scene had decided on an overkill approach in recovering whatever had been stolen. After all, given the significance of a previously unknown, hidden compartment in the Sovereign's Workshop, whatever had been pilfered might need to be recovered before the thief had time to figure out how to use it.

The Knights had gone in with seven members, to catch what turned out to be only four people, all but unaware and barely armed. The four were arrested humanely. None claimed to be the original thief, but the Sovereign's criminal rehabilitation team would question them in more detail later. All four were disarmed, bound, and led away by five of the seven knights, after minimal fuss and no serious injuries. Tersha arrived just as they were leaving. All four looked like regular folk to her, but what did that mean, anyway? Turning toward the building, Tersha saw it to be one of the truly ancient surviving structures of the Old Kingdom, reinforced for stability through stone-shaping, and internally redesigned to divide the structure into multiple small, simple residences. Tersha had been directed toward the southernmost door, which stood open with two of the Aldin Guard beside it.

She gave them a casual salute as she went past, which they returned, allowing her to pass after appropriate protocols. Inside, Tersha saw an oddly narrow little home, hugging the building's outer wall. It wasn't uncommon for these redesigned ancient structures to be a bit unusual in layout. About halfway down the hall, she saw evidence of a hasty departure in the form of an abandoned, half-finished meal spread across a simple wooden table lined on each side by even simpler benches, one of which had fallen on its side.

Tersha felt some sympathy for these people. It seemed unlikely that they really wouldn't know about thieves hiding out in their own basement, but they might well not have known the specifics of the criminals' activities or plans. Tersha wondered if they numbered among those she'd seen arrested.

As she continued on down the hall, a Rose Knight she'd known for several years, a fellow human named Burin, approached from the open trapdoor to a lower level. He nodded toward the abandoned food.

"Those two were helpful at first," he said. "Total cooperation until we found the trapdoor. Then they tried to run. We'd probably have just taken their parole and let them go if they'd stuck to their story." He sighed. "Oh well."

Tersha didn't see what else could have been done, but she found herself all the more curious about the circumstances that had led them to live above a thief's safehouse. She kept her senses alert in case of unexpected visions, but all she got were flashes of recent fear, presumably from having Rose Knights track a criminal to one's home. She couldn't get anything earlier, or more detailed, not without looking deliberately.

She'd do that if she had to, but it tired her faster, so she would wait until she'd assessed the entire situation before prioritizing what to read first.

She couldn't shake that strange, not-roses scent, either. It clogged her mind, getting in the way of other insights. Had she read something once about a scent that was almost like roses?

Descending into the basement below, Tersha found what appeared to be an additional living area, scattered with bedding and small, ordinary-looking workspaces for knitting, spinning, and simple woodworking. Again, she felt fear from the objects here—fear of a habitual variety, like that of refugees hiding from oppression. Tersha couldn't see how such a circumstance could apply to any citizen of Aldis, but that scent demanded she remember. Was it something with arcane properties? She wondered what she would learn when she gathered the full report of those already on the scene.

Other than the two guards on the door above, only three Rose Knights were present, including Tersha and Burin, so it fell to them to search the lair and recover whatever had been stolen. Tersha approached the third knight for his report, recognizing Hirell. Her shoulders loosened in familiar comfort while her stomach fluttered girlishly. He didn't seem to notice her response to him, however, too busy examining what appeared to be a blank wall.

While Tersha debated whether or not to approach him for a greeting—in case, for example, he was engaged in psychic communication or some other arcane activity—Hirell made a motion with one hand, causing a loud click and the appearance of a door outline in the wall beyond him.

"There it is," he said happily.

Of course. He'd been hunting for a secret door—there were a lot of them in older buildings. Tersha sometimes suspected that stone-shapers occasionally went through fads wherein they competed with one another over who could make the secret-est secret passages.

"How did you know that was there?" she asked, partly to flatter Hirell. Finding hidden things was a bit of a specialty of his—without using arcana, no less!

He turned and grinned at her, with that distractingly-charming grin in his bronze-featured face. Tersha had sustained a mild crush on him for years.

"Hello, Tersha!" he greeted, and went back to work on the door, perhaps examining it for hidden dangers before opening it any farther. "I wish I could take credit for finding this one, but we caught the two downstairs in the act of closing it when we arrested them. They did get it closed, but I'd already seen enough—it was only a matter of finding the catch."

Well, Tersha was impressed with even that much, and once again questioned her own utility on this case. She'd gleaned precious little so far with her abilities.

A scent that was almost-but-not-quite-like-roses? What was the utility in that?

Hirell gave her his report as he checked the doorframe. He'd shadowed the thief to this location after the other teams had failed to detain her on palace grounds. Considering her too agile to catch by himself, he'd instead opted to follow her in secret to see what he could learn of her motives and circumstance. She'd suspected nothing and led him right here. His commander had remained in psychic contact, and backup surrounded the building almost as soon as he'd found it.

"Did you get a look at the stolen item?" Tersha asked.

Hirell shrugged. "Half a look. Might be wooden. Might be leather. I thought I saw a round part at the end, maybe like the end of a scroll-case? Could be anything, though."

With that, he seemed to decide the secret door was safe to open, and pulled it toward them. An acrid, smoky smell wafted out as the door swung wide.

And there, in its wake, came the not-rose scent. It was here in the room this time, not in Tersha's mind, she was sure. And she *had* read about a smell like this. Where? Tersha liked flowers, but she didn't remember reading about any rare ones recently. No, she felt like it was in a letter? Who did she know who would have written to her about a rare flower?

Tersha hoped she could get more context from beyond the open door.

The smaller, dim space was filled with shelves upon shelves of interesting objects and mysterious locked chests and boxes, along with a small library's worth of books and scrolls. Tersha groaned. If whatever had been stolen had been left in this room, then she and her two companions now had the task of rifling through absolutely everything in this chamber—not only to learn what had been taken but also to determine how much else in this hoard should or should not be confiscated as unlawfully gained booty.

Though, if this was a thief's long-term loot stash, it seemed an odd array of stolen property. Nothing leapt out to her as particularly valuable. Most of it wasn't even shiny.

Of course, Tersha thought with a shudder, if it was a hoard of arcane artifacts, perhaps it made sense that it wasn't shiny.

Hirell whistled at the sight, and Burin, coming up behind the two of them, grunted a similar sentiment.

"Why don't you check it out first, Tersha?" Hirell suggested with a teasing bow.

Tersha sighed. She hoped she would get more from this place than she'd gotten from the rest of the objects in this case so far.

But she didn't—not on the first pass, at least. It was always so disappointing when the visions failed to volunteer themselves. Spontaneous readings were so much less exhausting. After her initial, fruitless scan of the smoky-, dusty-, musty-smelling space, Tersha asked Hirell for some light.

An accomplished light-shaper, he summoned a cheerful globe

of illumination to hover above them, lighting the strange storage room in a way that felt weirdly incongruous with its contents. Tersha peered around her. Despite the place's various aromas, the shelves looked to be well-maintained. Everything was tidy, with like items largely grouped together and footstools tucked into corners, presumably to aid in reaching higher shelves.

"If none of those prisoners turn out to be the thief," said Burin, "we're looking at a room full of junk. The stolen property is long gone."

Tersha wouldn't have used the word "junk," but he made a good point. They didn't actually know that *any* of this was either stolen or related to their case.

"You all got in here pretty fast after I tracked this place down," replied Hirell. "I don't think anyone had a chance to escape. She really had no idea she'd been followed, and you heard the way they were arguing when we banged down the trapdoor. They thought they had time to wait for their leader to get back."

"Maybe *we* should have waited, too," Burin said. "Now we'll never know who the leader was."

"We couldn't risk it," Hirell countered. "We still don't know if what they stole was dangerous. Besides, are you even using your second sight? This room is *full* of arcana."

Right then, Tersha caught a visionary whiff of urgency, and of rushed activity from one of the cave-like room's still-shadowed corners.

"Both of you, look." She pointed to a tipped over brazier, possibly the source of the sooty smell. She bent and brushed her fingers over the pot's edge, and sounds and images flashed through her mind. They were vague and hurried, but she was able to piece them together. "Someone tried to burn this room while you were battering through the trapdoor." She heard raised voices. The two in the room hadn't agreed on the plan, which might have been why the brazier was knocked over before they got themselves caught with the secret door still open. "There's information in here they don't want us to find."

"What do you know, he's right," Burin said, followed by a brief awkward silence from both Hirell and himself. "*She*, sorry Tersh! I'm practicing I swear. I'm just . . ." He trailed off unhappily.

Tersha was snatched back to the present, inwardly crushed by this reminder that she still didn't look as feminine as she wanted to, despite her efforts. Perhaps she should seek flesh shaping after all. But she did trust that Burin meant well. It hadn't been that long yet, since she'd told her companions in the Order how she identified. "You'll get it," she said. Then, tiredly, regretting the loss of whatever information she might have gleaned without the unfortunate jolt to her concentration, she told the others, "Back to work. You two, start looking at books and boxes. I'll take a pass through the whole place, see if anything else jumps out at me."

Burin scrambled gratefully to his task, while Hirell managed to make Tersha feel slightly better with a playful wink on his way to his own pile of mysterious loot.

"Make a note of everything," Tersha reminded them both. "Even if it's not what we're looking for specifically; we need to check every item in here, in case we have to return it to a rightful owner."

"Got it," Burin said, overeager to please.

Of course, everyone forgot the entire incident upon Hirell's next words:

"Ow, listen to this!" he said. "First book I pick up: *A History of the Usurper Sovereigns and the Corruption of the Cursed Hart*. Yikes! Who are these people?"

"Let me see that," Burin demanded.

"Does it really say that?" Tersha felt scandalized.

"It really says that." Burin snatched the book from Hirell and stared at it. He was dumbfounded.

Tersha noticed something on the floor between Hirell and Burin. It must have fallen out of the book when it changed hands. She picked it up. It was a small sachet of herbs, smelling strongly of the not-rose scent. Belatedly, she scanned it for arcana and found lingering traces of some sort of enchantment. She showed it to her companions.

"Do you think they used this to make the book seem more . . . reasonable?" she asked.

"If so, we probably shouldn't touch it," Hirell said. "The arcana looks mostly used up, but better to be safe."

Tersha agreed. She should have checked it before touching it in the first place. She set it in its own pile and made a note of it. "Keep an eye out for more like it," she said. "and touch them as little as possible."

The others agreed and kept working.

"There's another one in this book," Hirell said, setting the new sachet with the first. "And the book is just as wild. I flipped to a random page and found, 'It was then that we came to understand the scepter's true nature.'" He read with mocking drama. "'For all who touch it, the foul artifact seeks to enchant them to its corrupted will. Those it masters, it labels as nobility, for these are the bewitched slaves who can be safely trusted to serve the Hart-beast's goals. Those of wills too strong for the scepter to bind, however, are cast aside as mere commoners, wrongly labeled as flawed and untrustworthy.'"

"That . . . is a truly terrifying passage." Tersha felt chilled.

"Sounds like horse shit to me," said Burin.

"Of course it's horse shit," Hirell agreed grimly. He snapped shut the book and scribbled in his investigation notebook.

Most Rose Knights assigned to the capital carried investigation notebooks these days—a useful new fad—with little charcoal pencils tucked into their leather bindings. Tersha's notebook had pink flowers embroidered on the cover, which were already smudged, *again*.

The more dangerous little book in Hirell's hand also had a beautiful cover, leather with *Harsh Truths* skillfully tooled amid a tangle of vines and spiderwebs. Someone had taken the time to artistically decorate the cover of a book full of this kind of—as her companions so indelicately put it—horse shit.

That was what made it dangerous. Someone *cared* about this book. "If people believe that, it undermines all authority in Aldis," she said. "It distorts reality as we know it, all the way to the foundations of who we are."

"If people believe it, maybe," Burin said. "But who would believe that tripe?"

Hirell, however, regarded Tersha with some of the mockery drained from his handsome face. "I hadn't considered it that way," he said. "It seems absurd to us, but to someone who *did* believe it, our dismissal would only strengthen the perception that the Scepter has misled us."

"We should catalog every last thing here," Tersha said. "We're going to have to go over it all in detail."

After delivering the four prisoners, the other Rose Knights involved in the case sent back a team of the Sovereign's finest, as well as clerks, scribes, and porters, which certainly made the subsequent cataloging go faster. Burin left to interview the residents of all the other homes in the building. Hirell remained in the loot room with Tersha, joined now by Uwynne, a bespectacled envoy and expert on criminal behavior.

They'd uncovered by now quite a pile of false histories, conspiracy accusations, and what appeared to be a stash of fake arcane artifacts in a locked box in one corner (enchanted to radiate arcana to those with second sight, and nothing else—a common scam). Many of the books and "histories" they opened were copies of one another, and each copy they uncovered proved older than the last, some dating back generations. Only the newest copies contained enchanted packets of herbs, but all such books were painstakingly cared for and kept in excellent condition, such that even the oldest scrolls were oiled to unroll without a single tear or crack in their parchment.

And then there were the truly strange items. They looked like survival gear for a brutal journey—eyewear and something like armor, as well as a sturdy but portable shelter, Uwynne thought, perhaps against sandstorms. All was well-worn and bore faint traces of skin-crawling corruption, as if they'd been carried through . . .

The Shadow Barrens? The thought seemed far-fetched, but it tugged at a memory Tersha couldn't quite recall. She left it to steep in the back of her mind.

She still hadn't begun deliberately reading the objects she touched. There were too many, and she'd be exhausted too quickly; however, hoping for visionary volunteers, as it were, had brought Tersha precious little. She'd learned what they already knew: the people caring for these books really *cared* for the books. They seemed to have been held in reverence. Even some of the fake artifacts spoke to Tersha of devotion and honor.

"This isn't a criminal organization," Uwynne declared fairly early in their process, based on what she'd seen and what Tersha had shared with her. "This is a religious sect. Look here." She showed a passage in another copy of the same *Harsh Truths* book Hirell had read from earlier. "They think they're preserving the will of the gods in face of a Shadow plot."

Tersha asked, "How can this be so old without us having heard of them before?"

"Oh gods," Hirell cut in. "This isn't the only chapter house. Look!"

The box he'd opened most recently had been from one of the upper shelves, and was not only locked but also trapped with a tiny dart. Fortunately, Hirell was skilled at both picking locks and disabling dangerous mechanisms. After setting the probably poisoned implement safely aside, he clicked open the lock so quickly it was as if he'd had a key. Though a major asset in urban reconnaissance, Tersha found herself pondering that if the man wasn't a Rose Knight, no one would trust him at all.

Which said something quite relevant to the very cult they were discovering. As Hirell showed Tersha and Uwynne the hand-drawn map he'd found, depicting what appeared to be several different "safehouses" and "knowledge shelters" throughout the city of Aldis, Tersha found herself considering Hirell.

He was handsome, charming, quiet as a cat when he moved, and could bypass every security measure she'd ever seen him encounter. He had basically every skill required for a world-class spy and assassin. So why did she trust him so much? Was it really just because she trusted the judgment of the Scepter?

She'd known Hirell for years, of course, and couldn't recall a time when he'd done anything she felt to be out of line, but then . . . take the current situation. Everyone had only Hirell's and one other tracker's word that the thief had come here. If they had lied, would it not be a terrible violation to arrest four people simply minding their own business in their own basement? Would it not be profoundly oppressive to be rifling through their things in such detail, without any evidence of a crime?

Tersha did believe Hirell and the other tracker. Many in the palace had seen the yellow-haired thief on her way out past the guards, and Tersha believed she really had come here. She also believed that this secret chamber they'd uncovered was full of dangerous misinformation and tools of chicanery. She believed they did have reason to arrest and question the four people they'd taken into custody, and that all four would be released unharmed if they turned out to be innocent. She believed that their property would be returned to them, save for any pieces that provably turned out to have been stolen, or were too dangerous to leave in the hands of common citizens.

She really believed that she and her companions were handling this odd situation as best they could. But why did she believe that? It had to be more than just the Scepter, hadn't it?

"How did these people get this crazy?" Uwynne asked, staring at the map of "knowledge shelters."

"You only think they're crazy because of the Scepter's hold on your mind," Hirell said.

Tersha glanced sharply at his expression, and saw the tight irony there. He didn't believe this nonsense either, but he saw, as she did, the depth and breadth of the implications.

How do we know that we are who we think we are?

"Ha ha, very funny," Uwynne said. "I'm serious, though. Where does this come from? That enchantment on the herbs is too small to make a regular person swallow all this poison."

Just then, an object Tersha had grabbed down from the shelf sang out to her of cruel, cackling malice—the first such feeling she'd had in the entire secret chamber. She looked down to see an ornate scroll case of polished silver in her hand. It radiated no arcana, but corruption seemed to drip from it, like it had been steeped in forces of Shadow for a long, long time. Its latch appeared too simple to be trapped, so Tersha—careful not to touch it with bare skin—slipped it open to find the oldest scroll she'd yet seen, this one damaged here and there despite obvious signs of painstaking care.

"That's foreign work on the scroll case," Hirell offered. "Southeastern Jarzoni, if I'm not mistaken, and very old."

Southeastern Jarzon was right on the border of the Shadow Barrens. Had it been brought back with whatever expedition had required the gear they'd found? Glancing between the case and the gear, Tersha thought the traces of corruption felt similar, even if those on the scroll case were much stronger. Perhaps it had lain hidden in the Barrens for a much longer time?

Tersha glanced over the scroll in her hands and saw it was a memoir, claiming to date all the way back to the death of Seltha, Aldis' first sovereign.

"'Great Seltha, in her wisdom,'" Tersha read with some surprise, "'knew that her heir could not be chosen in the conventional sense, by mere bloodline. It was always understood by her companions and her companions' companions, like myself, that her relatives were not to succeed her unless they proved themselves to be the best candidates for rulership. To lend weight to this contradiction of traditional assumptions, Seltha chose an heir from among her most trusted advisors and friends, someone with the strength, wisdom, objectivity, and moral courage to carry on her vision for Aldis.

"'That heir was my beloved mentor and dear friend, Rileb Sworddancer.'"

Tersha knew the name from legends, of course. Seltha had many companions, and as Tersha wasn't an avid history student, she tended to confuse which was which, but Rileb Sworddancer was not an unfamiliar name to her. Other than Seltha having chosen an heir before her death, there was nothing so far in the scroll that ran counter to anything Tersha had been taught.

But it went on.

"'No possible heir could have been better chosen, and the glory and righteousness of Aldis would have been assured under her reign, for she was, indeed, Seltha's equal in all but age and experience, and might even have one day surpassed our fair founder had she been permitted to fulfill the destiny Seltha chose for her.

"'Alas, the enemies of Aldis knew that the moment of Seltha's death would be their one opportunity to disrupt the rise of Aldis' sun, the light of which would by now have vanquished all Shadow from the face of the Earth, to the glory of the gods forever. When our sublime first sovereign breathed her last breath, they summoned a beautiful monstrosity to enchant and befuddle the people of Aldis. Contrary to what all the edited history books now say, this was the first appearance in Aldis of Shadow's loveliest messenger: the Golden Hart.

"'As gentle Rileb lay weeping at Seltha's side, this heretofore unknown being strode among Seltha's loved ones, seeking one whose will was weak and timid enough to be easily overpowered. Those watching were transfixed by the creature's beauty and suspected nothing of its hideous true nature. It stopped before Varti, a simple craftswoman with small children to protect, and easily broke her spirit to its own will. It marked her as its own, the brand of the usurper sovereigns, and as soon as it departed, Varti stood and moved to the Rose Scepter, still clutched in Seltha's dead hand.

"'The Rose Scepter was merely a sculpture then, a gift of love from the people of Aldis to their ruler, and its rose was an innocent pink, carved from simple quartz. When the bespelled Varti touched it, however, the corruption of Shadow ran down her limbs and into the scepter, tainting it to the deep blue color it remains to this day.

"'Varti then spread the lie for the first time—though the histories now wrongfully claim the words came from Seltha—that the scepter was enchanted to read the righteousness of one's soul, and thereby to sort the nobility from the commoners. She used the scepter on all present there at Seltha's side, and so great was their confusion, in this time of grief, that all succumbed to the scepter's foul sorcery, save for pure-hearted Rileb, who saw through the corruption being visited upon her companions and warned me not to touch the befouled artifact myself.

"'Rileb and I fled as best we could, but Varti knew the passages better than any of us, for she was the architect who had designed so much of the city. Within mere days, Varti and her followers tracked us down and surrounded us, and Rileb was slain in cold blood by those who were once among her dearest friends.

"'I escaped with my life due to Rileb's heroic battle prowess, and because she specifically asked me to do so. She begged me to find a way to record the truth of what had occurred, so that one day, the hold of Shadow on Aldis could be broken once more, and Seltha's glorious dreams could yet be achieved. Though grief has dogged my every step since that day, I have done as Rileb asked. All I can do is preserve the truth, and hope.'"

Tersha sat staring at the ancient scroll, unable to find words for the way the tale seemed to set her world spinning. She didn't believe it. She was sure that if she knew more about those historic events, she would be able to point out a million ways in which this version of history didn't make a lick of sense, but . . . The fact was, Tersha *didn't* know that history. She didn't have the arguments on the tip of her tongue. And she didn't know what to say in the face of this revision of everything that mattered about Aldis.

Before she could show it to Hirell and Uwynne, she received another psychic communication from back at the palace.

We can't hold these detainees much longer, came the crisp, oddly bluish thoughts of a senior Rose Knight named Vrenn. Something about the flavor of Vrenn's thoughts jogged a memory for Tersha, but she couldn't place it just yet.

Rehabilitation team can't find evidence of criminal behavior, Vrenn went on, *and the prisoners won't consent to mind delving.*

That last is disappointing, Tersha replied. *It's more suspicious that they tried to burn the contents of the secret room before we found it.*

But none of that is illegal, if it's all their own property, Vrenn reminded her, *and none of them matches witnesses' descriptions of the thief, anyway. Two were bearded men to begin with, but even the other two are a long shot. It's hard to mistake yellow gold hair, and we're not seeing an arcane disguise. Tell me you've found what was stolen.*

We still haven't, Tersha admitted, with some frustration. *Just more weird ramblings about this anti-Hart cult.*

That's so bizarre. Everything about this is bizarre. These prisoners are terrified of all of us, too, no matter what we do. It's surreal! Since when are Rose Knights scary? We're Rose Knights! *And that cult you're talking about . . . I mean, people are allowed to hate the Hart if they want, but . . . why?*

Tersha had no answers for her senior knight, but her memories coalesced and she suddenly found she had a question. *Vrenn, remember a few years back, when I was pestering you in your room while you were trying to study for a mission?* The reply came back, a wary affirmative. *Was that for that trip into Jarzon?*

Another affirmative.

Do you remember anything in your briefing that I might have seen over your shoulder, about something that smelled like roses, only not? The memory was clearing now, but Tersha knew that memory could be twisted by too much imagination. Was she taking this in the wrong direction?

I'm not sure, Vrenn said, *but I know where that briefing is filed. I'll check.*

Thanks, Tersha offered. She hoped she wasn't wasting his time. She gave a more detailed update, not that it helped her or Vrenn to better understand how any of this cult's beliefs would be plausible to the average Aldin citizen. Vrenn thanked her in a bewildered tone and cut communication.

Tersha turned back to her companions. "They don't think we've caught the thief yet," she said. "She wasn't among the four we brought in."

"That doesn't make any sense!" Hirell protested. "We got here too fast for her to slip by us. She has to be on the premises somewhere."

Footsteps on the stairs alerted them to Burin's return. "No one in the rest of the building knows anything," he said. "I got a strange feeling from the folk in the third home down, but nothing to connect them to any of this. The folk next door say a lot of strangers come and go at this end of the building, but they just thought their neighbors were particularly friendly, or were offering space in their residence to displaced people from outside the city." His face and tone made no effort whatsoever to disguise his bewilderment.

"I didn't get the wrong house," Hirell said. "This is definitely where the thief came, and we would have seen her leave."

Tersha hated that she'd been so useless throughout the process. She wished any other object-reader among the Rose Knights had been available in her stead—someone skilled enough, perhaps, to be able to soldier through deliberate reading after deliberate reading, not needing so many rest breaks or to rely on chance. After so many hours, Tersha honestly didn't know why she hadn't been removed from the project and replaced by someone more competent.

Just then, however, an assistant who'd begun to sweep up the soot around the upended brazier in the corner, said, "Oh! What's this?"

He held up a simple brown scroll-case, covered in soot and scorched at one end. It glowed faintly to Tersha's second sight, as if it had been recently affected by a minor enchantment. Squinting, it appeared to Tersha to be a harmless but improbably old arcane working, perhaps in the process of failing.

"I found it inside the brazier," said the assistant.

"Let me see it," Tersha said. She slipped the scroll of lies back into its silver case. Setting it in her lap, she reached for the other scroll.

As soon as the old leather of this scroll-case touched her hand, Tersha knew it hadn't been in this room long. A closer second-sight inspection told her that the fading enchantment on the object matched what she'd seen on the secret compartment in the Sovereign's Workshop. This time, Tersha decided a deliberate reading was worth the fatigue that would probably follow. Breathing deeply to focus her concentration, Tersha yet again gathered arcana, sculpting it in her mind and senses, then pushing it outward until it enveloped the object in her hand.

What can you tell me? she asked it with her mind.

A vision filled her closed eyes: an elderly vata'an with the pale sovereign's crest upon his brow, and kind, worried eyes. He placed a scroll into this leather case, and the case itself into the very compartment that had, just today, been robbed.

Swaying with the effort of her divination, Tersha announced, "This is what was stolen. It belonged to one of our sovereigns, a vata'an king."

"Rannath?" Hirell asked.

Tersha shook her head. Rannath was *laevvel*, sort of like herself, so she'd studied him a little. The man in her vision didn't look anything like Rannath's portraits.

"Wait, Lartik then?" Uwynne asked. "That's centuries ago!"

"The last scroll I read claimed to be that old as well." Tersha was glad she was sitting down, as the room continued to spin a moment longer. If she was going to be assigned to this sort of mission regularly, she would really have to get better at object-reading. It drained her too easily, every time. "This organization dates back almost to the founding of Aldis."

"I just learned in the journal I'm holding," Hirell said, waving a small, hand-bound, recent-looking volume, "that this particular 'knowledge shelter' doesn't have its own 'silencer,' so 'initiates' must visit another 'shelter' to have their 'tongues bound' upon initiation."

Tersha and Burin blinked at him.

Uwynne said, "You mean they're using some sort of arcana to *force* members to keep their secrets?"

Hirell shrugged. "It would explain how they've kept their mice under the floor so long."

Tersha shivered. "It also means this could be much, much bigger than we even imagine. If no one exposed to these ideas can speak of them, save to fellow initiates, there's no way of telling how far it's spread over the centuries."

"Well," Burin replied, "it also means it wouldn't be easy for them to spread their ideas or recruit."

"Still, they've had hundreds of years, apparently," Uwynne said. "What's our stolen treasure, Tersha? The arcana on it looks like a simple preservation enchantment, probably taxed to its limit by being set on fire. We'll need to re-preserve it soon, if it's something the queen wants to keep."

Good preservation enchantment, to have lasted this long. Then again, locked in that little compartment for centuries, the enchantment probably hadn't been tested much, until now.

"All I got from my reading was that there's a scroll inside, and who placed it in there," Tersha explained. "Should I open the scroll here or later?"

"It might give us context we need to decide how to handle the rest of this hoard," Hirell said. "This is such a weird case."

Tersha nodded and slipped open the remarkably new and supple leather of what had to be a nearly three hundred-year-old scroll-case. Inside was a similarly well-preserved scroll, a bit dry and crisp near where the fire had burned its leather container, but otherwise as pristine as if it had been penned yesterday.

In a graceful and tidily dexterous hand, the author did indeed identify himself as King Lartik, third sovereign of reborn Aldis. The scroll, as Tersha unrolled it, was a great deal longer than the last one she'd read.

"'On this 20th day of winter in the 35th year of the reborn Aldis, I, King Lartik, have chosen to pen an account of a tale I have promised to never tell anyone. I am uncertain that this is the right thing to do, as I was uncertain at the time I made it that my promise was the right promise to make. Nevertheless, as the chosen of the Hart to guide this land, I feel compelled to at least make a record of the truth, in case my tale should ever be needed by my people.

"It is my sincere hope that my fears are unfounded, and that none shall ever read these words. Should they be found by accident, I beg the reader to consider carefully what lies within before sharing its contents. It is truly not my story to share, but the women who could have told it rightfully are years dead now, and I worry that my dear friend's choice of silence was based too much on humility and too little on practical concerns, despite her ever-practical reputation.

"'Nevertheless, I would have trusted her judgment in this matter to my grave, had I not today experienced an encounter that chilled my blood in a way I have not felt since before Aldis' founding. Walking in a park with my great-grandson, I saw an old man watching me with what appeared to be open hostility. Neither I nor my rhy-bonded hawk, Lustre, recognized him, but that meant little. As a king, it is not impossible that I have simply made some decision with which he intensely disagreed. However, something made me wish to approach him, ask him what I had done to incur his ire.

"'I took a few steps toward him, but Lustre reminded me that, as king, I should probably inform my bodyguards before entering striking distance of someone who openly loathed me. I turned away to address the young warriors who'd accompanied my great-grandson and myself to the park. When I turned back, the man had already risen to leave, and was striding away with surprising vigor, soon to be out of sight.

"'It seemed undignified to pursue, and uncalled-for to send guards after him. All Aldins and even foreigners are welcome to glare at the sovereign as much as they like, after all. The last thing I wanted was to make a disgruntled citizen feel even worse. I suppose I could have asked Lustre to follow him instead, but a rhy-bonded creature can be used to threaten a sovereign as surely as any family member, so I chose not to risk him over an encounter that might have been nothing.

"'After the man was gone, however, his face stayed with me, ringing in my head until hours later, alone here in Varti's workshop, when I remembered who he reminded me of: a face from nearly twenty-five years ago, belonging to a man named Wesren. The two looked nothing alike, of course, but the expression on the man's face and a certain flavor of arcana in the air made me wish

I had questioned him after all. Twenty-five years is a long time to hold a grudge, but I found myself wondering if Wesren could be alive, and if the old man I saw could have been manipulated in his hatred by some sort of enchantment.

"'The notion sounds farfetched as I write it, but if the man I saw is in arcane contact with who I fear he may be, I certainly made a mistake in not sending guards after him. Wesren is a man who fell to Shadow long ago, who slew one of my dear friends before my eyes and has evaded capture all these years. Whatever arcana he might be working, from wherever he has been hiding all this time, I feel certain that it will harm Aldis somehow.

"'And so, I will go against Varti's wishes, just enough to record the truth, of what really happened when Rileb died.'"

Tersha fully intended to read further, but at that moment her mind was enveloped by the longest, clearest vision she had ever experienced.

Three Hundred Years Ago

Seltha was gone. It was hard to believe. She'd always seemed larger than life, and far too vibrant to be mortal. Lartik was older than most of her companions, old enough that Seltha had always seemed young to him. He'd lost friends before, and family, and he understood that he was just in shock, but even for him, the reality of the situation hadn't sunk in yet.

It was nearing sunset, mere hours after her death. Most of her closest companions, just over a dozen, had gathered together at Lartik's home, because for some reason his young husband Monti had invited them all. Lartik decided this must be some kind of debt he owed the universe for having accepted the gift of such a young and handsome husband. An older man, Lartik was sure, would have known better.

Then again, as Lartik gazed around at the other grieving faces huddled together or separately on every single chair, bench, stool, and sturdy crate his home could drag together, he saw how desperately they all needed one another right now.

Monti brought everyone hot tea, causing Lartik to wonder how they'd even acquired that many mugs. As his husband passed Lartik his own warm, steaming, ceramic container, and the wholesome smells within filled his nostrils, he met his beloved's eyes and saw the love, the worry, the sorrow, and . . . the intent.

You need them, too, Monti seemed to say.

Well, perhaps Lartik did. He wasn't as alone as some here. He had Monti and Tekti and the children, and Lustre dozing fitfully on his shoulder, but . . . none of them had known Seltha the way he had—the way some of these others had.

Perhaps there was a level on which he needed to be with people who truly *understood* what Aldis had lost in its Founding Sovereign.

"So . . ." Talani said. "What do we do?" She was one of Seltha's newest close companions, a young protégée of sorts. She wasn't in on all the secrets yet.

"She chose a successor, years and years ago," said Drell the sculptor, a man Lartik believed to be a former lover of Seltha's, and still one of her best friends. He looked as numb and disoriented as Lartik felt. Lartik hoped he had someone to hold tonight.

As for the successor, Lartik had known, of course. It had been only half serious, but not a terrible choice. He and everyone else in the know now looked across the room toward Rileb Sworddancer.

She was a pale woman, with skin like cream and hair like the purest golden honey. A cinnamon sprinkling of freckles dotted a divinely symmetrical and wide-eyed face. Tall and strong, with a rich, confident voice and—as her appellation implied—a dancer's grace in battle, Rileb had once been asked by Seltha to be prepared to carry on the dream of Aldis, in case of her own death.

The decision had been logical at the time. The budding nation's capital had lain under threat of constant bandit raids back then, before they'd built up the fortifications and population to discourage such things. Rileb was a natural commander, even as young as she was. People looked to her as a hero, almost as if she were Seltha herself. She spoke well in public and didn't flinch from the responsibility of leadership. Compared to her, most of Seltha's companions felt woefully underqualified.

Lartik had never quite agreed with Seltha's choice, though he'd never been able to articulate, even to Lustre, exactly what bothered him about the woman. Nor had he ever thought of someone who seemed better suited to the role.

Everything about Rileb screamed that she should be queen. Even to Seltha's companions, Rileb was like something out of legend. It seemed unthinkable that a person like her, acknowledged by the Blue Rose Scepter, could possibly bring anything but glory to Aldis.

And yet, Lartik disliked the thought of her following Seltha as sovereign. Perhaps he was simply tired. Perhaps he needed time to believe Seltha was . . . gone . . . before he could consider her successor. He gazed over at Rileb, pondering. Everyone else seemed to be doing the same.

She sat in a corner now, gazing solemnly out a window at the setting sun. Golden light painted her pale skin a warm yellow. She looked like a picture of dignified sorrow, grief. Lartik wondered if it made him a terrible person that the whole tableau looked false to him—too perfect to be real.

An odd scraping came at the door, and Lustre was suddenly awake. Tekti moved to answer what technically might have been a knock, but as the door opened, she fell back in wonder, golden light spilling over her features as well.

Everyone's gazes were dragged from Rileb to the door, where they saw the soft, sunset glow of the Golden Hart. Gasps sounded throughout the room, and tears began to flow freely.

The Hart's beauty was so different from Rileb's—so much more otherworldly, and at the same time so unquestionably real.

No one had seen the Hart since the day, nearly a decade gone, when it had come to bless the reign of Queen Seltha, first sovereign of the reborn Aldis. Lartik, and many others he knew, had believed that appearance to be a final miracle of the end of the rebellion, a divine blessing that would never be seen again.

But now the Golden Hart stepped into Lartik's home, its softly-glowing hooves tapping gently on Lartik's floors. Like for many others here, it seemed, the Hart's presence made suddenly, terribly real the loss of their beloved Seltha, and most of the faces—Lartik's included—were soon wet with rivers of clean, natural grief.

Had the Hart come to comfort them? To honor Seltha and share in their grief? That seemed unlikely. People lost loved ones to the ravages of mortality every day. There was no reason the Golden Hart should need to appear just to help them engage in something as natural as mourning a departed friend.

It had a reason for visiting.

Everyone watched it as it stepped silently though the room. An odd anticipation grew within Lartik as he followed its movements with his eyes. He remembered the day it had touched Seltha's brow with its antler. He remembered the sober peace that had suffused Seltha's face, as if that one touch had filled her with both a terrible burden of responsibility and, at the same moment, an unshakable understanding that she could rise to meet the tasks she had been set.

A thought occurred to him: Had the Hart come to do the same for the next sovereign? Was it here to bless Rileb as it had blessed Seltha? Its trajectory through Lartik's crowded front room could well be taking it toward Rileb's corner.

Lartik saw others glancing in Rileb's direction as well, clearly leaping to the same conclusion. After all, they had only seen the Hart upon that one occasion in the past. No one had context to know what else the holy creature's presence might mean.

Rileb stared at the Hart with what appeared to be genuine confusion, and perhaps a touch of fear.

Lartik decided he liked her better if she understood the reality of leadership enough to be afraid right now. He still had his doubts, but if the Hart were to bless her . . . well, perhaps that blessing alone could make up for whatever subtle lack Lartik had sensed in Rileb's heart.

Except that didn't happen. Before the Hart ever reached Rileb's corner, it stopped at the stool of the very last person in the room Lartik would have expected.

Little Varti was as dark of skin as Rileb was pale, her cloud of fluffy black hair cropped practically short, but these differences of painter's palette had nothing to do with the ways the two women were nothing alike. Where Rileb was improbably beautiful, Varti was pleasantly ordinary. Where Rileb was tall and stately, Varti was short and plumpish. Where Rileb shone with the solitary authority and the confidence of a natural-born queen, Varti was a shy and bookish mother of three, as normal as leaves falling in autumn.

Everyone stared as the Hart bowed its head before little Varti, brushing her brow with its antler. The crescent mark appeared where it had touched, just as it had nine years ago on Seltha's brow, though it stood out more against Varti's dark skin.

The Hart raised its head and looked at her with such compassion. Lartik looked at her as well. He'd always liked Varti. They had much in common, the two of them: both quiet craftspeople, doting parents. These days, they'd even started sharing childcare between their two families. Unlike Lartik, however, Varti had never seemed at home out on the road, adventuring with Seltha. He'd never been entirely certain why she did it.

Oh, the little architect was a great deal stronger than she looked, a tireless worker and honestly not bad in a fight. Her arcane abilities were top notch as well, if focused in only a few areas. She'd always been an asset to the team, especially in constructing fortifications and other defenses. Varti understood how materials worked—wood, stone, and metal in all their varieties—and how to combine them together in the most practical ways possible.

Seltha had commissioned Varti to build . . . well, most of the city, once they'd grown stable enough to entertain such plans. When granted the freedom to craft permanent, beautiful structures, Varti had proven to be something of an artist as well as a craftswoman. She was quite religious, too, Lartik recalled. And innocent. Lartik, much older than most of those here, had long seen Varti as almost a kind of niece.

The Hart . . . didn't intend to make her queen, did it?

Judging by the look on Varti's face as the Golden Hart regarded her, however, Lartik began to believe that the creature intended to do exactly that.

Varti looked terrified, but determined and brave. Lartik had seen that look on her face before, on the eve of battle. He thought now that he would feel similarly if the Hart told him he had to pick up where Seltha had left off.

"I understand." For all the fear in Varti's eyes, her voice was steady. "I will do my best."

Apparently satisfied, the Hart turned and tip-tapped its way back to the still-open front door, leaping into a run as soon as it was outside.

It had never even looked at Rileb.

Everyone turned to stare at Varti again. She stared back, her expression stunned.

"It chose you." Drell wasn't asking a question. He sounded certain. Where he was seated, the Hart's pathway through the room had been very narrow. Lartik wondered if the holy deer had brushed him in passing.

Varti nodded mutely. Lartik thought he could see, on her face, her desperation to flee his home, hurry back to her three young children and her father who lived with her. Lartik didn't blame her for such a response, and he admired her force of will as he watched her steel herself to remain.

"I have no desire to go against Seltha's wishes," Varti said. "Or against the wishes of my companions here, or the people of Aldis." She did not sound as shy as Lartik knew her to be. Varti never did when she spoke. Her tone was soft but clear, and unhesitating. "But the Hart has told me that I am chosen to rule." It was the voice of an architect and builder, not a queen, not exactly. But she did sound more competent to lead than Lartik knew she must feel.

Indeed, though she would never have occurred to him as a candidate to succeed Seltha's rule, now that he considered her, he found he could think of no reason to protest the choice. She was ordinary, yes, unlikely to be hero-worshiped or romanticized, as Seltha was, as someone like Rileb would surely be, but Varti was solid. She would keep things together and get things done.

Lartik checked the faces of their other companions, to see most of them grown thoughtful, glancing back and forth between Varti and Rileb.

"Why would the Hart pose us this dilemma," asked Gerrol, a vata'sha adept and refugee to Aldis, who had made his way into Seltha's inner circle through use of his cool head, far-reaching perspective, and constant compassionate public action (required, he claimed, by his ethic of rational objectivity). "If Seltha had selected no heir, I would understand the Hart's visitation, in order to prevent wasteful conflict between Scepter-sponsored nobles. But why would the Golden Hart risk *creating* such conflict? What message are we to take from this act?"

Everyone looked to Rileb, who, as always, looked perfect. Her expression was schooled to a carefully unreadable dignity, and Lartik could see that she knew she could not possibly win this argument by appearing hungry for power. Indeed, were she to abdicate to Varti, without question or protest, it would have improved Lartik's sense of her considerably. He couldn't be the only person in this room who felt that way.

Pondering her in this moment, her dignity and her silence, made Lartik realize one of the reasons he'd long questioned her fitness for rulership. They weren't here tonight, because Monti had the sense not to invite them, but Rileb was constantly surrounded by . . . people Lartik could only think of as sycophants. There were two or three of them who followed her around like puppies, Lartik thought, but one in particular who had always disturbed him—a slimy little toady.

Lartik believed in being kind to everyone, even slimy little toadies, but sometimes he suspected that Rileb didn't just compassionately tolerate the man's presence. Sometimes she seemed to actively enjoy his company. Lartik wasn't sure if he judged the man too harshly—after all, Lartik didn't even know him well enough to remember his name—but the old vata'an had never thought it spoke well of Rileb to have a friend like that.

And if he'd been here with her—praise be to Monti that he wasn't—Rileb wouldn't have needed to look power-hungry to get any point across. She could have sat silent and let her toady protest for her, and then looked humble when she gently shushed him . . . *after* he'd said everything she wanted the group to hear.

Was Rileb that calculating a person? Lartik wondered how would she handle this moment, without her little gaggle of followers to cheer her on.

"I'm sure the Hart does have a reason, and a good one," Rileb said, "but we should certainly not be hasty in leaping to conclusions about what it might be. The choice of leadership is a task at which most nations fail, leading to downfall or oppression for nearly every group of people in history. The Hart challenges us to choose wisely, and to set a precedent that will serve Aldis for generations to come."

Listening to Rileb speak was, as always, a joy. Her voice was honey-rich, soothing in cadence and musical in tone, and her vocal and facial expression, combined with her bearing, made every word both interesting and inherently reasonable.

"We cannot assume," she went on, "that a miracle will come to us in the flesh every time one of our sovereigns is laid to rest. Nor can we assume that every sovereign will be given the opportunity to name an appropriate successor. We are presented with two options, neither of which is sufficient on its own to lay our future's foundations. Let us discuss where we go from here."

"The Hart *will* come to us every time," said Dari, a respected healer and another companion seated near the middle of the room, where the Hart might well have brushed her physically on its way to Varti. "It told us this. We can rely on this method of choosing."

Dari was perhaps the most trustworthy person Lartik knew. When Drell and—humbly—Varti nodded their agreement to Dari's claim, there was no mistake that the Hart had spoken to them all. Two other companions touched by the Hart in passing murmured agreement as well.

Rileb frowned slightly but didn't speak. Korrel, sitting closest to her, near the corner, said, "That doesn't mean our job is blind faith, or that Seltha's wishes should be thrown out without due consideration. I see no harm in Rileb's suggestion that we formalize a decision-making process."

"Yes!" said Fresta, a known skeptic of the idea that gods had any reason to mean ordinary people well, or that worshiping and revering them was of meaningful use. "Even if we accept the Hart's choice as an interim sovereign, while we deliberate, that doesn't require us to invest her permanently with a sovereign's rights and responsibilities. The Hart could be letting us know that it will always arrive to grant us the stability we need to make a proper decision regarding the next sovereign, however long that may take us. For such an endeavor, I can think of no one better than Varti, after all. She'll keep us together while we work this out, am I wrong?"

Varti frowned, clearly troubled, but she did signal her agreement. "I don't think we should distress ourselves with this question today. We've lost something none of us can ever replace. We need time to feel before we force ourselves to think."

Much of the room murmured approval. Lartik spoke up: "But to be clear, we agree on Varti as the interim sovereign until a final decision can be made. Can I get ayes and nays to make sure?" This room didn't represent a full quorum of Aldis' scepter-acknowledged nobles, so their decision wasn't necessarily legally binding, but Lartik still felt like a clearly stated temporary agreement would be helpful, at least until a full quorum could be assembled.

Lartik heard a chorus of ayes (including Lustre's) and no nays, but it did not escape his notice that several in the room remained silent, including Rileb.

"Sovereign Varti," Lartik said, "before everyone leaves tonight, will you give us all tasks to smooth this period of transition, as best you can on short notice?"

Varti was deeply involved, Lartik knew, in many inner councils. She had a wider breadth of practical knowledge about the current state of Aldis than nearly anyone else, maybe even including Seltha herself. Varti was just one of those people who quietly made happen the things that needed to happen.

People like that are usually secretaries and assistants, Lartik thought. *They rarely get put in charge.*

That's the problem with everything everywhere, Lustre replied in Lartik's mind.

The more Lartik pondered the idea, the more he agreed.

He wondered what Rileb would do next.

At the end of the evening, Varti had made simple, practical requests of each of the guests as they left, all of it well within each person's normal talents and responsibilities, but all of them the sorts of things that can tend to be forgotten in crises. She stayed far longer than Lartik was sure she'd wanted to, to make sure she spoke to everyone, and to make sure she did so privately so as not to co-opt this gathering of grieving friends by turning it into a political meeting.

Varti also took time to care for everyone emotionally, sharing her own grief with each weeping friend, the warmest companion one could hope for.

Lartik couldn't imagine where she found the strength. *Thank all the forces of life itself that the Hart knew better than to pick me*, he thought.

Lustre laughed inside his mind. *You're stronger than you think.*

Lartik supposed that was probably true for everyone here, but he remained grateful to be watching Varti exhaust herself instead of the other way around. Though most of Seltha's companions sought Varti's advice and coordination before taking their leave of Lartik's home that evening, Lartik noticed that Rileb almost managed to slip out the door without speaking to the interim sovereign.

Varti caught her near the door. Lartik was in no position to eavesdrop on what they said, but he found himself struck by the image of the tall and stately warrior staring down her perfect hero's nose at the shorter, rounder, plainer woman.

Everything about Rileb's posture and expression was dignified and calm—difficult to read, yes, but in no way deserving of reproach. She still looked like a queen. Varti's posture was diplomatically humble and warm, companionable and ordinary, equally beyond reproach and yet . . . something about that image, of the two of them side by side, convinced Lartik completely: Varti was his queen. She was not in any way queenly, and it made her somehow perfect beyond words.

Rileb left moments later, followed soon after by several other guests. Once they were gone, a tension Lartik had barely noticed seemed to dissolve from the room, and what remained of the gathering turned to fond tales of the old days, interspersed by tears and comfort from loved ones.

It was hours before the other guests departed and only Varti remained, having stepped up to help Monti and Tekti with hosting—more effectively, Lartik noted, than he himself was managing in his own home.

When the house was quiet again, Varti turned to Lartik. Without a word, both of them slumped into two of his comfier chairs. Lustre—in part out of sympathy and in part to tease Lartik—landed on the arm of Varti's chair, and bowed his head to have his neck-feathers ruffled. Varti obliged with a grateful smile, having always got on well with Lustre.

Monti and Tekti brought the kids in from the back to say good night (those who weren't already too old for such things, of course, his children from his first marriage already adventurers in their own right). Lartik gratefully gave the required kisses to his little ones, and smiled as some—those the same age as Varti's two youngest—hugged Varti good night as well, calling her "auntie." Apparently, their childcare-sharing system was working out well enough, in the children's minds at least.

Once the little ones had been herded off to their bedrooms, Tekti checked in silently with their spousal signal code: *You want me to politely kick her out?* Lartik declined the offer. As tired of social interaction as he was, he knew Varti wanted to go home to her family even worse. She wouldn't have stayed if this wasn't important.

Tekti's next signal: *You two need privacy?* It was usually used to ask if one partner or another wanted romantic time with a new lover, but by the look on Tekti's face, Lartik knew she didn't mistake his relationship with Varti that way. She just wanted to know if this was official business. Lartik nodded, and trusted Tekti and Monti to make sure no one overheard whatever would be said next between himself and the interim sovereign.

When he turned back to Varti, she was ruffling Lustre's neck-feathers again. "You'll spoil him," Lartik said.

Don't ruin this for me, said Lustre, in his mind.

"He deserves to be spoiled," Varti replied.

See.

Lartik laughed. Then silence fell again—long and awkward this time. Lustre eventually hopped away to his favorite perch in one corner, sharpened his beak for a minute or so, and then fell asleep. It was quite late for him.

Finally, Lartik broke the silence. "Queen Varti, eh? Unexpected."

"It's stupid. Why me?" She shook her head. "But it was clear as the summer sky in my head. The Hart didn't ask me to look after things while we make a decision. It bid me to rule. Rule!"

"I think you're the only one who can," Lartik said, surprising himself but still meaning every word. "The Hart chose wisely."

Varti narrowed her deep, brown eyes at him. He could tell she wasn't sure if he was making fun of her. He tried to show his sincerity but wasn't sure if he succeeded.

Varti frowned and looked away. "I'm just an architect," she said. "I'm not a hero."

"I don't think Aldis needs another hero right now." Lartik realized the profound truth of it as he said it. "No one can replace Seltha, and it would be hubris to try—an insult to her legacy. What we need is not a would-be Seltha the Second but someone completely different, still fit to rule. You're perfect."

"And if everyone else disagrees with you? If they decide to crown Rileb instead?" Varti asked. "I don't want a fight over this. I don't want to dishonor Seltha's memory by sowing bitterness and conflict between her dearest friends."

"Rileb shouldn't want that either," Lartik said. "If she's willing to fight over this, it just shows she's not fit to rule—not in a place like Aldis."

"So, cowardice in the face of conflict is a queenly trait now?" Varti was only half-serious, but Lartik took that half to task.

"It is reactionary violence and needless war that are acts of cowardice, as well you know," he said. "Remaining calm and compassionate in the face of a cruel world takes true courage."

Varti bowed her head. "I know. I just . . ." She fell silent for a long while, and when she looked up again her face was wet with tears. "I don't want to do this, Lartik. My babes hardly see me as is! I have so many projects underway, and there's so much to coordinate, and the last thing I want is to be in *charge* of it all."

Lartik wouldn't want that either. He didn't know what to say, so he just lay a hand on her arm in sympathy.

Varti covered her leaking eyes with her other work-callused hand. "I wish Seltha were here," she said. "She'd know what to do."

"She would listen to the Hart," Lartik said. "Rileb may have been what we needed when Seltha chose her, but our departed sovereign would choose someone different now, I'm sure. Aldis' needs have changed."

"You really think I can do this?"

"Not only that, but we'll make sure you still get time with your little ones, too."

Varti let out a tiny moan and clutched Lartik's hand with her own tear-wet grip. Lartik found himself weeping, too. Seltha was gone. It felt to Lartik as if the brightest star in the sky had suddenly winked out.

It was too soon for them to be thinking about these things. It was too soon for anything but grief. And yet.

Aldis needed them. Seltha's nation—a nation of peace and justice for all people—couldn't run itself. Not yet. Their grief was not as important as providing stability to Seltha's people.

"It should have chosen you," Varti said. "You're much wiser than me."

Lartik laughed, but felt alarmed at the very thought. "I'm far too old," he said, waving the idea away with some vigor.

"I know you better than that." Varti's grin soon melted, however, and she stared thoughtfully into the distance past Lartik's shoulder. She sighed one last time. "I'll do my best. Thank you, Lartik. I don't know what I'd do without you."

"Papa, is this yours?" Varna asked. She held up a clever contraption Lartik recognized. He'd made it, but it wasn't his. He took it from his daughter's hands and shook his head. "It's Auntie Varti's. She sat in that chair the night . . ." The night of Seltha's death. "The night everyone came over." He tried to hide the tremor in his voice. It had only been a few days. Of course it was normal to still be mourning the loss of so great a hero and friend as Seltha. Lartik was simply tired of feeling sad. He wanted a break from it, for a few hours at least. "Varti must have dropped it. She'd been meaning to bring it over for repairs."

Lartik looked over the little device. It was designed to hold a common charcoal pencil and had delicate moving parts that could be arranged to help one draw a short length of straight line, any angle of one's choice, or a small perfect circle with only a few quick adjustments. Lartik had invented it after watching Varti work on her architectural drawings. Now she used it so often she'd worn out one of the joints on the mechanism.

In Lartik's grief for the loss of one friend, it meant more to him than usual to have been able to give so useful a gift to another. To his great annoyance, he found himself forced to once again brush away tears in front of his children.

They understood, of course. They missed Seltha, too.

Lartik slipped the contraption back into his pocket and went to breakfast with his family. Afterward, he went down to his corner of the cellar, summoned a light, and went to work on the little drawing tool, replacing one of its tiny hinges with a new one, and bolting a tiny splint to the piece. He fiddled with it until satisfied and slipped it back into his pocket.

Returning upstairs, Lartik encountered Monti, who graced him with a sweet and spousely kiss. "Back to the adepts' guild today?" he asked.

"No, they've moved on to smooth running without me, I think" Lartik said. "My next job is the artisans, but first I need to find Varti and return something she left here."

"Oh good!" Monti said, giving Lartik a squeeze. "You've been wanting an excuse to check in on our interim sovereign."

Lartik glanced sharply at his young husband. How had Monti known that?

Monti's grin told him not to ask. Lartik's spouses knew him too well. Reesto and Krin had been like that, too, before they'd died.

Protecting Seltha.

Who was also now gone.

In yet another surge of inconvenient emotion, Lartik found himself leaning forward to kiss Monti more passionately than was typical for late morning in the middle of the front hall. Monti returned the kiss, but not without some surprise. When Lartik pulled away, he felt Monti searching his face with a, "Really? Now?" sort of expression.

Lartik gave him a regretful smile. No, he had things to do. He just . . . "I'm so grateful you exist, Monti. You, and Tekti, and the children . . . Thank you."

The words seemed to leave Monti speechless, though he did squeak out a, "Have a good day!" as Lartik took his leave.

It was some time before Lartik managed to locate Varti. When he asked after her whereabouts, it quickly began to seem that she was everywhere at once, single-handedly holding the kingdom together. Finally, with Lustre's help, Lartik heard that interim-sovereign Varti was scheduled to have some time for lunch between a meeting with foreign diplomats and a meeting with Seltha's minister of finance, whom Varti seemed likely to retain for her own advisors council as well.

Lartik considered the locations of the two meetings, as well as the location of the palace kitchens, and chose a nice alcove to wait in on what he predicted to be Varti's route, where he thought he himself would want to stop for lunch, if it were him. It was a sheltered little atrium full of flowering vines, comfortable benches, and a truly elegant series of petal-like arches—some of Varti's loveliest work on the palace design. The whole atrium was, of course, shaped like a rose.

Lartik asked someone from the kitchens to bring him a pair of sandwiches and cups of iced tea, as well as water and strips of meat for Lustre, and he sat himself down with a nice angle to contemplate a shaft of sunlight gleaming down from above, and the way it caressed the leaves of the currently blossomless vines. Lustre quickly finished off his lunch and began to bathe with what remained of his dish of water, ever mindful of the state of his every feather.

I just realized, Lartik told his friend, *I haven't directly asked you. What's your stance on this sovereign question? You've been helping me help Varti, but . . .*

It's not even a question, Lustre replied, without pausing his grooming. *It won't be for most rhydan. The Golden Hart made a decision. I trust that, even if Varti wasn't already my friend. We rhydan understand the Hart better than other people, I think. It speaks for all of us, sometimes in ways we don't even realize at the time.*

Lartik found himself surprised by this perspective, but strangely comforted by it as well. He was glad he'd asked.

Sandwiches and tea untouched, Lartik fell then into something of a reverie, watching Lustre preen himself in the pretty little space, until they both heard footsteps approaching. Three or four pair, Lartik thought. He didn't have a good angle from where he sat to know if one of the people coming was Varti, but before he could stand to find a better vantage, he heard Rileb's voice, echoing among the arches.

"This is dragging on too long," she said softly. "It's hurting Aldis, and you know it. The people deserve a proper coronation ceremony. They need to know who to look to for long-term decisions." Her tone was calm, utterly reasonable, but Lartik imagined he heard a thread of irritation hidden underneath.

"What exactly are you asking me to do about it?" Varti sounded tired, pained.

"As if you don't know what you could do about it," said a third voice, low and masculine, purring and oddly reasonable. Lartik found it both strangely charming and condescending.

This must be that toady, he thought.

Oh yes, confirmed Lustre, who never mistook a voice. Post-preening, Lustre's feathers were—as always—perfect. *He doesn't like animals,* the rhy-hawk added.

Where did you hear that?

Lustre regarded him steadily. *I just know.*

"What I could do about it is no different from what Rileb here could do," Varti said. "You know as well as we do why we don't. She's trying to honor Seltha's memory, and I'm trying to honor the Golden Hart. Don't pretend this is simple."

Lartik feared that this interpretation of Rileb's motives might be unrealistically generous, but he liked Varti better for giving their friend the benefit of the doubt.

"We already have the explanation as to why the Hart did this," the toady insisted. "Korrel and Fresta hit upon it the first night, from what I was told. Are we to assume now that the Hart was wrong in choosing you as interim sovereign? Are you prepared to threaten the very stability we all believed you to have been selected to uphold?"

"You go too far, Wesren," Rileb said, though she didn't sound displeased to Lartik's ears. "We are all grieving a great leader. It's understandable that this decision is taking time. But, really, Varti, we can't let it continue much longer. You see that, don't you?"

"The last I heard," Varti said, "we planned to convene the Noble Assembly next week to ratify a final decision. So long as everything remains organized in the meantime, I don't think less than two weeks is too long to make the people wait. They're mourning Seltha, too."

"You can't possibly believe that everything will be neatly formalized and packaged with a bow after one meeting," Wesren declared. "If we let it come to that meeting at all, we're looking at months of drawn-out arguments—or worse."

"The entire deliberating body will be nobles acclaimed by the Blue Rose Scepter," Varti said. "I think we can trust that we will all be prioritizing the needs of Aldis' people."

"And you would risk creating lasting rifts in such a group? Why has ruling Aldis suddenly become so important to you?" Wesren asked.

Are you sure you want to just sit here and listen? Lustre asked inside Lartik's head.

Lartik remembered where he was. He stood and brushed himself off, gathering up the food he'd brought for his luncheon with Varti.

"I don't want to rule," he heard Varti say. "I'm busy. But the Hart has called me, and I will not ignore my people's need. But what I want to know is, why aren't you asking the same questions of Rileb here? She has every bit as much power as I do to end the debate before it starts."

"We all do what we feel we must for the good of Aldis," Rileb said. "I only hope that we are all truly keeping the Aldin people forefront in our hearts."

"Exactly," Wesren said. "I'm very concerned about what's going to happen to Aldis' future if this debate turns the way I fear it may."

Lartik stepped out where the other three could see him, Lustre flapping up to land on his shoulder. As soon as everyone had turned to look at him, he said, "It sounds to me like you know you don't have much support among the nobility, Rileb. The Hart's arguments are persuasive, as it turns out. Here's your lunch, Varti. Where did you want to sit and eat?"

He handed the interim sovereign her sandwich and tea, and steered her away from the other two as if they were irrelevant.

If Rileb ended up queen, such an undiplomatic action would probably cost Lartik, but . . . well, it was done now, and he didn't feel like he'd erred in breaking up the tension between the two women and this "Wesren."

Varti accepted both the lunch and the offered escape with gratitude. "This way," she said. "I'll show you one of the recently completed gardens."

About an hour before sunset that same night, Lartik found himself with three of his closest friends, waiting at the top of a hill, just outside the city limits.

Lunch with Varti had been largely an exercise in listening and offering sympathy. Foreign diplomats were all vultures dressed as griffins, and why did everyone else feel the need to talk exclusively to Varti instead of each other? Didn't they know she needed to sleep now and then? Lartik thought he'd helped her, but the take-away at the end of the conversation was still a deep morass of self-doubt on Varti's part.

She didn't want conflict. She didn't want ugliness. She was not remotely power-hungry.

Without Seltha's leadership, she didn't actually have much experience at standing her ground in the face of an opponent.

That was the first flaw Lartik had considered, within Varti's character, that might prove any sort of argument against her being fit to rule; however, he knew her to be no coward, and to harbor a will of steel beneath her accommodating exterior. He remembered her leadership among the fortifications teams saving lives during the Shadow-empowered bandit siege of Reborn Aldis' first autumn. He remembered also the way she'd kept him and a dozen others alive with her unshakable practicality in the winter when that storm had pinned them down on their way home from the Ice-Binder expedition. She'd kept everyone together, organized construction of a shelter and the rationing of supplies, and kept everyone warm and safe until the skies cleared long enough for them to make it down out of the pass.

She could be assertive, plenty assertive. She just needed to figure out how to do it in the face of manipulative toadies and, well, imposing friends.

Finally, as they finished their food in the newly planted garden she'd led him to, Lartik had suggested, "Look, if you're really that worried about whether or not you're doing what Aldis needs, why not ask the gods? They're wise, right?" Lartik himself wasn't particularly religious, but he knew Varti was. Maybe it would help her.

To his surprise, she'd grown very calm and thoughtful at the suggestion, promised to consider it, and then several hours later sent him a note for where to meet her for a ritual.

Lartik had little desire to participate in a religious ritual, and far more desire to get home to Tekti and Monti (as Lustre had done—the rhy-hawk truly hated to be outside after dark), but Lartik didn't feel he could abandon Varti at a time like this. If she needed him at her side through this challenge, well, here he was. Drell and Dari were present as well. Varti had apparently invited no one else.

The hilltop was a lovely one, with a grand view of the setting sun over the valley beyond and a crown strewn with old ruins that had discouraged trees from obstructing one's vision. Lartik found he could see for miles in all directions, even though they were less than an hour's walk from the half-finished Azure Plaza. This place wouldn't remain untouched by the city's rebuilding efforts for long, the way Aldis was growing. Lartik felt a pang of sorrow that such a hilltop would eventually be covered with houses or shops.

"I want to build a temple here, to all the gods," Varti said, almost as if she'd read his thoughts—which was not, as far as he knew, among her talents. "I had Seltha's approval before she died, but I've been too busy to get started."

"A temple would be wonderful here. I'm already getting lovely ideas for statues of the gods," Drell said. "Let me know if you want me to draw up plans."

"Please," Varti urged, "assuming they choose me as queen."

A short silence fell.

"Will people still be able to see the sunset?" Lartik asked. "And the stars?"

Varti nodded. "It's a mostly outdoor design, for just that reason."

Of course it was. She knew what she was doing. Varti's artistry would enhance almost any natural setting. Lartik foresaw a truly beloved temple in Aldis' future. Drell and Dari also gazed around them in apparent approval, undoubtedly picturing the place as it might look adorned with one of Varti's architectural achievements.

"But I've been coming out here to pray for a long time," the little architect added.

"I can see why," Dari said. "So, what do you want us to do?"

"The three of you have supported me from the beginning. Drell and Dari seem to have felt at least part of the Hart's message to me as it passed through the room." Varti looked around at her friends. "I don't know what I'm looking for tonight, other than guidance. I know that what I want is to step down and let Rileb be sovereign. I have always admired her, and I don't want to fight with her, or to take away something important to her. I do see concerns with her behavior the last few days, but we are all grieving in our own way. I don't think the Rileb I have known for years would make a poor queen."

Lartik, again, felt that this interpretation was perhaps too generous, but reassessed his own opinion when he saw Dari and Drell both nod their agreement. He realized that they and Varti had all met Rileb somewhat earlier than he had, during the pirate conflict en route to establish better trade along the coast. Perhaps they knew a side of her he hadn't yet seen.

"It would be the easiest thing in the world for me to pretend I misunderstood the Hart's calling, or the message of this new mark on my face," Varti went on. "I have children to raise, and buildings as well. I didn't have time for half the things Seltha was asking me to do before she died, and now I'm doing her share as well. Who could want that? Of course I'd rather let Rileb do it."

Lartik did feel sympathy for his friend, and another surge of gratitude that at least it hadn't been him.

"But I know what the Hart has asked of me," Varti said. "Like it or not, I can't lie to myself about this. The Golden Hart who came to bless Seltha, at the founding of Aldis, came next to me and laid upon me the burden of responsibility to lead Aldis as its second sovereign."

Again, Drell and Dari nodded. Lartik envied them a little, the glimpse of clarity they'd had as the Hart brushed past them.

"So," Varti said, "If this is still what the Hart wants of me, I want to know how I'm supposed to achieve it without harming Aldis more than stepping down quietly would achieve. And if it *isn't* what the Hart still wants of me, I'd like to be informed as soon as possible, so I can go home and go to bed."

"Makes sense to me," Drell said. "May the gods be with us in this quest for wisdom."

The ritual that followed was simple and quiet, mostly just the four of them holding hands in a circle and meditating together. Both Varti and Drell murmured prayers out loud now and then, to various gods it seemed to occur to them might have useful input. Dari uttered a soft prayer to the Golden Hart itself at one point. Lartik, being the least religiously inclined of the four, held silence, content to clear his own mind with deep breathing and focus, and to wait for the voice of his own inner wisdom.

Partway through the ceremony, he noticed that Varti was crying. Drell's face, too, was marked with subtle tear tracks on both cheeks. Lartik himself had no such transcendent moment, but he did feel very calm, very open of heart, and the most relaxed he'd been since long before Seltha's death.

The sun finished setting behind the distant hills, and darkness settled around them. The birds quieted and the bats came out. Crickets chirped in nearby bushes. Bit by bit, everyone in the circle began to stir.

Varti uttered a final prayer of gratitude in a soft, thick voice, and hands were released. The ritual was done.

"It's true what I told everyone," Drell said, as they all pushed themselves back to their feet. "The Hart will always return to choose our sovereign, until Aldis becomes so perfect that we can choose the right sovereign for all of its people, even without divine guidance. I believe the Hart to be an incarnation of both the will and the deeper needs of the Aldin people."

Dari nodded. "I think it would be wise to choose a method for selecting a sovereign just in case the Hart somehow does not appear, but I'm convinced now that such a method should only be used in the Hart's absence. Anything we concoct will be fallible. The Hart is not."

Varti nodded. "Though, I do agree with Drell," she said, "in the hope that one day we will grow beyond the need for the Golden Hart as a people and as a nation, I don't believe that blind faith is true faith, and I dislike relying on a system that encourages people not to think for themselves about who should and shouldn't lead."

Lartik had experienced no mystical revelation, himself, as the other three—to all appearances—seemed to have had. Nevertheless, he did feel clear and untroubled. "Until that day, we are lucky to have a messenger like the Hart, to guide us when our own common sense fails," he said.

The others nodded, though Varti's was somewhat bashful.

"So," Lartik said. "Now we just have to convince everyone else."

"We will," Drell said. "The Scepter has chosen them. They will hear us out and make the right decision. I know it."

"I don't think the conflict will be bad," Dari said. "Most of us were convinced by the Hart. I've been talking to everyone since that night. Rileb herself may end up feeling a bit disappointed, but she's a good person. She'll move past it."

"I'll talk to her again." Varti's tone was confident, determined. "This is a challenge I must meet. Rileb is our friend."

"Aldis needs her," Dari agreed, "just not quite in the capacity she expected."

Varti nodded again. "What I think she doesn't understand yet, and Seltha did, is that the sovereign is the servant of Aldis, whether or not that sovereign is also a hero. We aren't chosen to lead from above. We are chosen to lift up our fellow Aldins, every one of them our equal."

As Lartik heard these words, he understood with a strange clarity that it was not merely his dear friend who spoke then but also his queen.

Varti did not waver again in her quiet certainty that she was Queen of Aldis—at least not that Lartik saw. She carried herself with calm confidence and the humility of grave responsibility, and she kept the kingdom together without Seltha. Everything continued to run more smoothly than anyone could possibly have guessed.

On Lartik's own insistence, Varti even gracefully delegated several of her duties to other qualified nobles of the realm. In each case, she appeared to choose wisely, and the average Aldin felt no interruption of the common order.

Seltha's funeral service was grand and moving, attended by a truly startling throng of people. All crowds were handled with a gentle practicality that was remarked upon by foreign dignitaries. Lartik caught several watching Varti with shrewd appraisal; he predicted improved trade arrangements on several fronts after Varti was officially declared queen, as wealthy foreign merchants reassessed the relative risk of business ventures in Aldis. Under Seltha, the nation had been little more than an upstart collective in their eyes, but after such a smooth and stable transition of power, Aldis would begin to appear to the rest of the world like a real sovereignty.

But through all this, Rileb did not at any point choose to withdraw her claim to the throne. She made no public fuss, nor did any observe her in seeking to undermine Varti's authority, but she did privately approach many nobles, both within and without Seltha's close circle of companions.

Due to this interference, the council that convened to establish the long-term regulation by which all Aldin sovereigns would be selected, was an unexpectedly large and therefore poorly organized meeting. Everyone talked over everyone else, with occasional descents into shouting and rancor. Lustre and, Lartik suspected, several others became irritated enough to remove themselves from the room, long before any decision was reached. Even Scepter-chosen nobles get tired and frustrated after four hours of fruitless debate. Wesren, along with Rileb's other two disciples, were eloquent and passionate, and Rileb—much as Lartik had suspected she might—sat quiet and dignified, and let them do the fighting for her. As predicted, she gently shushed them when they said something inappropriate, skillfully warding off the stain of impropriety from her own reputation, but without sacrificing the convenience of having had the assembly hear what she wanted heard.

After six grueling hours, a decision was reached by a better-than-two-thirds majority of those present. It wasn't quite the consensus everyone had hoped for, but it was close enough that the remaining dissenters—including even Rileb—honorably conceded to the prevailing will: If the Golden Hart chose a sovereign, the decision would be ratified by the Noble Assembly and that person would reign until death, or until the Hart chose someone else. If the Golden Hart did not arrive to select someone, candidates could be nominated through what Lartik considered an overly complicated process, but which did take into account the departed sovereign's wishes, ultimately ending with an election among nobles present for the vote.

It wasn't a perfect ruling, but it only mattered if the Golden Hart failed to appear.

And the Hart had appeared. Varti was affirmed as queen.

Wesren stalked out of the meeting in a fury. Rileb was, as always, unreadable, but she kept her dignity and refrained from an early departure. She did later brush past several would-be well-wishers, however, leaving in a hurry as soon as the council ended.

And who could blame her? It had been a long and frustrating day, and it hadn't ended the way she'd wished it to. Anyone in that situation might want some time alone to think. Lartik and several others encouraged other attendees not to think ill of her. She was still Seltha's companion and friend. She was still a hero of Aldis.

Varti took some time to accept everyone's congratulations, listen to everyone's concerns, and even to begin the planning of her official presentation to the Aldin people as their queen. When her eyes began to dull and lose focus with fatigue, Lartik and a few of the others reminded her that she didn't have to do everything herself, and that she certainly didn't have to do it all that night. Bit by bit, Varti bade her farewells and made her way to the door of the theatrical auditorium into which they'd had to cram the unexpectedly gargantuan council.

Lartik found himself walking beside his new queen, along with a few of their close friends. Varti led them by a route Lartik hadn't known existed—first down into the bowels of the palace, and then out through the corridors. Lartik wasn't certain by then where en route they'd lost the rest of their companions, but by the time they emerged from the unfinished library, it was just himself and Varti striding through the Aldis streets. "This is the fastest route from where we were to Rileb's house," Varti said. "I need to talk to her." Her tone was tight and tense.

Lartik glanced sharply at her face. She looked worried.

"Why?" he asked. It had been over an hour since Rileb had left the hall. What could have changed in that time to make Varti need to speak to her so urgently?

"I realized something, when you all came up to make me stop working," she said. "I have so many dear friends helping me through all this, but I haven't been there for Rileb. I don't know if any of us has. And when I thought that, I just had this horrible feeling come over me." She looked up, meeting Lartik's eyes, but didn't slow her pace. "I feel like I'm about to be too late."

Lartik saw such concern there, and such weight of responsibility—deserved or no—that it never occurred to him to argue. He stopped where he stood, and then had to trot to catch back up. "Are you sure we should be doing this alone?" he asked. "As sovereign, you do have some responsibility to be mindful of your own safety."

"Safety!" Varti said. "Lartik, you really are an old man. You think someone will try to hurt me?"

"Someone might try to hurt *any* ruling monarch," Lartik said. "And, meaning no offense to Rileb, one's very recently defeated rival for a throne is not *traditionally* considered to be the person least likely to wish one ill."

Varti waved a hand and kept walking briskly, toward Rileb's modest residence a few streets over. "Rileb doesn't wish me ill," she said. "She's still one of us—will be until the day she dies. I'm more worried that her disappointment at this rejection could fester, push her away. Her friends have to show her we still care. As queen, despite her protest, it's *my* responsibility to reach out first."

Lartik admired this logic from a moral perspective, but he still wasn't convinced they were handling this wisely. "We should at least go back for Dari and Drell, and a few of the others," he said. "You and I alone make a terrible questing party."

She shot him a look, then smiled, beneath an eye-roll. "I think Dari and Drell stayed back to prevent others from following," Varti said. "They probably realize a small group is better. More sensitive. And this might be the last chance I'll have in a while to speak to Rileb privately." She shook her head. "I can't let it wait. If it's just you along for the ride with me, I'm sure that will be enough."

Lartik wasn't remotely sure of any such thing. He checked that his mental shields were properly in place and patted himself for weapons. He didn't carry as many these days, but he still had that dagger the unicorn had blessed, when he and Varti and . . . now that he recalled it, also Rileb had participated in rescuing the creature at Seltha's side. It was his favorite dagger, just as he knew Varti's unicorn-blessed sword from the same incident was her own favorite weapon.

Lartik wasn't ancient yet, but he was older than he had been, and not exactly in the best fighting trim of his life. He hoped very much that Varti was right and they would not encounter any sort of danger—either at Rileb's home or in the streets. But just in case, he was glad of the weight of an arcana-imbued blade at his hip. He unclipped the fastener on the sheath, making sure his scholarly robes weren't in the way of him drawing at a moment's notice. He hoped he remembered how to fight in long robes, without tangling them around his legs.

Then, reaching out with his mind, he called to Lustre, who was at home for the evening.

I'm not going back out, Lustre said, before even a greeting. *It's dark, and wet.*

Varti and I are headed to Rileb's home, just the two of us, Lartik explained. *She thinks she has to do this now, and in private, to preserve Rileb's feelings and their friendship, but . . .*

But it might be better for everyone if a lot more friends showed up soon after? Lustre asked. *Just in case?*

Lartik offered the psychic equivalent of a nod. *Just in case.*

There was a pause, and then Lustre replied, *Fine, I'll go back out, but you owe me for this. Stall as long as you can. I don't fly as well in the rain. Weighs down your feathers if you're not a duck, you know.*

Thank you, Lustre, Lartik thought. He felt much better knowing that someone would be coming to join them. If things went as well as Varti hoped, having more friends arrive to let Rileb know there were no hard feelings could only be an added bonus. And if things went as poorly as Lartik feared, having other friends arrive to disrupt the tension would be all the more important.

Even after this, however, Lartik still couldn't relax at Varti's side. He considered raising an arcane ward, but he wanted his mind to be clearer than the concentration a ward would require. Besides, Rileb wasn't known for her arcane abilities.

Instead, as a final preparatory touch, Lartik pulled his mind into clarified focus—an old adventuring ability with which he was *not* out of practice—and drew arcane energies from the world around him into his own limbs and body, enhancing his speed and agility to levels approaching those of a much younger, tougher man. It might take a toll on him later, to enhance himself this way, but

Lartik was healthy for his age, and had decades of practice at keeping it going for periods beyond what many adepts could manage. He hadn't used such enhancement for combat in years, but combat was its intended purpose.

With these precautions in place, Lartik continued to keep pace with the short-limbed but surprisingly quick-moving Varti. As Lustre had noted, it was a gray, drizzly day, and near enough to sunset that the shadows of the surrounding structures were lengthening. Few citizens were in the streets, as the public announcement of Varti's confirmation was yet to be made—between the dim light and drear weather, none even noticed Lartik's and Varti's passing, much less troubled them on their way.

Rileb's home was one of several small dwellings that had been fitted into the sturdy remains of one of the Old City's surviving structures, making it both a forbiddingly grand edifice and a humble place of residence at the same time, as if—like seemingly everything else in her demeanor—it had been deliberately chosen to demonstrate Rileb's fitness to rule.

Lartik hadn't visited here in quite some time, but Varti knew exactly which door was Rileb's, and approached it with the same courage Lartik had always known in his friend. She wasn't confident, socially gifted, or in any way fearless, but she was practical. If something needed to be done, Varti just did it, whether it was hard or not, whether she liked it or not—whether or not she even thought she could do it. Necessity was her guiding star, no matter what got in her way, even her own self-doubt.

Lartik knew himself to be much more fragile. It was, he suspected, why he surrounded himself with so many partners and so much family. He liked to have a lot of support when he was down.

Varti had never seemed to need that, and Lartik admired her for it.

But he still felt nervous when she knocked on Rileb's door.

One of the fawning disciples answered, to Lartik's increased anxiety, though in her defense it was the fawning disciple he disliked the least—a sweet-faced young woman named Shinda, with golden skin and starling-black hair, who seemed to be trying to make herself a hero under Rileb's guidance. She struck Lartik as less obsequious than merely infatuated. When she recognized Varti and Lartik, she tensed all over and flashed a smile so nervous it was almost a grimace.

"I, uh, will tell Rileb you're here?" Shinda asked, then fled back inside.

Varti and Lartik waited in taut silence on the front step. They didn't wait long.

Rileb's pretty admirer returned with the third of the three primary fawning disciples in tow, a plump little man who otherwise looked like Shinda's brother. Each gave an awkward and excessive obeisance to Varti, and the maybe-brother babbled, "Lady Rileb Sworddancer is waiting inside. Go on in. We were just leaving." With that, they both ran out the door, black curls bouncing behind them.

Varti spared a worried glance after them. "I hope everyone doesn't start treating me like that."

"They'll adjust to your style in time," Lartik replied, though they both knew Seltha had harbored similar complaints to her dying day. "That's the least of our worries right now, isn't it?" Lartik was far more concerned with the wild-eyed excitement in the plump young man's face, as if he'd known something shocking was about to happen.

Perhaps the young man was simply an excitable sort of person. He had certainly seemed so to Lartik, especially in recent weeks. Perhaps he was the sort who always expected a shouting match, tears, and broken friendships. Lartik knew Varti and Rileb too well to consider such theatrics likely, but perhaps this boy had a different impression of the two women.

Or perhaps he knew something he wasn't saying.

Lartik was of half a mind to chase him down and question him before they went any farther, but just then Varti sighed and nodded.

"You're right," she said, in answer to something Lartik had already forgotten saying. "Let's go." She stepped into the shadows of Rileb's front hall.

Lartik forgot all about the mysterious expression on the boy's face, and dragged his mind back to high alert. Rileb's home appeared to have no candles or lanterns burning anywhere within—the only light came in through the few windows. Of those, only the front window faced the setting sun, its golden light streaming under the rainclouds and through the stylish glass panes in eerie patches that painted the whole hallway with Lartik and Varti's own long, distorted shadows.

A vata'an, Lartik could see fine in darkness, of course, but this sunset half-light, with sharp contrast between patches of bright gold and dim gray, had him jumping at every sound, feeling as blind as a human might at night.

"I guess she's feeling down," Varti said. "I don't think she usually keeps her house this dim."

Lartik loved Varti for worrying so much about her friend's disappointment, but he wished for the ten thousandth time that she was a bit more suspicious. This situation didn't feel right.

But Varti already hurried on ahead, apparently insensible to the poor visibility of their circumstances. It didn't look "dark" of course, with the sunlight painting everything gold. Perhaps she hadn't noticed the depth of the shadows. Or perhaps human eyes didn't work quite like vata'an eyes, and she, for once, could see better than Lartik. He wondered if he should try again to convince her to wait for their friends to join them before proceeding. Peering forward, and into each room they passed, he followed Queen Varti through not-queen Rileb's house.

As was often the case with homes built into the remains of the old city, Rileb's residence was a bit oddly shaped, long and narrow in layout. The front hall led past a cloak nook, an empty but sumptuous sitting room, and a similarly appointed dining area with a deeply shadowed archway in a back corner. Lartik squinted back there, and thought he might spy a small kitchen area. Before he could point it out or suggest they explore it, Varti was already moving away, down the hall toward the rear of the house.

Lartik trotted to catch up to her, just as the hallway took a sharp turn into a staircase leading down beneath a low, diagonal ceiling—undoubtedly the upward staircase of a different home in the same building.

Here in Rileb's home, flickering lantern light spoke of possible occupants downstairs, but Lartik didn't find himself particularly comforted by the cheerful glow.

He paused at the top of the stairs. "We don't know what's down there. Varti . . ."

"Shinda's a good girl," she said. "If Rileb meant us ill, she'd have warned us on her way out." Lartik wasn't certain that Shinda was capable of seeing past her feelings to Rileb's true intentions. Varti laid a gentle hand on Lartik's arm. "Rileb needs us. I know she's been acting strange. I know it started before Seltha died. I should have reached out to her months ago. She hasn't told any of us what's wrong, and that's her right, but we can't leave her alone after a day like today. Whatever's troubling her, we have to help her through it."

Lartik wanted to trust Varti's judgment. Listening to her, he found he liked her much better than he liked himself. Where Lartik was withdrawing from Rileb in suspicion, Varti was believing the best of her friend, no matter what. He wanted to be that person.

But he wasn't.

With a last, troubled sigh, Lartik resolved himself to giving up convincing Varti. He didn't want to be right about Rileb. He in fact hoped very much that he was wrong.

"Let me go first, at least," he said.

Varti rolled her eyes but gestured for him to go ahead. "Just be polite," she cautioned.

Lartik studied her face one last time as he passed her. Up close, he could see how anxious she was. He knew her stomach must be tied in a thousand knots; that she was forcing herself through this out of duty and loyalty. But at least she'd said he could go first.

Of course, it would have been nice had they someone better suited to the task of playing bodyguard to a queen.

Lartik again considered an arcane ward but found that he preferred to maintain his physical enhancement. His body was still keeping up with its demands, for now, and the enhancement didn't require his constant attention as the ward would. With that, he braced himself for the unexpected and stepped onto the stairs.

The first few steps were the worst, as he descended without a clear view of what lay below. After that, he was able to duck down low enough to see into the room beneath. It was the largest room so far, lit indirectly by the flickering light of a lantern in another room beyond. It stood as empty as all the other rooms had been, but nowhere near as well-appointed. Full of elderly chairs, simple stools, and even a few empty crates arranged as seating, it appeared to be a room dedicated to discussion among peers.

It smelled of incense. Rose? No, something else. He'd smelled it before, long ago he thought. It gave him a bad feeling.

Lartik wondered what it meant that Rileb kept the upper floor of her house—including a receiving room—so pristine and wealthy-looking while still maintaining this much-larger discussion space in such a humble, simple state. What message was she trying to send, and to who?

"Is it safe?" Varti called down.

"Not sure yet," Lartik replied. "Give me a moment."

The flickering lamplight was dim, the lit parts of the room not much brighter than the shadows. The relative lack of contrast was easier on his vata'an eyes than the streaming sunlight had been, allowing him to properly adjust to the low light. He was able to scan the shadowed corners and crannies quickly. The room looked lived-in but clean, cozier than the rest of the house. He couldn't explain what about that lingering incense sent shivers down his spine.

With second sight, he noted traces of fading arcana, all of it too old and minor to read without intensive study. He wondered what sorts of things Rileb and her sycophants discussed here, and why the use of arcana might be part of their discussions.

Moving on, the room beyond appeared, from what Lartik could see through the half-closed door, to be a bedroom. He approached the door with caution, even putting his back to the wall beside it before calling out. He would feel foolish if Varti turned out to be right about Rileb's intentions, but better foolish than skewered.

"Rileb? Are you here?"

"I am," came the reply. "Come in."

It was, indeed, Rileb's rich, aristocratic voice. Lartik misliked her tone, but felt he had no reasonable option than to enter. He double-checked his psychic shields, which seemed strong as ever, made certain his physical enhancements would remain active, and steeled himself to face whatever awaited him in Rileb's room.

Lartik pushed open the door.

Immediately, Rileb had the point of her sword to his throat. Even with his enhanced agility, his exaggerated caution, Lartik never saw her coming.

Well, she had always been the better fighter.

"So, you're who Varti sends to do her dirty work." The satin beauty of Rileb's voice seemed surreal in the face of both her words and actions. "I'll admit I'm surprised. I didn't think you were the type."

Lartik left his dagger in its sheath and raised both hands to show they were empty. He tried to speak, but no words emerged.

"Did you think I wouldn't defend myself?" she asked. "You should have known you'd be no match for me at close quarters."

Finally, he found his voice. "Rileb, I don't understand. What's going on?"

Sword still at his throat, she moved toward Lartik, backing him into the larger room. "Don't play stupid," she said. "Everyone knows you aren't. I know why you're here."

Lartik heard footsteps on the stairs behind him. He didn't turn from Rileb and her blade. "Don't come down!" he called out. "Something's wrong!"

Rileb struck out at him, and Lartik fell backwards while avoiding her strike. The footsteps didn't stop, and he heard more than one pair.

Hope surged. Lartik wanted to call out to Lustre's mind, to confirm his hope, but with a sword in his face, he found himself a bit too preoccupied to effectively channel his thoughts. However, if Varti's company had arrived because the rhy-hawk was here with backup . . .

His enhancement holding, Lartik twisted as he scrambled backward, away from Rileb, to give himself a glimpse of who it was coming down the stairs.

And hope sputtered.

It wasn't reinforcements. Lartik saw Varti's boots backing awkwardly downward as another pair advanced on her. He rolled back to his feet to face Rileb once more, but he was sure he knew what had happened. Someone had been hiding in that kitchen-looking nook they hadn't explored. Whoever it was—Lartik's bet was on Wesren—had emerged once Varti was alone, and now forced her at the point of a blade to join Lartik and Rileb in the basement.

"I'm here in friendship," Varti said, backing down another step. "I thought Rileb might need a friend right now."

"An obvious lie," Wesren hissed.

Lartik watched Rileb's face through this exchange. As always, he couldn't read her expression, though her pale skin did seem strangely flushed. A human might have dismissed it as a trick of the light, but with Lartik's better night vision, he was sure she showed signs of some kind of exertion. Her breathing, too, seemed accelerated. If she was ill, she didn't show it in her stance, or in the steadiness of her blade. As it covered Lartik's every move, he noticed that it, unlike his own and Varti's blades, was not the one that the unicorn had blessed for them. This was a fancier piece, with an elaborate hilt-guard complete with three rosebuds in blue enamel and gold leaf.

Of course it was.

"Why did you come yourself, Varti?" Rileb asked, still covering Lartik with her blade. "Why dirty your hands with this?"

"How could caring for a friend dirty my hands?" Varti replied, still backing downward. She stumbled a little at the bottom of the stairs. Lartik could see her now past Rileb's shoulder, and

Wesren, too, menacing his new queen with his own ostentatious sword.

"What's happening here, Rileb?" Varti's tone was as low as always, practical and reasoned, but Lartik heard a thread of alarm adding a hint of a tremor, especially to Rileb's name. Knowing Varti as well as he did, he understood by even this subtle signal that his friend was more upset than he'd heard her in years.

For her own part, Rileb was silent. She kept Lartik guarded with her sword and waited, though for what Lartik was afraid to guess.

"You know perfectly well what's happening," came Wesren's taunt. "Lady Rileb is a threat to your rule. She's Seltha's chosen heir! How can you play queen knowing Aldis' rightful sovereign breathes right under your nose! We know what you and your lackey have come for."

Lackey! As if Wesren were one to talk! Then again, Lartik thought, right now it seemed almost as if Wesren were the commander in charge of this strange confrontation. Rileb only stood there—with a sword that she still pointed most skillfully and discomfitingly in Lartik's face, but . . . such an action did not imply the leadership that Lartik would have expected of her. She seemed almost distracted. A sheen of sweat glistened on her brow.

Lartik took a chance that she wouldn't threaten his concentration for the next half a moment, and finally reached out to Lustre again.

Things are bad, he said. *Hurry.*

On my way, Lustre replied. *Don't die.*

"What are you talking about?" Varti asked Wesren. "The decision is made! And Rileb is a Scepter-chosen noble who gave her word in concession to that decision! Why shouldn't I trust her?"

Well, Lartik thought, *she does have a sword to my throat.* It had, perhaps, begun to waver. Lartik noticed that Rileb's heavy breathing had increased, as had the pink in her otherwise especially pale cheeks and nose. Her eyes, he now noticed, were showing a slight glassiness, like someone in pain.

"What have you been telling her?" Varti asked. "Who even are you? How long have you been poisoning her like this?"

Something clicked in Lartik's mind.

Who was Wesren? He'd been at Rileb's side for years, but where had she met him? He'd been at the council, to which supposedly only nobles had been invited, but was he a noble? He'd certainly never acted like one, and Lartik couldn't remember him being tested by the scepter.

He hadn't been present for the testing of every noble, of course, but . . . had everyone just been assuming all this time that Wesren belonged among them? Lartik racked his memory for evidence in any direction on the subject and found all he knew of the man was his ubiquitous presence at Rileb's side since—now that Lartik thought about it—not long after Seltha chose Rileb as her emergency successor.

Lartik understood then, with no small dismay, that he'd been making a terrible mistake all along. Rileb was so strong, so independent and naturally authoritative, it had never occurred to him that poor judgment on her part could possibly come from any source but herself. That assumption had led him to miss everything important.

"It's not what he's telling her," Lartik all but whispered. "He's done something to her." As he spoke, he looked at her again with his second sight and saw the evidence of it right before his eyes: sorcerous arcana rippled around her.

The scent of that not-rose incense seemed to have intensified.

Sorcery didn't explain everything. Lartik wished it did, but this was far too obvious an arcane control to have gone unnoticed all this time. Even if Lartik himself had failed to check Rileb for corrupted influence until now, *someone* would have.

But a psychically talented sorcerer, who'd spent all day with Rileb every day for months or years, could have warped her mind ever so subtly in that time—shifting an emotion here, altering a memory there, little by little until even a hero worthy of Seltha's highest trust might begin to twist toward Shadow.

Varti had been right. All this time, their friend had needed them, and Lartik hadn't offered her any help at all. He'd sensed something was wrong and pushed Rileb away instead of reaching out.

Seeing on her face, however, how hard Rileb appeared now to wrestle with herself, Lartik risked a glance at Wesren. He saw hate there, and rage, and desperation. This hadn't been his plan, Lartik guessed. Rileb wasn't done being corrupted yet. She was supposed to have been chosen as queen while she was still mostly her old self. The corruption was supposed to be completed after her ascension to the sovereignty.

Wesren, or whoever lay behind this, hadn't counted on the direct interference of the Golden Hart.

Lartik steeled himself against his own guilt and shame at Rileb's plight. It was late-coming, he knew, but he could still be useful to her now. Whatever his flaws as a friend, he could at least feel better about himself as Varti's choice of companion on this dangerous mission. If they were up against a sorcerer, Lartik knew just what to do.

His own arcane talent, apart from his bond with Lustre, didn't lie with psychic abilities that might have let him restore Rileb's mind. Nevertheless, he could certainly make it harder for Wesren to control Rileb in this moment. Now was the time for Lartik's arcane ward, and he didn't cast it to protect himself. Drawing arcane energies through his own body and soul, he channeled them outward, toward Wesren, enveloping the other man in a wall of arcane power.

No sooner had his wall of arcana finished closing itself around Wesren than the sorcerer's hate-filled gaze switched toward Lartik. The contest of wills had begun. Lartik saw Rileb's sword waver, point drooping; saw her stagger back a step and shake her head in disorientation, but Wesren hadn't given up yet. Lartik could feel how the man threw himself into his corrupted arcana, drawing on his own life force to strengthen himself against Lartik's ward.

With Wesren's attention pulled toward him, and Rileb grappling with whatever had been done to her mind, Lartik put his trust in Varti to keep their confused friend occupied while he faced off against their true assailant.

Lartik had skill and experience on his side, but the sorcerer had youthful vigor and seemed unafraid to spend it cracking open the shell of Lartik's ward. Lartik had to find some way to get the upper hand, or he'd pass out before young Wesren was even tired.

Beside them, in his peripheral vision, Lartik saw Varti reaching out toward Rileb, as if to catch her from falling. Rileb rounded on her before she could, sword still wavering but high once more.

"Stay back!" she warned. Even now, her dignity remained remarkably intact. "Whatever you're doing, it won't work!"

"I'm a stone-shaper," Varti reminded her, with patience only a parent can learn. "I *can't* do anything to your mind. What you're feeling, it isn't me."

"Don't patronize me," Rileb muttered. "No more words. Draw your sword."

Lartik pushed harder to defend his ward from Wesren's assault. He had to keep Rileb's mind as clear as it could be. If she realized who'd betrayed her, she might be able to shake off some of what had happened. Wesren's sheer force of will was strong, however, and Lartik—handsome new young husband notwithstanding—was an old man. He'd managed a lot of arcana without paying a price in fatigue, but shoring up a ward was a whole other matter. He stumbled to one knee.

"I won't draw steel against you!" Varti's tone remained soft, even now, but the intensity of her emotion could not be missed. "I am your friend, Rileb. You've been lied to. I'm guessing now that even your memories have been changed. I'm so sorry I didn't realize sooner how bad this was. Please, we can get you to a mind-healer."

"I'm not crazy!!" Finally, Rileb's voice cracked. Finally, she showed vulnerability. Varti was getting through to her. If Lartik could just hold out until help arrived . . .

But just as he thought it, he felt Wesren winning. The ward fell. Rileb staggered again, then straightened her stance, her sword steady once more. She pointed it at Varti's heart. Lartik had failed them both.

Two hundred yards, came Lustre's voice. *Dima, Drell, Talani, and Gerrol. Will we be enough?*

Yes.

Their friends were coming. New strength flowed through Lartik's soul. He pushed himself back to his feet and summoned a new ward, flinging it at Wesren with all his might. It was too much power to channel into a ward, but that was the point. The leftover arcana spilled inward from Lartik's mystical wall, slamming into Wesren like a wave of pure force.

Lartik felt the sorcerer's spell dissolve under his arcane might. It was Wesren's turn to collapse to his knees. Trusting Varti to handle Rileb, Lartik drew his blessed dagger and stepped forward, placing it to Wesren's throat.

"He's been controlling you, Rileb," Lartik said, without taking his eyes off Wesren. "I was wrong about you, and Varti was right."

He couldn't see Rileb anymore; he'd put her behind him when

he moved to cover Wesren. Even now, his spine tingled with fear that she would strike him in her confusion. But it wasn't just Varti he was trusting to keep him safe. Rileb wasn't fallen yet. If she were, Wesren wouldn't be so desperate now.

Rileb had always been a hero. She wouldn't strike a friend from behind.

Which door is hers? Lustre asked. *Drell and Talani are arguing.*

The distraction came at a bad time. *Far right,* Lartik replied, as quickly as he could. *The blue one.*

But even that brief lapse of attention was too long. Lartik had barely blinked, but it was all the distraction Wesren needed. He lurched away from Lartik's blade and rounded on Varti.

"I won't let you beat her!" he cried. And unleashed a barrage of sorcery.

Lartik was instantly in motion, though he didn't know what he planned to do.

It didn't matter anyway.

Rileb got there first. She threw herself between Wesren and Varti, catching the blast to her own chest. Waves of arcanely amplified hate exploded outward after hitting her—even Lartik reeled in their wake. Rileb, however, absorbed them at full force.

She fell to both knees and vomited blood.

Wesren screamed. Varti caught Rileb in her arms.

Lartik dove toward Wesren, but the younger man flailed outward and caught him in the throat. Gasping, Lartik staggered to the wall to brace himself. Wesren scrambled back up the stairs and flung open the trap door.

"I'm sorry," Lartik heard. It was Rileb's voice, but ruined and made ugly by whatever Wesren's blast had torn apart inside her.

Lartik steeled himself and lurched after Wesren, up the stairs.

Where are you? he thought to Lustre. *He's getting away!*

Having trouble with the lock, Lustre said. *Should we break the door?*

The lock? Who in the world had managed to lock the door on them? *Surround the building*, Lartik replied. *Catch Wesren.*

Behind him, just before he reached the top of the stairs, Lartik heard, "I should have trusted my friends."

Yes. Lartik should have, too. He shook off a welling of tears and pushed after the sorcerer. As he raced down the hall, Lartik saw Drell and Lustre rushing in through the front.

"Where is he?" Drell asked.

He didn't come this way, Lustre added.

Lartik grunted and turned toward the dining area, to the archway in the back corner. It did, indeed, lead to a kitchen.

He searched around him. If Wesren hadn't come this way, what other way could he have gone? He could easily have hidden here when Lartik and Varti entered, since the two had bypassed it completely, but now that he was searching it properly, he couldn't even see a proper place to *conceal* an adult human, much less allow one to escape.

After sending Lustre off to fetch Dari, in case Rileb could still be saved, Lartik searched the kitchen space while Drell went to hunt for secret passages in other parts of the house. All Lartik found was one large cupboard with its door ajar. It looked large enough to crawl through, but inside it was just an empty cupboard.

Drell was similarly unsuccessful.

"They'll catch him outside," Drell said. "Even if there's some passage we can't find, he won't make it out of the building."

Lartik nodded, though he didn't feel so confident. "I just hope Dari is having better success with poor Rileb," he said. He didn't feel much hope there either.

"Me, too," Drell said. "In the meantime, we keep watch here, in case he doubles back."

Lartik nodded. *We were too late,* he said when Lustre returned, silent and grim. *Varti practically jogged here when she left the assembly, but even she realized the danger too late.*

And he was right. There was nothing Dari could do to save Rileb. Whatever harm Wesren had done, Rileb Sworddancer had been gone before the healer even knew what was wrong.

The next several hours passed in a daze for Lartik.

Varti told everyone else that only Wesren had tried to kill her and that Rileb had taken the sorcerous blast in her stead. It wasn't a lie.

Wesren was either hiding in the building somewhere or had somehow escaped past their cordon and out into the city. A full search was in effect, but no one seemed to have seen anything.

As soon as more soldiers and healers had arrived on the scene, Varti was forbidden from continuing the hunt for Wesren herself. Lartik, far too tired to keep running around after mad young sorcerers, stayed in Rileb's upstairs sitting room with Varti. A rain-wet and disheartened Lustre had already gone home to sleep, on Lartik's urging. Hawks of his species hated nighttime, so even if Lartik could have used his companionship, he couldn't bear to keep his friend out any later.

He turned instead to the friend still beside him, Varti, second queen of reborn Aldis.

"Why didn't you tell them everything?" Lartik asked, soft enough that the nearby guards wouldn't overhear.

"Rileb was wronged," Varti said. "I'd rather keep things simple, so she can still die a hero."

"You were right—we should have been there for her," Lartik said. "We lost her because we withdrew instead of trusting her. I won't forget that lesson, but . . . she did choose to surround herself with fawning admirers instead of real friends. She chose not to come to us for clarity when he started to play with her mind."

After Dari had declared her gone, Lartik had done a thorough arcane reading with his second sight. He'd been right about Wesren's methods. They'd been subtle and had been building for *years*. Traces of similar sorcery lingered in the downstairs discussion room where she'd died, along with that oddly too-sweet incense. Had he smelled it before, in that merchant's stall in Jarzon?

Lartik wasn't sure, but he wondered how many people had joined Rileb there, in her basement, and how they too had been affected by Wesren's influence.

"He found a vulnerability in her mind, and he exploited it," Lartik said aloud. "He's the villain, not her, I agree, but . . ."

"That's just my point!" Varti said. "I don't want anyone else to say what you're saying, Lartik. We *failed* her as friends. Let it end here. Wesren fell to Shadow. Rileb was Seltha's chosen heir. If people wonder why the Hart chose me and not her, let them think it knew she would die before she could rule."

"What if Wesren contradicts you when we catch him?" Lartik said.

"I won't lie to the people of Aldis, but I will still do what I can to protect Rileb's memory," Varti replied. "It's what Seltha would want, I'm sure."

Lartik still had misgivings, but he hoped that catching Wesren would render them moot. For now, he let the subject drop. After all, Varti had been right about Rileb all along. Perhaps they could have saved her if Lartik and their other friends had trusted Varti's judgment on the matter and thought to reach out. The gods knew, poor Varti herself simply hadn't had time.

And Varti was chosen by the Hart for a reason, after all. Lartik didn't believe for a second that it was because it knew Rileb was going to die. Varti had been the better choice all along, with or without Wesren's interference. Aldis didn't need another hero; it needed a builder, an architect.

Besides, Varti wasn't just Lartik's friend anymore. He had to remember that. She was his queen. He needed to take her instincts seriously.

"Are you recovering all right?" Varti asked him then. "That arcane struggle looked . . . impressive."

"I'm not as young as I was," Lartik admitted, "but I'm not *that* old. It was tiring, but I'll be right as roses by tomorrow." Still, he told himself, now might be a good time to start playing with his children more, and taking longer walks. He had a lot of years left in him, as a vata'an, and a wonderful family to share them with. He needed to be sure he could still keep up with the people he loved when they needed him.

He needed to be sure he could still protect them.

And not just that. No, Lartik had a strange feeling that Aldis wasn't done with him yet.

Now

Tersha's vision ended with dizzying abruptness. She swayed where she sat and stared around her, utterly disoriented. Never before in her life had she gleaned such prolonged detail from an object. To remember where she was—even *who* she was—and what she was supposed to be doing, she stared down at what she held in her hands. It was a scroll, with writing she now unquestionably recognized as King Lartik's. Tersha remembered it now. Had she continued to read the thing while her vision unfolded? She seemed to be almost to the end of it.

She read on.

"'We never did track down Wesren,'" it said. "'We never learned his motives, where he'd come from, or who had taught him sorcery. We never learned what allies he might have had in his unknown long-term goals, or even whether he was a fallen noble or an impostor from the beginning. Shinda and the young man who turned out to be her cousin both needed a small amount of mind-healing, due to Wesren's meddling, but seemed otherwise completely uninvolved, and were able to shed no light on our mysteries.

"'Shinda did share the names of others who'd frequented discussions at Rileb's house, but had apparently never participated in any untoward conversations herself. Those on her list that we were able to find seemed similarly innocent, but there were several that we never did locate.

"'Shinda inherited Rileb's property, and she and her cousin both lived there, though Shinda traveled a great deal after that. Neither cousin ever seemed to recover from the death of their idol. After Shinda died with honors, defending a northern village from bandits, the cousin withdrew into near-seclusion, and I'm afraid I can't for the life of me recall his name. I should probably have kept closer track of him over the years, but when he'd had no new contact with Wesren or other suspicious characters after ten years, it seemed cruel to keep reminding him of the tragedy that he, like myself, had stood by and failed to avert.

"'As for Wesren's escape from justice, it was Varti who discovered how he'd done it. Poring over the original plans for turning Rileb's building into homes, she found a discrepancy that led to us learning where Wesren had hidden. The suspicious cupboard in the kitchen had indeed housed a secret passage—one whose latch had been cleverly broken on Wesren's way through, to keep me from finding the trick.

"'The passage inside led to one of the other homes, which had contained a secret cellar that none of the residents had known was there. When Varti looked there, she found evidence that someone had prepared the tiny space with emergency rations, and later used it as a living quarters for months or more. He'd left it a mess upon his departure. With the patience of a spider, Wesren had crouched in that dismal little hole, waiting out our search until it was finally called off.

"'Varti never withdrew her request that I uphold Rileb's perfect reputation to the end. I didn't think it mattered much, as Rileb's memory soon paled in Seltha's shadow. Oh, she was honored with a grand-enough funeral and a small monument in one of the palace gardens—I don't recall which—and today she's mentioned here and there, in histories and songs, but my grandchildren can't keep straight the difference between Rileb, Drell, and any number of other heroes of that era, all passed on now. Varti's kindness did no apparent harm, so I simply let it stand. Even if we didn't know what Wesren had been plotting. Even if we didn't know what sort of conspiracy might have used Rileb's home as its base of operations.

"'But now Wesren—or at least his influence—has returned to Aldis. I would assume that he has aged at a human rate, making us more evenly matched in vigor this time. I only wish I knew what he was planning, and why he'd risked letting me see his arcane influence on that old man. He has a reason. All these years, though, and I still don't know what, or who, he serves.

"'I fear there is so much more to learn. And we could have learned it all decades ago if we'd simply taken the time to stay close to a struggling friend. Wesren is, in retrospect, a huge part of why I rejected Rileb when she grew cold and distant. Reaching out to her would have meant reaching out to him, since the two were always together. He drove me away by being unpleasant and ever-present. And I'd judged Rileb for that, and let her go.

"'Whoever is reading this, I beg you, pull your friends back from the brink before they fall into Shadow. Varti was right that Rileb deserved to be saved, but she was wrong to hide this lesson from Aldis. Even heroes can go astray, when Shadow is persistent and subtle. It is up to those who love us to catch the problem early and bring us to our senses.

"'As for Wesren, well, I hope that for you, unknown reader, he is long-since apprehended and his plans laid waste, but if not . . . My advice is this: Expect him to have taken a longer view than anyone else would. Expect subtlety and planning, far better organization than he showed before. Expect truly inhuman patience. Wesren has kept himself alive and free for twenty-five years, despite his status as a wanted assassin. He'll have learned from his mistakes, and from his years as a fugitive. His plans for Aldis this time might even take as long as centuries to unfold.'"

Lartik's words rang in Tersha's mind as she wordlessly passed the scroll to Uwynne. She knew where she was now. This little house, this strange basement in which she'd spent an entire day rifling through stacks upon stacks of lies, misinformation, and subtle manipulation was the same house she'd seen in her vision.

Rileb had lived here.

Tersha motioned for Hirell and Burin to follow her and mounted the stairs to the floor above. She ignored Hirell's shrugging exchange with Burin behind her and continued on to what the current residents had made into their main living area.

Much had changed from what she'd seen in Lartik's memories, but the basic structure remained, as did the corner archway into a tiny kitchen, with a truly ancient oven here, passage to a scullery there. And in the back, an elderly cupboard, strangely empty.

Tersha turned to Hirell. "Find the latch," she said.

His eyebrows shot up, but he didn't question her. It didn't take him long, either. Unlike Wesren, this thief hadn't chosen to break the door on her way past—or maybe the new latch was just harder to break than the old one had been.

Hirell slid open the hidden door to reveal a surprisingly large, wholly unlit stone tunnel beyond.

"They're right over at rehabilitation," Tersha said to her companions. "None of those four we captured is the thief. There's a concealed chamber in another part of the building. She's been hiding there."

Hirell looked impressed. "You're getting better at this vision thing," he said.

Tersha didn't feel like she'd done anything. The vision had just come, unbidden—and she still reeled from having someone else's thoughts and feelings in her head, in such detail.

"Maybe," she said, "but Lartik wasn't present when they found the chamber. There are five homes in this building! Where do we start? We can't just barge into the homes of innocent people searching for random secret doors."

"I'll go get the assistants working on digging up those old plans Lartik mentioned at the end there," Hirell said. "Maybe they're still preserved, or have faithful copies on record."

"Too slow," Burin replied. "It's the third house down."

"We can't invade someone's home because you didn't like them," Tersha protested.

"Maybe they'll help us if we just ask them?" Hirell suggested.

Burin shook his head. "They won't," he said, "but we do have a reason to barge in. I saw some of their layout, it makes sense for the passage to lead that way."

"We'd still need a queen's writ . . ." Tersha began, but Burin put up a hand to show he hadn't finished. She waited.

"The thing is," he said, "This place doesn't work as a hideout unless the organization owns both houses at either end of the secret passage. Lartik's story may not be public record, but the pursuit of the assassin was. That means they probably bricked all this up ages ago. Someone's *restored* it, and you're not going to get away with that kind of work on a person's home without the residents knowing."

Tersha and Hirell glanced at one another.

"And if the people on the other side are friendly to our thief . . ." Hirell began.

Then as soon as the cordon around this building was lifted, she'd be helpfully smuggled out, rather than needing to cower in a hole for weeks as Wesren had.

"Honestly," Tersha said. "The guard didn't even know what to be looking for. If she was really brazen about it, we might already be too late."

Tersha and the other two Rose Knights just stared at one another for a pair of heartbeats. Then all three broke into a run.

Halfway to the third house, they saw a young woman outside, talking to one of the guards in the remaining cordon. The knights changed course to intercept them both. The guard, Fim, a friend of Tersha's, was smiling and chatting with the younger woman, though Fim's eyes looked concerned and uncertain. The woman faced away from the three knights.

While avoiding the appearance of doing so, Tersha and her companions moved carefully to surround the pair. Tersha ended up on one side, with a good view of both people's expressions. The face of the young girl shocked her. She wasn't just short—she looked adolescent, barely more than a child, and as pale as mashed potatoes, like she hadn't seen the sun for most of her life. Her eyes held the strange blend of innocence and world-weary cynicism typical only in the faces of war refugee children. She'd seemed shy, speaking to Fim, but when the three Rose Knights approached, her little face paled further, taking on a sickly, greenish cast. She looked ready to cry.

Also, Tersha noted, under the girl's unnecessary rain hood, her hair looked freshly and clumsily dyed a flat, dull brown.

"What's up, Fim?" Tersha asked.

"Ah, nothing much," Fim said. "This young lady just needed a friendly ear."

In Tersha's mind came a request for psychic contact, which she granted.

She's having a family issue, so she wants me to let her leave without noting her name or what time she left, Fim explained. *Do you think an exception would be all right?*

Did you notice she fits the description of the thief perfectly? Tersha shot back. She glanced at Hirell for confirmation. He nodded—he recognized her; Hirell had gotten one of the better looks at their thief.

Then Hirell and Burin, noting the signs of psychic communication, tried to strike up a conversation with the girl. It didn't seem to Tersha to be likely to succeed, but she hoped it would at least distract the frightened little thing from the tableau of Fim and Tersha just silently staring at the walls.

Oh wow! Fim responded, sounding shocked. *How did I not notice that terrible dye-job! Her poor hair! But Tersha, really, this pup feels more like a victim than a criminal. Just look at her!*

Tersha could only agree. This was a situation for delicacy. If the cult couldn't easily recruit outsiders, they probably relied heavily on the indoctrination of their own children. This little girl had possibly been lied to her whole life, taught to believe that the Golden

Hart was a Shadow-agent, the Blue Rose Scepter corrupted, and that the Rose Knights were puppets controlled by Shadow-wrapped enchantments. Of course she was terrified.

Arresting her now would only make that worse.

It went beyond that though, Tersha guessed. The same people who'd raised her that way had most likely used her to do their dirty work. However they'd found out about Lartik's hidden scroll, they'd sent in their fastest thief to steal it, regardless of her tender age and what consequences she might face. And if she was caught, they would simply use that fact as fuel to frighten more children like her into continued fanatical isolation.

Given what Tersha had seen in that cache of books—in what, long, long ago, before the addition of the secret door, had been the bedchamber of Rileb Sworddancer, hero of Aldis—Tersha had no reason to suspect King Lartik had overestimated this enemy. And if her nation's third sovereign had been right about Wesren's methods, then the Rose Knights would have to take just as subtle and long a view in rooting out this misinformation.

On the other hand, they definitely couldn't risk compounding the abuse this girl had already suffered. They couldn't use her as her abusers had. They couldn't send her back into whatever had caused a girl her age to wear such world-weary despair.

They had to take her into custody. Just then, Tersha received contact from Vrenn:

I found your smell, Vrenn said. *You were right. It's a threat in the Jarzoni underworld market called shadow rose incense. It comes from the actual Shadow Barrens.* Vrenn sounded inappropriately impressed. *Apparently, there's a cultivar of roses from ancient Austium that has somehow survived but become twisted by Shadow. It's used as an ingredient in rituals of memory-warping and mind control. We were warned to be on guard against a too-sweet scent that was like roses but unpleasantly so. Are we dealing with actual shadow roses? The briefing says they're a creepy shade of blood red.*

But Tersha didn't have time to chat about creepy flowers. *Thank you,* she sent back, *I'll keep you informed.* She cut contact and gave the signal. Fim and the Rose Knights stepped in to make their arrest.

The girl struggled and cried out, but there was nothing she could do against the overwhelming forces surrounding her. They had her bound in moments.

Tersha performed the search of her person. She found a small knife, barely usable as a weapon, and a bundle that looked like some sort of smoke bomb.

And then, in a pouch on a leather thong around her neck, held close to the poor girl's heart, she found a sachet of sickly sweet rose-smelling herbs. The crumbled flower petals inside it, Tersha noticed, were the precise red-brown shade of dried blood.

How do I counter it? Tersha sent back to Vrenn.

If they're fresh, there's a whole, long—

They're dried.

Oh, Vrenn sounded disappointed. *Run a bit of warding arcana through some clean water and dump it on the dried roses. Should disrupt the ritual casting until they're dry, at least.*

"Clean water," Tersha demanded. With a knife, she cut free the leather thong. The little thief whimpered and squirmed, but her bindings held. Someone handed Tersha a canteen.

"Help me fill this with warding arcana," she said.

All three Rose Knights touched the canteen, while Fim kept watch on their bound prisoner. Tersha felt Hirell and Burin's arcane efforts blending with her own. Burin's warding skills were particularly strong, she knew.

When the canteen hummed with charged arcana, Tersha tugged

open the little pouch and poured the canteen's water inside, drenching the herbs and crushed flower petals within.

They all felt the arcana melt away—even Fim seemed to sense its passing. The little thief stopped her struggling and stared around her in confusion.

Tersha felt her shoulders relax. "You're safe now," she said to the girl. "We have to question you about the theft, but I promise, you'll be treated justly."

The girl's eyes widened. She didn't make a sound.

"What's your name?" Tersha pitched her voice to be as gentle as possible.

"K-Kesso." She still sounded frightened. As confused as she must be, who wouldn't be? But the flavor of her fear had changed. Tersha thought there might be room for hope now.

"No one will ever hurt you again, Kesso," Tersha promised. "We won't let them. You never have to go back there."

And with that, their thief burst into tears. Tersha laid a hand on her shoulder and let her cry.

Find the herbs on your four prisoners, Tersha sent back to Vrenn. *The water trick worked. Maybe you can get them to talk after they're free of the sorcery.*

"I think we should let them all go," Tersha said.

Hirell, Vrenn, and Felba of the rehabilitation team frowned at her.

"Are you sure that's even safe?" Hirell asked.

"No," Tersha admitted. "I'm terrified for them, but if it's what they want, I don't think we should detain them any longer."

"We have to at least keep the thief," Vrenn said. "She committed a crime, inside the palace."

"Kesso stole an old scroll that we already have back," Tersha said. "This is bigger than that."

"That scroll has extreme historical value," Felba said, "and one of those people we arrested tried to burn it to ashes."

"And failed," Tersha insisted. "Besides, Kesso was already away and hiding by the time the brazier was lit. She'd never have made it from the basement to the kitchen if she'd only run *after* we banged down the door."

"We're getting off topic," Hirell cut in. "Tersha, I can see letting her go, but only if we follow her." Everyone shifted uncomfortably. "This cult undermines Aldin security from within," Hirell went on, "and it does so by tricking good people into believing lies about other good people. It's deeply insidious, and I do see your point, Tersha. Force is the worst way to solve it."

"We need more information," Felba said, though she didn't sound convinced.

Tersha wasn't sure about Hirell's suggestion, either. She'd promised to keep Kesso safe, which made having her followed appealing, but when she considered the possibility that the girl would use her freedom to head directly back to her abusers, she found herself questioning her entire line of reasoning.

"This operation was a major mistake on their part," she pondered out loud. "The cult handled it clumsily, in a way they haven't done in generations or we'd already have known about them. We can't miss this opportunity to catch up on three centuries of plotting, especially when we don't know when or if they'll slip up again."

Hirell nodded. "We still don't even know if Wesren was the original author of this plan, or if someone or something was controlling him from the shadows, as it were. That's especially likely now that we know there's some connection to the Shadow Barrens."

"And maybe even Austium," Vrenn put in.

Tersha sighed. It was true that the people they'd arrested hadn't known anything not already gleaned from their stash. They'd all been willing to answer questions, once their tongues had been loosened, but they'd knownn precious little and their memories had been blurred to be more like fever dreams.

Tersha felt for all of them. They'd been living such a nightmare for so long.

"You're thinking these people could lead us to someone with real authority," Felba said. "Even if they've told us everything, you think the cult might contact them again once they're free."

"I don't want to use them," Tersha said. "They've been used against their own wills for far too long."

Hirell sighed and nodded. He even looked a little embarrassed. "We need to take this to the queen," he said. "It's is going to be a long process. And you're right. We need to help these people, expose them to the truth, break the hold this cult has on them."

"Vrenn and I will bring our recommendations to her Majesty," Felba said.

Vrenn nodded and gave Tersha a hug before following his team-mate away toward the palace.

Tersha turned back to Hirell, who met her eyes with a troubled expression. The bewilderment of the long, strange day suddenly bubbled to the surface of Tersha's heart.

"How do we know, Hirell?" she asked her friend. "You were joking earlier, when you said we only think they're crazy because the Scepter's controlling us, but . . . I saw into Lartik's mind. I felt the sincerity of his emotions, and I still don't have proof. How do we know *for sure*, that Lartik's account is the real one, and Wesren's is false?"

"We don't," Hirell said, shocking her to her core. "Words can always be lies, and visions can always be illusions. There will never be proof to satisfy these people, and that's why you're handling this right."

"What do you mean?" Tersha asked.

"We'll win them with patience, kindness, and care. Force would only make things worse." He looked away, toward where the prisoners were still being held. "In a contest of lies, it's our actions that matter. We know the side of justice by its works."

Hirell surprised Tersha then by taking her hand in a decidedly more-than-friendly way, almost as if it were something he'd been wanting to do for a long time. "Thank you for being you, Tersha," he said. "This could have ended much worse without your insight."

"It isn't over yet," Tersha replied. She didn't want to reclaim her hand, but now was not the time for such things. She accepted the gesture at face value, returned his clasp, and let go.

Hirell nodded. "I know someone I should ask about how those flowers are getting into Aldis. I'll see you soon."

Tersha watched him jog away around a corner. As she admired for the thousandth time the perfect grace of his every motion, Tersha reflected on his words.

He was right. It wasn't the Scepter or the Hart that really mattered, in the grand scheme of things; it was that the people of Aldis knew kindness, and justice, and as much well-being as the sovereign's servants could manage.

This cult they'd discovered was a danger, yes, but they knew now how to undo its spell, and they knew where to start looking for the source of this centuries-old corruption. It may have been tainting their fair city since its very re-founding, but it couldn't much longer. Shadows always melted away when exposed to light.

Tersha hoped they could destroy Wesren's plan—or those of his hypothetical unknown master—by simply cutting off the illegal supply of these Shadow Barrens roses into Aldis. But Tersha and the other Rose Knights, she knew, would rise to whatever challenge Aldis faced, be it even the dark lord of Austium.

No one could win in a contest of lies. The people would believe what they would, and hearts twisted by sorcery could believe some truly terrible things. The answer was as it had always been: to rise above the corruption. To be worthy of the people's trust, come what may.

LIKE SMOKE IN MY MIND

Tiffany Trent

A wolf howl echoed through the caverns of Oritaun. Disturbed in his healing trance, Cenin opened his eyes and listened.

His fellow healers were also pulled from the Heartward Meditation, looking around in confusion. Some turned their gaze on him.

"Toh Yah," he whispered. He rose from his cushion, made apologetic bows to those who looked perturbed, and left the Heartward. The echoes of that singular heart-rending howl had not quite died away before another sounded nearby, in the direction of the Goiaeneum.

He said the wolf's name under his breath again as he ran.

When Cenin arrived, a small crowd had formed around the rhywolf, who had fallen on his side in the market where toys had been sold. This place, once so full of life and color, was now ghostly, faded ribbons blowing in the cavern breeze, its market stalls empty. Long ago, arcana caused the cavern ceilings to mimic the passing of days, but no more. Such power could not be spared now. All was fed directly into keeping the wards of Oritaun strong against the massing of Austium.

Cenin pushed through the crowd as politely as he could. The great rhy-wolf had sunk onto his side and was panting into the dust. Cenin slid a hand into Toh Yah's ruff.

"Old friend," Cenin said.

There was a twitch of recognition.

"Does anyone know what happened here?" the vata'sha healer asked.

The ten or so people who stood there shook their heads.

"We were drawn here by the howling," one vatazin woman said, "but when we got here, he slumped down on his side and didn't move. He wouldn't allow us to come any closer."

Cenin did a quick examination, digging his fingers deep into the silvery fur. The wolf's pulse galloped a bit. There was something . . . just the merest shadow that clung to the rhy-wolf and unsettled Cenin. Toh Yah didn't seem to have hurt himself physically, but his mental anguish was clear.

"He needs to return with me to the Heartward," Cenin said. Toh Yah was a large wolf; the healer knew he couldn't lift him alone. "Would someone please help?"

A vata'sha sentry, her skin the ebon of the shadows between caves, lifted her hand and the wolf floated just above the ground.

Cenin breathed a sigh of relief. A sentry who was also a shaper.

"Kemri," she bowed to his unspoken question.

"All will be well, old friend," Cenin said to the wolf. "You'll see." He addressed the shaper. "Thank you for taking the trouble."

"But of course," Kemri said.

Soon, they were directing the wolf's body down the corridor toward the Heartward. Cenin avoided the alcove that housed the vatazin spies and their healing staff, and tilted his head toward another alcove, against the far cavern wall. "That way," he said.

Kemri nodded and followed his lead.

At last they got the wolf settled on comfortable blankets.

Kemri bowed to both of them, hand to heart. "I must return to my post, healer. The last phase of the moon is upon us. We must be prepared."

Cenin nodded and bowed in return. "Thank you for your aid. Strength to your shield arm."

Even as he said the words, Cenin hoped this would not be the time when Austium came calling. No major military maneuver had happened yet, but that didn't mean it wouldn't this time. The Heartward had nearly doubled its patients in recent moons, with vata who had been compromised by darkfiends. Austium was certainly on the move, whatever some of the councilors might say.

Kemri saluted and departed with a smile.

Cenin turned his attention to Toh Yah. The wolf was still largely unresponsive, but nothing seemed visibly wrong. The healer decided what was probably needed most was rest. He sang a soft sleep chant, heavy soporific power flowing through his fingers to blanket the wolf in comfort and rest. Soon, the wolf's eyes closed fully and he began to snore.

Just then, a shadow darkened the alcove, and a familiar hand pushed back its curtain. "Cenin?"

Heat rushed to his face as the vatazin poet Kel Abremil stepped into the space. She glanced down at the wolf. "Will he be well? I heard . . ."

Cenin stood. "He'll be fine. I think he just needs rest." He took her darkening hands. They were cool and slender, with long, strong fingers that he loved to watch compose the lines of poetry for which she was famous.

"It seems more of us fall under the Shadow as the dark moon approaches," she said.

Cenin wanted to soothe away the apprehension in her tone. He cupped her cheek, which he knew would soon be the color of a moonless night sky. "All things are cyclical, love. The moon, the predominance of Light or Shadow. You taught me this."

"Yes," she said. "Yes." Her eyes took on that drifting gaze they so often held when she was on the verge of composition. "But I would far prefer that we were living in the cycle that took us away from the Shadow rather than toward it."

He laughed softly, drew her closer. "But you must admit, there are advantages to the darkness—things we can do then that we cannot in the full light of the moon."

She fell prey to his kiss. "It seems I have much to teach you, sweet boy."

Toh Yah stirred then, and Kel stepped back. "Come to my cave when you're finished?"

The wolf's amber eye focused on him. Cenin said, "Yes. It would seem I have work to do."

"I'll leave you to it," she said. She kissed him softly between the eyes, and the skin there tingled with all the magic of words left unsaid.

Cenin, the rhy-wolf said as the healer knelt next to him. *You are still with the poet then?*

Yes, old friend. Still. This had been and continued to be a point of contention between them. Toh Yah did not like the vatazin poet and thought she had no business fraternizing with a vata'sha half her age. He had said as much on many an occasion.

But Cenin, after probing Kel's mind when she had once been suspected of harboring a darkfiend spy, had not been able to resist the feelings that had grown between them in the Heartward.

You know how I feel about her, Cenin, the wolf growled.

You know how I feel about her, Toh Yah. Cenin's mental tone grew stiff and formal.

Yes, the wolf said, *but will you not listen to me, for once?*

Cenin half-smiled. *Only if you tell me something first.*

If a wolf could roll his eyes, Toh Yah would have done so.

What happened back there? As he spoke, Cenin reached for Toh Yah's muzzle. *If you'll allow me.*

Toh Yah knew what the healer wanted and obliged by opening his jaws wide and lolling out his tongue. It was pink and healthy. Cenin tried not to think about the deadliness of the wolf's yellowing teeth.

Well, you haven't been bitten by a cave spider, I guess, Cenin said, *but I'd still like to know what happened.*

The wolf pushed himself up on his front feet, then shifted his hindquarters so that he was fully sitting. It took a little effort, which Cenin assumed was due to age as much as anything else.

I just suddenly felt sad, Cenin, walking through the old markets where my bondmate and I used to frolic. He would buy ribbons and flowers to tie about my neck. We would play together through the stalls of the Goiaenium, much to the merchants' dismay. I miss him. The wolf hung his head.

I know, the healer said. *But are you really saying you fainted from sadness?*

The rhy-wolf tilted his head. *Are you saying that isn't possible?*

Cenin shook his head. *It is, but . . . everything about you suggests you're too healthy for this to happen.* He reached to cup both sides of the wolf's face, to initiate a reading of his psychospiritual being, but the wolf jerked away.

Will you let me read you, Toh Yah? It's been a while. Maybe there is more to this than being sad.

The wolf stood, stepped out of Cenin's reach. *Thanks to your ministrations. I feel fine now, Cenin. I don't think that will be necessary.*

But—

The wolf pushed the curtain aside with his nose, but paused and glanced back over his shoulder at the healer. *Thank you, Cenin. I'll see you again soon.*

If you are feeling sorrowful, remember, this is a place to heal hearts as well as bodies and minds.

I will remember, the wolf said. *If you will remember that we still must discuss your poet friend. You promised.*

Yes, Cenin said, trying to keep the reluctance from his mental voice. *Another time. If you are truly well enough, I have other patients to see.*

I am. Farewell. The wolf bowed his head and slid fully from the alcove.

Cenin sat back on his heels. He quelled the impulse to recall Toh Yah. He'd felt something as he'd tried to take the wolf's head in his hands—like the remotest wisp of shadow, like smoke in the mind.

He took several deep breaths to clear the uncertainty he felt. One of the more difficult things about being a healer, he'd found, was that one often had to trust one's patients on their journeys to wellness. Even if he felt they weren't as well as they said they were, they had to be allowed to make up their own minds.

"Cenin! Cenin!"

A young vata'an woman whom Cenin did not know well, but who clearly knew him, pushed into his alcove. "You're needed—come!"

As Cenin followed the young vata'an deeper into the Heartward, he saw that a crowd had formed around one of the central patient beds. Here, a number of psychic patients were grouped together in a ward where a dedicated group of healers monitored their health.

Their newest patient, though . . .

"Sikredh Yis!" Cenin gasped.

Sikredh Yis was the Councilor of the Arcane Arts and had served in the Pinnacle for several seasons. The vatazin Spirit Dancer's face, though darkening with the waning moon, was ashen, their eyes wild. They did not seem to see the concerned faces about them, but kept thrashing wildly, as if trying to tear something from within their own skin.

"Cenin!" Elenzen, the elder healer of the Heartward, gestured for him to join the circle of healers forming around Yis. "We just calm them before their distress radiates to our other patients," Elenzen said.

Palm to palm, they stood and chanted the Heartward meditation, soft and low at first. Contacting the Heartward, they channeled the energy into a circle of protection and calm that steadily slowed Yis' thrashing and helped send them deep into a healing trance.

Elenzen did not break the circle or meditation but used his arcana to speak into the minds of those who supported him. *I will seek to determine what ails them.*

There was an absence and a pull as though Elenzen had rappelled into a deep cave, going beyond the usual forms of communication. He had left a tether, though, something he could be hauled back with, should he need it.

As Cenin's arms trembled with the force of feeding energy into the circle, he glanced at Yis. Though the councilor was still now, their lips were gray, cheeks drawn.

There was a heavy tug at the line of Elenzel's consciousness as he climbed deeper into the mind of Yis. Cenin remembered the time he had gone spelunking with his mothers, how Narus Molvan had very nearly fallen into a dark hole when one of her lines had snapped.

It was like this with Elenzel—the feeling of something snapping, of falling away into a vast space. Cenin saw Elenzel's mouth twist into a silent scream.

Elenzel!

Against the internal protests of the others, Cenin plunged in after his leader. In the caverns of Sikredh's mind, Cenin sensed the shadow of a malevolent presence. It had nearly devoured Sikredh already, and now it reached out hungrily for Elenzel and all the healers who stood with him.

Darkfiend, Cenin relayed to the others. And they were there with him, joining their strength with his.

Elenzel didn't have time to warn Cenin or the others away. They turned their thoughts as one on the darkfiend. They surrounded it with the pure light of the Heartward, through which no defiling spirit could pass. Slowly, the thing withdrew into itself, collapsing until it was forced to relinquish its grip on Elenzel and Sikredh entirely.

It winked out in a heavy thrum of darkness that sent them scrambling back into themselves, shoring up their individual defenses and leaving the darkfiend unhoused and curdling into nothingness.

Cenin slumped against the bed, arms drifting down to his sides.

Sikredh was awake; their cool gaze perused the ring of exhausted healers. "Another darkfiend?" they whispered.

Elenzel nodded. "Unfortunately, Councilor, you are a preferred target."

"And a far too easy one," the councilor sighed. They stared sightlessly at the ceiling for a moment. Cenin saw a light shudder over their body.

"I never even know how it happens," they said. "One moment, all is well, and the next . . ."

"You are not alone in this, Councilor, I promise you. Look around, you see I speak truth," Elenzel said.

"I have no doubt," Sikredh said. "I just want to know how I can become stronger."

Elenzel grimaced. "That is a mystery we are still working to uncover."

The healer looked up and seemed to notice all those who swayed or leaned against the bed platform, including Cenin.

"All is well for now. Go home and rest."

The councilor sat up with Elenzel's assistance. Though no one could quite say they looked at them directly, still their words felt deeply personal. "I appreciate that you sacrificed vital healing energy to ensure my safety. It will not be forgotten."

They all bowed, hand to heart, and left the councilor with Elenzel.

Feeling bruised, Cenin wasn't sure where his steps were taking him until he ended up not at his own home but at the door of his mothers. Narus, in her usual way, seemed to have sensed him coming, for she was at the door when he arrived. She took his arm and said softly, "I made sure there was dinner enough for all of us."

He slid rather than sat into his seat at the table, tried not to feel guilty when his other mother, Ersid, dished out the stew of roasted tubers and ground beans, and tore the thick, hard-crusted bread into pieces for him as if he were still a small child.

"Thank you, Mother," he said. "I—"

She waved her hand at him before he could apologize. "Eat."

After such massive energy depletion, he did so, ravenously, as his mothers spoke around him, gently asking one another about their days. Cenin only heard half of what was said, so deep was he in the clay bowl of stew. When he suddenly realized he'd finished, he looked around wistfully and noticed both mothers staring at him in consternation.

Cenin blinked.

"We wondered how your day was," Narus said.

"Difficult," he said. He told them of the darkfiend infecting Sikredh. Ersid put her hand over mouth. Narus' dark brow creased. "Another one?" she said.

Cenin nodded. "Nearly got all of us. It was very powerful."

"Poor Sikredh. How are we going to stop these things?" Ersid asked.

Narus frowned. "More importantly, when are we going to do more to actively prevent them instead of allowing them to attack us?"

"You sound like Bruclun Ahngorha, with all his talk of mounting offensives instead of shoring up our defenses," Ersid said, rising and taking a few empty dishes over to the sideboard.

"He's not entirely wrong," Narus said. "As it stands right now, we are vulnerable. We need to rise up and make them fear us!"

Cenin could see by Ersid's face that she did not like this line of thinking. "Dessert?" she asked brightly, clearly hoping to change the subject.

"Yes, please," Cenin said.

Soon, he was spooning warm pear mold custard into his mouth and trying to forget the darkfiend he'd helped eliminate from Sikredh's mind. He couldn't stop thinking, though, of how similar it had felt to what he'd sensed with Toh Yah.

"That wasn't even the strangest thing that happened today, though," he said.

"Oh?" Narus looked up from her bowl, poking at it as if there should be more custard. Cenin knew the feeling.

"Toh Yah fainted in the Goiaeneum today."

A faint look of mistrust crossed Narus' features.

Ersid spoke from across the dining room. "Was he all right?" Years ago, Toh Yah's bondmate had saved Ersid's life. She'd always been grateful and quite fond of the rhy-wolf.

"He seemed to be," Cenin said, lingering over the last bite on his clay spoon. "But I felt something really strange in his mind—well, as much as he would let me feel. Reminds me a bit of the darkfiend we encountered."

"Hm," Narus grunted. This too was a point of contention between her and her wife. She didn't share her wife's feelings for the wolf, despite her gratitude to him.

"I know how you feel about him, darling . . ." Ersid began.

"How I feel is irrelevant," Narus said. "If Cenin senses something of the Shadow about him, then he should submit to examination. End of story."

"He really didn't want me to do that," Cenin said.

"I'm not sure he should have a choice."

At her wife's words, Ersid made a noise somewhere between a gasp and a snort. "Really, Narus? You'd take away the wolf's free will just because of a hunch?"

Narus looked at Cenin. "I'd say our son has more than a hunch, *cariad*."

Cenin pushed up from the table. He didn't think he could stand even what amounted to gentle ribbing between his mothers tonight. "If you don't mind, dear mothers, I'm very tired. May I sleep in my old bed? Assuming you haven't converted my room for something else, of course."

"Oh, by all means, son," Ersid said. "Probably best to sleep here where we can take care of you. You look like you're about to drop."

Cenin forced a smile on his face. "I am."

As he retreated to his old room, he could hear his mothers still discussing Toh Yah. He climbed into bed and pretended he couldn't hear. His last, startled thought was that he had forgotten to go see Kel as he'd promised, so tired had he been.

Her name was the last sigh on his lips before he fell into darkness.

In the morning, the news was everywhere that another assassination attempt had been made on Sikredh's life. Rumors abounded, the biggest being that Sikredh would step down now and seek a quiet retreat back to the Hithaeum, where the other spirit dancers surely missed them.

But the truth was that no one new had been interested in taking up council seats after the standard season of service. No one wanted to put their own lives on the line. Everyone was worrying only about themselves.

As Cenin hurried to the Heartward, a familiar shadow kept pace with him through the deeper shadows and lichen-illuminated *felis-arns* of the mountain.

Good morning, Toh Yah, Cenin said.

And to you, the rhy-wolf said. *I trust you slept well.*

Like a stone in sand. And you?

Not as well as I would have liked.

What troubles you?

I think you know. The rhy-wolf tilted his head to look up at him, and Cenin could almost believe he was smiling rather than grimacing.

Truly, friend, tell me.

Your poet friend.

Toh Yah, for what reason do you worry about whom I choose to love?

The rhy-wolf sighed. *I don't want to see you hurt. It would break your mothers' hearts, you know.*

Cenin chuckled. *Sometimes I think Narus wouldn't mind seeing me get my comeuppance so much, but then she feels that way about everyone.*

Even me?

Cenin felt his face flame, remembering the conversation from last night. He tried to pass it off lightly. *Oh, probably.*

Toh Yah grunted but pressed on. *Listen, Cenin, do you really think it's a good idea for you to be involved with a vatazin of her age?*

'Of her age'? Cenin repeated. *What has that got to do with anything? Should I not be friends with you because of your age?*

We are not romantically involved, Cenin, Toh Yah grumbled.

Fortunately, eh? Because that would surely be awkward, age notwithstanding. Cenin laughed.

This is not funny, though you seem to think so. I am merely trying to make certain you don't get hurt. There is something . . . not right about the poet.

Cenin frowned. *What do you mean?*

Well, have you read any of her recent verse? It's very dark.

Much is dark these days, wolf. What's your point?

Merely that perhaps you did not scan her as well as you think you did.

Cenin stopped in the center of the *felisarn* and the wolf stopped with him. The few people who were up at this hour moved around them, muttering in agitation. *What are you suggesting?*

I think you know. Toh Yah's amber gaze was level and unblinking.

Cenin stared back at him until the rhy-wolf turned his head, uncomfortable with such direct gaze from a friend.

It wasn't only me that scanned her. Many others did and found nothing. She just . . . probably shouldn't apply to be a spirit dancer again any time soon. Cenin laughed softly at this, remembering how Kel had been scanned because her spirit dancing was so awful that people feared she'd been infected by shadowspawn. She had gone back to her poetry and *khumeii* directly after.

You think what I say is little more than a jest, healer, Toh Yah said, affronted. *You will surely think otherwise when she has breached your or some other ward because you wouldn't believe me!*

With that, the rhy-wolf left him, slipping away as silently as he'd come, though certainly leaving behind a signature of anger and raw affront, accompanied by that drift of psychic smoke Cenin could not confidently identify.

So, like the darkfiend Sikredh harbored, he thought. *And yet . . .*

He could not admit to himself, when he resumed his post in the Heartward, that he was glad when Kel didn't turn up. He reminded himself many times throughout the day to send her a message, something to explain his absence. He had always been very chary of his lovers' time in the past. He meant to be no different with Kel.

But times themselves were different.

Yet another vatazin spy was ushered in, and healers needed to scan and remove a darkfiend that lurked within. This one was not as powerful as the one that had inhabited Sikredh, but it was violent and nasty, and Cenin knew he'd not fully recovered from its predecessor.

Afterwards, when he turned and saw her waiting at the mouth of the inner ward entrance, he was less than pleased. He was tired and cross and hungry again.

"Is something wrong, Cenin?" she asked.

All he could hear were the words of the rhy-wolf balanced precariously against everything he'd witnessed with his patients.

"Kel, I am sorry but now is not a good time."

Multiple emotions chased across her face before she drew herself up. "I see," she said. "Perhaps you are trying to say that no time is a good time?"

"Perhaps I am." The words snapped out of his mouth before he could stuff them back in.

"I'll be on my way then," she said. She turned. He reached for her wearily but missed.

Still, she felt the draft of his fingers passing and half-turned.

"Surely you can understand. The darkfiends, the healing . . . I am *tired*, Kel. But there is no time for that. We are going into the Shadow and . . ."

She half-smiled, wistfully. "And I fear from the Shadow you and I will not return together."

His eyes widened. She understood.

"Very well," she sighed. She departed then, seemingly having aged even beyond her already lengthy years.

"Cenin!" Ezrenel called from within.

He drew himself up and returned, too exhausted to feel much, too drawn by duty to go after her.

But deep in the eternal night of the mountain, as he lay alone, he wondered whether he had rejected her for the reason he'd given or whether it was because Toh Yah's words had dripped on his heart like acid, eating away at whatever had tried to grow there.

At last, he cast away those thoughts. The Shadow worked too well on the exhausted, fearful minds beneath the mountain. He would face these questions in the light, when the danger had passed, but for now, he would have to trust his instincts.

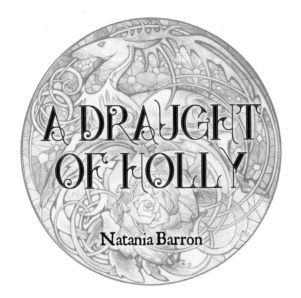

A DRAUGHT OF HOLLY

Natania Barron

Veda Nadiq clutched her field kit to her chest as the little boat shuddered to a stop on the shore of the mist-covered island. The contents were precious, and though the container itself was covered in wax and tied so tightly that the pages were dented permanently on one side, she could not be too careful.

This far out, finding more paper would be nothing short of a miracle. Even though she carried a sword, a dagger, and surveying equipment worth enough to feed a small family of four, it was the field kit that she could not bear to part with.

As the boat finally wobbled and stabilized, the sand grating across the hollow bottom, the stink of the place rose up around them. Veda sneezed.

"Is there any island you're not allergic to?"

Renn was just behind her, already poised to help the boat the last few paces, muscles flexing, white teeth flashing. He carried all the hallmarks of a young man who had flourished in childhood, having been given the best cuts of meat and the choicest vegetables. Unlike where Veda grew up, the faces she was accustomed to seeing in the remote Jarzoni village of her birth, Renn's cheeks were free of pox marks or the remnants of other childhood diseases. The rumor was that he was a lordling, likely disinherited or dishonored, and had given up all his titles to join the ranks of the Sovereign's Finest.

Veda didn't complain. Though he was occasionally a bit conceited, Renn made up for it with unflagging enthusiasm and genuine friendship. It didn't hurt that Renn had lively brown eyes, bold brows, and the kind of lips that begged to be touched, nibbled, kissed . . .

Still, Renn liked to tease Veda in a playful way. Unlike Renn, Veda simply hadn't grown as robust as many others selected for post as Envoys, and indeed, not even compared to those living in the Ring. She was often mistaken for a teenager, given her narrow shoulders and her small stature due to her twisting spine and weak, unreliable legs. But her deep voice and "ancient eyes," as Renn liked to call them, usually gave her true age away rather quickly. She was no child.

And certainly, the thoughts she had about Renn, on an hourly basis, were far from puerile. He was, quite frankly, the most beautiful creature she had ever seen. She treasured their friendship, but out here on the edge of the world it seemed indulgent, especially on an errand as somber as theirs.

Besides, it was difficult to make an impression on a man like Renn. Stature and physical shortcomings aside, Veda also had a frustrating habit of being allergic to nearly everything. Aboard their ship it had not been so much of an issue, but the closer they got to shore the higher the likelihood that she'd end up a sneezing, watery-eyed mess. Beauty and grace incarnate, to be sure, when one was constantly wiping snot from their nose.

Her weak constitution had almost cost her this post, and if it hadn't been for the intercession of Gadian Harbor, her teacher of ten years in the arts of archivist's skills, she would likely still be working at the herb warehouse in the city. The mildew and mold of that place, coupled with the intense proliferation of pollen, had made her life a misery.

But in spite of the physical limitations of the job, here among the Surveyors, Veda could flourish doing precisely what she excelled at: recognizing plants and drawing them. Her handwriting was poor, her physical form less than adequate, but no one in her class could come close to her when it came to recalling from memory the shapes and colors of flowers.

"Be careful, Renn," said Veda as she watched the strapping young man. "There is bladder-velvet algae over there, and if you get it on your skin, you'll end up with a terrible rash for the next few days."

Renn gave her that look, half-amused and half-annoyed, but eventually took heed and settled the boat a little farther away from the twirling mass of kelp. Veda watched the little fuzzy knobs of it bobbing up and down with the tides around them, trails like elegant veils beneath the surface, marveling at how the waning light illuminated them just slightly, like perfectly smooth—and hairy—emeralds. The kelp served its purpose, though; aside from being interesting to look at, Veda knew that it gave the local fowl of the island its distinctive citrusy flavor when cooked. But there was something about the enzymes in the birds' stomachs that rendered the rash properties inert once consumed.

Bladder-velvet: A kind of saltwater kelp. Inedible to humans, but commonly eaten by waterfowl. Grows anywhere from one to twelve handspans long; plants are one long, connected entity. Can cause allergic rashes with contact on human skin, but were often used in old herbal remedies for cough and cold once dried and boiled. Due to its scarcity, it is not currently used in such a manner.

They'd been to the other islands on the coast before this, on the edge of the Shadow Barrens, searching for their missing comrades: Grey's Surveyors. And each time, they had returned with nothing. Yes, they'd seen signs, but nothing recent and nothing that spoke of foul play. Some of her companions began to wonder if there were ghosts, ghouls, or worse plaguing the missing company. Veda didn't entirely discredit the arcane in their fates, but she liked to rule out the ordinary first. Yet in spite of all her categorizing and archiving of plants, Renn's observations of their tracks, and countless theories, what had happened to Grey's Surveyors remained baffling. Veda's company, Arunn's Surveyors—named for their infamous and rakish leader, Arunn Leftfellow—followed them from location to location, finding clues but never answers.

Then they'd found the first island. What was now considered an archipelago was more a chain of islands, and even an atoll or two, from long-ago volcanic activity. There were some ruins on the larger islands, but this far south, if any civilization had lived before, they left little trace. Renn, the resident expert on ancient peoples, couldn't properly place the architectural style they frequently saw in crumbled temples and tiles.

"Bladder-velvet algae," Veda continued, almost losing her footing on the soft sand but righting herself quickly, grabbing Renn's hand to steady herself, "only grows when the water is a specific temperature in the winter—not too cold, not too hot. So, it can't get much warmer than a good spring at home."

"Always with the astute observations," came Arunn's booming voice from behind them. Arunn was a man both broad and tall, his bright blue eyes twinkling out of his massively bearded face like burnished turquoise. He was large in every way possible, muscle and girth combining to create a truly imposing figure capable of smashing things to smithereens when the opportunity arose. He preferred a mace, though it wasn't standard issue. Come to think of it, Arunn preferred a great many things that weren't standard issue. That was probably why his team was full of such miscreants.

To say that Arunn's Surveyors was second-string was, perhaps, generous. Even among the Sovereign's Finest, there were those who, for lack of a better term, simply made up the last in line for a variety of reasons. For Veda, it was her size and health; her talent, however, made more than enough compensation, but the reality of her fragility could not go ignored. For Renn, it was his upbringing that set him apart. He had been coddled, groomed for greatness, but when he'd decided to scorn his family name and revoke his noble lineage, well, that hadn't gone over well with everyone.

Arunn himself was simply too much: Too loud. Too brash. Too reckless. He'd never met a rule he couldn't find some way to break. It was rumored that he'd run afoul of the queen, and that was what had precipitated such a fool's errand as this one, a rescue mission on the edges of the Shadow Barrens, off the charted edges of the world.

He didn't speak of it, but they all knew why he had insisted that his Surveyors go on this task: his sister, Hellaa Leftfellow, was among the missing.

Veda tried to keep out of the way as the rest of their crew, twenty or so in total, went about the same routine they'd had since departing over a month before. She could try and insert herself in the unpacking and the hauling and the tying of rigs, but she knew she'd be more of a nuisance than a help.

"The fog's so thick you can't even see our ship out there," came Kinna's voice. She was a small woman, but strong in a way that Veda would never be. And her voice always sounded halfway to burnout, like she'd just woken up from a hangover. Though, as far as Veda could remember, she'd never seen the woman drink. "But aside from that, it's like we're living the same day over and over again, isn't it?"

Veda wanted to say, no, it wasn't. It was hard to explain to the tracker that each island was its own ecosystem, that every place they'd stepped along the way was, to her, like meeting a brand-new person. But Veda learned, long ago, that her angle on nature was considered unusual. So, it was best to nod and give a shy little shrug.

"I hope this time, at least, we get some answers," Veda said. She smoothed her hands over the curling cover of her notebook, its supple texture comforting. When they had set out, this gift from the queen had been the most beautiful object she'd ever beheld. All the moisture, though, had given it considerably more character. Renn said it was ruined. He couldn't see beauty for its lack of pristineness.

"I've got a feeling," Kinna said, taking a swig of water from the waterskin a passing crewmate tossed her, and then wiping her face, "that we're going to get answers soon. And I don't think we're going to like them."

"What did you see?"

If there was anyone who could come close to understanding the way that Veda saw the world, it was Kinna. Tracking would have been a good option for her had her body been more robust. Though Kinna was not good at details, nor valuing independent plants for their unique contributions to the world, she could spot when things were off: cracked branches, moved logs, turned earth.

Kinna squinted across the water again. "They were here. Not long ago. I can already tell by the way the trees . . ." she trailed off, shaking her head. "I can just tell when people smash through the undergrowth, especially when it's been undisturbed for so long. We didn't see that evidence on the other islands, just that they'd made landfall."

"I wish the light was with us tonight," said Veda softly. "I'm always worried that we're just too late."

"We can't be any later than they are," joked Kinna, but no one laughed.

"But the forest here is dense, and it will be slow going," said Veda. "There are dozens of trees growing here that I've never seen before, and companion plants, too. This was once a garden."

"I suspect we'll find a high density of ruins," Renn said, plopping down next to Kinna and taking her waterskin without asking. "You can see the beginnings of a road over that way." He pointed. "Slightly different stone-stacking technique than we'd seen before. Perhaps we'll discover a lost civilization, and Grey's are just having the time of their lives, living as kings and queens among them."

It was a bright thought, but no one laughed. It was too cold, and they were all too heartsick and homesick to laugh.

The night passed without event. They had all so often slept beneath the stars, huddled together under their blankets and tarps, that no one complained. Kinna and Grycie sounded like they were enjoying themselves, their giggles rising into the night before Veda managed to fall asleep. It was good, she reminded herself, that people fell in love, that they enjoyed their company together. Even if no one ever felt the inclination to do so with Veda, it didn't mean she should resent others for such behavior.

Still, she couldn't help but think about Renn. The way, sometimes, she thought she caught him looking at her. The way he always rushed to help her when she was tiring. The way he always made her feel . . . seen. Not for the ways her body was different, but for the way her body was her own. Her eyes were "ancient," her fingers "deft," her ears "like cockle shells."

Lover's Lace: A large white, flat-leafed flower found living in marshy conditions along the Shadow Barrens' island chains. Produces prodigious seed-pods, which can be used to heal burns and thicken soups.

She hadn't slept much when the first, watery rays of sun rose, but that wasn't unusual. Veda was always one of the first ones awake and the last ones asleep. Though her body was stronger than it had been in a long time, too much sitting still made her bones ache.

Besides, there were flowers and herbs that only liked the earliest morning light, and if she was going to get any sketching done before they moved out, now was the time.

Renn and Old Born were preparing breakfast. Veda took a bowl of porridge before sitting down by one of the tide pools to observe what she could. She had only managed half a sketch—of some water beetles that had gathered on the long tubers—when Renn was hovering over her again.

"You're in my light," she said, not looking up.

"It's almost time to move."

Veda frowned. This was the worst part.

"I really don't mind," Renn said.

"I'm sure this is not what you envisioned yourself doing when you left your family and fortune for adventure," Veda teased.

No matter how she tried to joke about it, Renn always prickled at the mention of his personal sacrifice. "I know what I signed up for," he said softly. "And though, yes, my mother might raise her perfectly manicured eyebrows a bit to know that I'm serving my days in such a manner, I have no regrets, Veda. I mean that."

"I just . . . hoped I'd be better at this point," Veda said, angrily tucking away her pencils and rolling up the rest of her kit. The beetles would have to wait, no matter how lovely their gold-flecked markings.

"Well, judging by the fact you were up six times last night stretching your legs," Renn said airily, "I'd say that, even if you were feeling better, it's a bad harbinger of things to come. It was a hard crossing, even for those of us who don't live with pain every day."

Veda swallowed back the tears prickling the corners of her eyes. "I'm not an *invalid*," Veda said, standing and trying to look in some way whole and hale. But she was so much smaller than Renn. And her bony elbows looked impish at best.

Renn's handsome face softened. "Come on. I know I'm not as good at it as Festen was, but he's not going to be carrying anyone for a long time now."

"He's not dead. He just broke his leg. And he probably wouldn't have broken his leg if he wasn't carrying me," Veda said as Renn turned around.

They had fashioned a special halter for the long days of walking. Festen was considerably taller and wider than Renn, but he had a habit of ignoring Veda while they walked. In another survey group, they might have had animals—and originally, they did—but an unfortunate swine flu got most of them half a week into their voyage. So Festen was aboard the *Wistful,* and Renn had volunteered to carry Veda.

No one knew nature like Veda Nadiq. No one could draw it, measure it, understand it. And slight as she was, barely much larger than a girl just into her flowering, she wasn't much of a burden.

But Renn.

Anyone but Renn.

"That's nonsense. He was clumsy and hungover, and I'm quite certain your weight wasn't enough to drive him headfirst into the cask of ale," Renn said, turning around. He'd fastened the halter just right, to her specifications. Veda could get a foothold and then . . . well . . .

She couldn't make herself do it yet. When they were camped, when she could just wander in the tidepools, she could decide where her feet went.

She didn't move, and Renn knelt down, looking her in the eyes, taking her shoulders in his lovely hands.

"Veda, look at me."

She did. Reluctantly. And felt her heart skitter when their eyes met.

"You're the most brilliant botanist naturalist artist I've ever known."

"That's not my occupation—"

"And, yes, I know that's not your real title, and I know you doubt yourself constantly. And, lords, I know how frustrating this must be for you to have to be literally stuck to my back for hours. I probably smell worse than those donkeys after they died—"

"You don't, you—"

"—but Arunn, and the queen herself, have made it clear that we're to protect you. I may not be the cleverest or the most enterprising or the most handsome among us," Renn said, though Veda was quite certain on that last count he was wrong, "but I am honored to carry you."

"You just like taking credit for discovering ruins when I spot unusual undergrowth," she said.

"*And* I like taking credit for discovering ruins when you spot unusual undergrowth." His smile was wicked and beautiful, just like Veda's favorite plants. "Please. I can carry you."

Even though it was the last thing she wanted to do, Veda smiled, consented, and prepared for the trek deeper into the island. Damn that beautiful boy.

Red ferns: The oldest plants on record, red ferns prefer colder climates and are half the height and width of ferns found on the mainland. Red ferns, however, grow more densely, and their fronds have twice as many leaves. When stewed, they resemble spinach greens in flavor.

They found the roads surprisingly clear as they made their way deeper into the wood. The trees were similar to those they had seen on the other islands, and particularly akin to those on the second atoll they'd come across. Veda supposed they might have been on a similar current, and some of the seeds had simply migrated. She theorized that this would have been the origin, though, since the trees here were so much more immense: broad-leafed evergreens, twisting moss-covered conifers, and the ever-present red ferns that covered the forest floor as far as they could see.

It was colder, here, and the ferns were still in their fiddlehead state, but no less beautiful. Though she appreciated the view from Renn's back, and his reassuring strength beneath her, she would have loved to spend more time at the level of the fiddleheads so she could check them for spores and other insects.

"I can't believe this road is still intact," said Renn once they stopped for their first break. The weather was pleasant and the hike relatively easy, but poor Renn was bright-faced and still catching his breath. He was by no means the strongest of the survey crew, but he was certainly determined to carry Veda as far as he could. "I can tell by the construction that it's absolutely ancient—I don't know that anyone would know how to begin that layering and pattern these days—but it's pristine."

"You only tripped once," Veda said. Her joints ached, especially her hips. But given that Renn was doing most of the work, she hardly felt like complaining was appropriate.

"Do you think it was the vatazin?" Renn was half speaking to himself, but Veda didn't want him to feel as if she was ignoring him.

He always thought it was the vatazin.

"It could be," she said softly. "Could have also been some enterprising individual who found their way out here and had a knack for laying brick."

"It's more than that. It's a feeling," Renn said.

"Always with the feelings."

He frowned at her. "You know, you pester me for being genteel, but it does mean that I have a good deal more experience in this matter. In fact, it's because my parents traveled so much that I found my calling. Stones speak to me. Don't laugh, Veda. You talk to plants regularly."

"They don't talk back to you, do they?" Veda asked, trying not to laugh.

Renn shook his head, looking a little embarrassed. "My uncle Horol was a gentleman explorer. His methods were faulty, his conclusions offensively inaccurate, and his approach nothing short of destructive, but he let me tag along with him. And after a while, digging in the dirt and running your hands over stones . . . it starts to make sense. You can feel things from them. Maybe it wasn't the vatazin here. But I wouldn't be surprised if the rock was either repurposed or sacred to them. It just has—"

"A feeling?" Veda nudged him. "This is an island, Renn. There's only so much one can do with rocks. And if the civilization was ancient, transport would be a problem."

"I've been thinking about that," Renn said, picking up one of the cobblestone shards and turning it around in the dimming evening light. "What if these weren't islands at all?"

Veda was used to Renn saying absolutely bizarre things during their work, but this was a bit out of range, even for him. "Not islands?" she asked. "As if they just decided one day that they wanted to slink off of the mainland?"

Renn paused in his rock admiring and gave her a look. That look. The one that she somehow felt in her toes. Exasperation and amusement all mingled into one.

"You are too logical," he said. "No. I do not mean that one day these islands decided to go for a long walk and simply detached themselves from land. I was thinking, judging by the composition of this stone—which is so similar to what we've seen in some of the coastal quarries—that this might have been a mountain. Or a mountain range. And over time, somehow, the waters rose and cut them off from everything else."

"You have a very vivid imagination."

"I do. And that serves me well. Not everyone sees the world as an endless catalog of stamens and seed pods."

"If I didn't know you better, Renn, I might accuse you of flirtation."

Veda expected Renn to respond with even more wit, but he did not. He looked at her a moment and, as hard as it was for her to believe, he looked a little shy. Embarrassed. He couldn't possibly have been meaning to flirt with her; the idea that someone like Renn could fancy a woman like Veda was laughable, at best.

"Well, that clears things," Veda said, slapping her thighs and taking a few steps back, nearly barreling into Arunn as she did. She'd have fallen over if he hadn't steadied her with one broad arm. "Oh, Arunn."

The immense man gave her shoulder an affectionate squeeze. "Enough babbling," he said playfully. "I'd like to get a little farther in before we bed down for the night, if you two don't mind. It'll be a while before we can get tight beneath the blankets."

Veda was very glad of the dusky light because she was quite certain she was blushing seventeen shades of pink at that strange, suggestive line—and matching smirk—from Arunn.

"Hardly," Veda said, making it look like she was about to take some notes on the trailside vegetation. But her stylus was the wrong way. And she was open to a page with sketches of fish. "I mean. We are tired. I just have a feeling we're going to have a hard time getting to sleep tonight. The first night under the trees is always the hardest."

The first night was not, however, difficult at all. Veda slept heavily, sandwiched between Kinna and her pack. The climate on this new island was incrementally warmer than the last, or else the weather had shifted. She woke, amazed at how easily her joints moved and how little effort was required to get moving. One morning, a few weeks before, she had been completely numb from the knees down, and it had delayed the surveyors over an hour because she couldn't even get in the harness. It had been mortifying, and she'd tried not to meet the eyes of the entire company around her, full of pity and judgement.

But it was a good morning. And Veda had learned to revel in good mornings. To be grateful for the times that her feet didn't ache when she slipped on her boots, or her shoulders didn't burn when she reached up to grab her drying jacket from the branches.

"Any great observations from our resident botanist?"

It was Arunn. Veda wondered if the man ever slept.

"I'm not a botanist," she said, tugging on her cloak. The familiar warm wool smell was as comforting as its weight. "I'm just a surveyor with a certain affinity for green things."

"Ah, yes. And tall, noble growths," Arunn said as he picked his teeth and wiggled his eyebrows over to where Renn was helping with breakfast. Somehow, the man always had a plentiful supply of wooden toothpicks.

"I like attractive angles," Veda said. "And I'm hardly alone. The same could be said for more than half the crew. I'm devoted, if not a little stubbornly, to my passion."

"Hmm. Well. If I'd had anything to do with it, I'd have sent you to become a botanist. To a university, that sort of thing. You'd have made a spectacular alchemist, or a professor. Sometimes I think your talents are wasted on us, Nadiq. Not that I'm not glad of it. You've saved me from crotch rashes more than once."

"You, like me, have a particular sensitivity to some plants. It's essential to know which ones serve best as methods of . . . cleaning," she said, trying to be delicate. Which was always a challenge around Arunn—he tended to bring out the bawdy in just about anyone. "I wouldn't be able to travel so much," Veda said, even though the prospect of a life of learning had always been tempting.

"Well, my ass thanks you."

She laughed. "You're very welcome."

"I'm serious, though. About school. About taking up a professorship. You've got a way with teaching, sharing knowledge. Just, as time goes on, it might be something to consider. I've got connections," Arunn said, softly. He didn't mean to be cruel; he was trying to help her, protect her. But it cut the same.

"I'm doing just fine," said Veda, straightening herself as best as she could. "I promise, I'll tell you if it's too much."

Arunn, for once, looked a little embarrassed. "I didn't mean to offend, Nadiq. All of us have limitations, and you know yours better than anyone. Just, if we manage to find our way back home after this, I suspect all of us will want a little rest and replenishment."

The whole camp bustled as they spoke, and to her frustration, Veda noticed Kinna packing up both of their cots. It was a kind gesture, but not necessary.

"No offense taken," Veda said. "We're closer than we've been."

"I just . . ." Arunn drew his massive hands over his face, shaking his head. "I'm starting to feel lost out here. And I'm not sure if it's because I'm starting to grieve for her already, or if it's just being out at sea for so long. I'd never been out without her, you know."

Hellaa Leftfellow was a legend, somehow even a bigger personality than her younger brother. Her love of feasts and parties and grand gestures was without par, and her crews practically worshipped her for her compassion and generosity. They weren't twins, but they might as well have been. The only marked difference was that Hellaa's hair was always shorn short and had been gray since she was a teenager, hence her nickname. But there was nothing gray about Hellaa Leftfellow; she lived in bold color.

"Well, we're putting together the story of this island," Veda said, "And I have noticed slightly higher temperatures. Certainly, a noticeable increase in plant density. But the same signs we'd seen before. Grey's Surveyors were definitely through here, Kinna has confirmed multiple locations where they bedded down, or chased game; Renn has seen markings on the stones, too."

"Same as every damned island we've come to," Arunn said, voice flat, eyes askance. "Plenty of fowl to eat, though I could do with fewer beasts and more welcoming faces."

"We'll find her," Veda found herself saying, though she felt that crawling anxiety rise in her again.

"I keep hoping for some kind of bloody mess," Arunn said, wiping a hand over his face. "As if that might explain things. Can you imagine? Hoping for a trail of viscera? Hoping for a femur bone? Signs of struggle?"

"We all need closure," Veda said softly. "It's nothing to be ashamed of."

"A dragon would be closure."

"A dragon would be the end of us, too, because we'd be in an old tale of magical pools, blessed swords, and talking plants . . ."

Renn bounded over, cheeks flushed, eyes bright. He looked from one somber face to the other and said, "Are we talking about trails of viscera again?"

"Don't discredit good viscera, Renn. It makes for surprisingly good fertilizer," Veda said, and even Arunn had to laugh.

Lichen of Ruin: A type of lichen only occurring in the Shadow Barrens islands, attached to ancient ruins. Pale in color with white edges; sometimes flowers a light blue under the right conditions, but only at night. No known medicinal properties.

Just when Veda was ready to ask for another break, Kinna came crashing through the brush, red-faced from exertion. She'd scouted ahead with her small group of trackers.

"Arunn! They were through here," she said, barely able to keep her breath. She must have run unimaginably fast. "Oh, lords, were they through here."

"What did you find?" There was a note of desperation in Arunn's voice that Veda had never heard before.

"Everything," Kinna said. "And nothing."

It was the most advanced camp they had come across. In fact, as Renn had observed, it had the beginnings of a town—or the bones of one, anyway.

Grey's Surveyors had used what remained of an old ruin to act as the foundation for their settlement. There was a longhouse of sorts that must have been living quarters—these resembled the ones that they all were taught to build during training, only using the side of what might once have been a temple or perhaps an open bazaar. It was difficult to discern beneath the vines and crumbling rock.

There was a blacksmith's hut, hardly more than a lean-to but with a rudimentary forge. A blacksmith meant there must be a mine somewhere, or else a store of artifacts they could use for refashioning into weapons. There was a basic mess hall, with an immense cauldron in the middle that had to be a relic of the previous era. One of the houses was used for drying herbs, another for making baskets.

And it didn't take someone of Veda's skill to recognize that they had gardens, stalks of *havan* grain braids still shivering in the wind, indicating they had begun a life here. In spite of the overgrowth, remnants remained of their attempt to bring agriculture and order to the island. They had been harvested in the fall, but now, in the cold spring, all that remained were unkempt remainders.

Inside the living quarters, Arunn's Surveyors found the previous surveyor's packs, papers, weapons, clothing.

But no sign of another soul. No fresh footprints.

"It looks like they vanished," said Kinna. She was restless, uneasy, pacing back and forth. Veda knew that she took her job very seriously and, like her, tended to skew toward skepticism.

No camp they'd seen had been this comprehensive; yet, it was somehow worse.

"You don't think it could be beasts?" asked Grycie, eyes wild with fear.

"There are no monsters here," Renn whispered.

"Except the ones we make," Veda replied softly.

They did a clean sweep of the area and confirmed—no signs of predators, no signs of struggle. Just the usual fauna: pigs, some of the speckled deer common to this climate, and tree-rats everywhere.

Arunn, showing an unusual lack of composition, threw one of his daggers straight into the trunk of a tree and then stalked off into the nearby wood.

Havan grain. A large-kernelled grain that grows quickly and can be harvested to make a rough flour. Stalks grow tall and must be braided together to prevent toppling. Generally considered the grain of poverty, due to its poor flavor, it is still a preferred crop for the early stages of exploration and land establishment. It is mostly resistant to blights and much of the mold and mildew found during sea voyages.

The company agreed that they ought to use this camp as their new center of operations. What few clues were left behind were gathered together for future perusal. Wet conditions had rendered the few journals all but unreadable. And even though they were all slightly uncomfortable with the idea of sleeping where the dead might have been, no one argued about beds and walls to shelter under. They were too tired.

If the light had been better, and her body not strained past the point of return already, Veda would have gone straight to the cauldron, then to the gardens, to try and decipher what Grey's Surveyors had managed in terms of food and agriculture, what strains of herbs and plants they'd used in their daily lives. There could be answers there.

She'd almost convinced herself to go with a lantern and check when the rain started in earnest, and Veda took to her cot in the very back of the long barracks. Elsewhere, her companions were singing softly, drinking a little—they had, of course, found casks of beer from home and, in spite of her warning not to drink, they had decided otherwise—and offering their theories about where Arunn had gone off to.

Arunn, Veda knew, was probably off sobbing somewhere. He could read the signs as well as he could. Nothing would have sent

Grey's Surveyor's away in such a rush unless something truly horrific had befallen them. Be it biological or arcane in nature, it didn't matter much. They were gone. And if they found the company . . .

When Renn slipped down next to her, Veda was surprised to feel a sense of relief wash over her. She had a habit of withdrawing from the others, trying to make up for her lack of fortitude during the day by letting them have their fun at night. Arunn had told her dozens of times that it wasn't winning her any friends, but Veda had a hard time letting go of the bad habit.

But Renn felt different.

She couldn't exactly decipher when that had happened, when she began to feel relaxed around him, and settled, and grounded; even the pain in her hips and at the base of her spine dissipated the closer he got. She distracted him in a way, she realized, she was truly beginning to count on.

"We can't solve every problem with plant fibers," Renn said, picking at Veda's shoulder. Indeed, wisps of the *havan* grain husks she'd been rummaging around in earlier still clung to the wool there. Stubborn little things.

"You should go have fun with them," Veda said. "You've already had to spend an embarrassingly large amount of time with me."

"Maybe I just got used to it," Renn said, jostling her gently. "I feel rather empty without you clinging to my back."

"I just feel like such a failure, Renn."

"We all do," he said.

"But I'm . . . I'm broken . . ."

The words spilled out of her, and then the worst thing happened: Veda began weeping. She couldn't remember the last time such a thing happened—perhaps when her father had died, when she'd felt his soul leave this world in her frail arms. Since then, tears had felt a childhood indulgence.

Now, though, they rose up and flowed from her eyes, issuing deep sobs from within.

"Veda . . ."

When he said her name, it was like the sighing of wind through wheat in the summer.

"You are so much harder on yourself than anyone else," he continued, squeezing her. She couldn't recall when she'd allowed herself to be folded into his arms, but even through her tears she reveled in the feeling of his body around hers. "We need you."

"I'm so tired of feeling as if my body is failing me, as if I'm failing everyone," she said, voice low. "Renn, I'm just so tired."

"I know," he said, smoothing the hair at her brow. Those long, beautiful fingers felt so right there, so familiar. "I wish I could give you freedom from the pain. But I can carry you as far as you need. Whenever you need. Veda, I—"

Kissing him was so much easier than she had considered. Renn was one of those men possessed of beauty in such an unfair, elegant manner that simply envisioning the act of kissing such lips had always felt like an exercise in childish fantasy. One could not kiss a statue, after all, but one could *imagine*. And, lords knew, she so often did.

And yet, this kissing was *very* real. And Renn was, most certainly, kissing her back. Not like a statue at all.

That was the part that gave her the most pleasure, really. Veda had kissed people before; she'd had a lover or two when she was studying, and was no novice to affection. But those relationships were casual, passing; fierce and then done. They were lovers of a season, a passing time. Which certainly had their merit, but were not . . .

Here, though, this kiss, with this man she had known for over a year, upon lips she'd seen smile and frown and quirk thousands of times . . .

They were speaking, she thought wildly, as his hand lifted and traced the back of her neck, communicating in another language that they had been whispering to one another for months.

I've waited too long for this.

Now is just as good of a time as any.

I've held you so close for days now and I haven't been able to stop thinking, but—

I won't break.

Veda.

"Yes."

Permission granted, Renn's plaintive exploring became bolder. His mouth traced the length of her neck, and Veda shivered as cold air spilled down her breasts and stomach as he deftly pulled the laces away. Her eyes were still raw from the tears; she blinked as pleasure rippled across her body.

She pulled him to her, no hesitation in her movements, no question in his. The passion was bright enough, obliterating all other thoughts, that she did not think about her withered legs or twisted spine. Veda, entwined as she was with Renn, thought only of the sensation of him moving inside of her, the ripple of his muscles under her fingers, and the very pleased, almost relieved sounds that came from his beautiful throat.

Later, she lay with his head on her chest, playing with his long chestnut locks, and marveling at their softness and spring. They'd all managed baths that night, but she would have taken him in any state. His scruffy cheeks tickled her stomach slightly, but she did not want to move him. Her whole body still sang with excitement and release.

"If we were home," said Renn, his fingers tracing the curve of her thigh, "I would have courted you more properly."

"If we were home, you'd be courting more proper women," Veda said, teasing through some of her darkest worries. "You'd be going to parties, dancing all night, and eating figs with every meal."

"I don't really like figs," he said. "Not when I can have these ripe dates . . ." He moved his hand up her stomach, but she batted him away.

"I'm serious, Renn. It's . . . hard for me to accept that you . . . that this . . . could even work. I grew up impoverished. I didn't even know what a fig was until I visited the queen two years ago."

Renn breathed deeply, then he pulled himself up, propping his head on his hand to look at her more directly. "And that isn't fair. But, Veda, I can't help the world I was born into. You can think all you want of me, but I left that life behind a very long time ago."

"Why would you?" Veda asked.

"Because this is who I was meant to be. And this is where I was meant to be."

"It still seems strange to me that you would eschew your birthright to gallivant across the sea with a group of miscreants."

"Miscreants are my preferred company," Renn said with a wicked grin. "And this particular miscreant is my most prized."

She wanted to tell him that she had grown up starving on the streets, that her father had been so addicted to alcohol when she was a child that, even though he died terribly, she wrestled with the guilt of feeling relief afterward. Veda wanted to tell him that she would have done anything, absolutely anything, to have been able to live without constant worry over food, over shelter, over what she needed to live. That she had thought dying was a better solution on some nights than living as she had.

But he did not need to know that. Not yet. Not when he was looking at her like that. Her anger melted away like the snow off of Golvan's lilies in the spring.

"This miscreant isn't quite ready to sleep yet," she said softly, running her small fingers over his bottom lip and almost moaning in response.

"And that's also why you're my favorite," he said as he closed her mouth with his own, and they began anew.

Golvan's lily: a small, early spring lily, that only blooms after the first snow. It is small enough that it is most often trampled upon, and only grows on the southern-facing side of hillsides high in lime. The lilies have a unique structure that freezes completely in cold temperatures but thaws within minutes when exposed to the sun, without loss of structure or blossom.

She did not want that night to end, but in the morning, the aches returned, and so Veda meandered her way back toward the gardens in search of clues for what had happened to Grey's Surveyors. Renn slept on, and she kissed his cheek.

So, off she went to spend some time among the plants. She was just trying to decipher some of the root balls she'd unearthed when Arunn appeared, face pale and streaked with tears, at the edge of the forest not far from her.

"Arunn . . ." Veda began.

"Rouse everyone," Arunn said. "I've found Grey's Surveyors. Or what's left of them."

They had not been dead long enough to spare Arunn's Surveyors from recognizing the familiar shapes of their bodies. The cold, dry climate on this side of the island had reduced most of them to leathery bits—what hadn't been taken by scavengers.

And that was relatively little.

Grey's Surveyor's ship, the *Haven*, listed out in the distance. Forty-six bodies remained on the shore, clustered together in little groups.

"We'll burn them," Arunn said.

"No!"

It was Renn. He came up in front of Arunn, and everyone exchanged uncomfortable looks.

Arunn looked furious. "Get out of my way, Renn."

"This can't be the end," Renn said. "There has to be another answer."

"The answer is that they got sick," Kinna said. Even she was red-faced from weeping. "There isn't another explanation."

"Probably some kind of rot," said Uvenne, who had the most experience among them with treating the ill, having once apprenticed as a healer. "I've heard of some that make you so thirsty you drink water, any water, until you burst. Maybe that's what happened here."

Veda stared at the bodies nearest to her. They were curled up like dried husks of squash.

She couldn't argue with Kinna or Arunn. All signs pointed to an illness, and the best course of action would be to burn them—and the ship—and get on with their lives. They would return to Aldis with the sad news, but that would be the end of it.

"I don't think so," Veda said at last, the words coming slowly as she tried to piece things together. "The bodies haven't been scavenged anywhere near as much as they ought to."

"You even said this island was unusually bereft of animals," Arunn said, and this time it sounded accusatory. "This is just the ass end of nowhere, and we're all better if we leave and never come back."

"That's not the pledge we all made," Renn said darkly. Veda felt afraid for him in that moment. No one had ever challenged Arunn like that.

Veda cleared her throat, taking a step toward Arunn. The ground was spongy and it was difficult to keep one's balance. "If there is a chance it was not an illness, nor something that could befall us, shouldn't we at least take a day to ensure that we're not putting ourselves at risk?"

"No," said Arunn. He did not look at her.

"Arunn," said Kinna, eyes full of remorse and pity for the man. She'd had friends among the dead; they all had. "What is a day? A few hours?"

The large man clenched and unclenched his fists. The sea stink and the reek of death rose all around them. In the distance, Veda thought she could almost hear the ship creaking in the distance.

"It won't change what happened," Renn said.

Arunn looked out to the ghost ship, then back to the assembled Surveyors. "You have six hours. Those who want to help in this useless errand can stay. The rest, come to camp and prepare to make haste homeward." He turned then and walked back to the camp. Alone.

Kinna and Renn stayed.

The bodies felt closer, somehow, when the rest of the Surveyors were gone, even though Veda hadn't moved.

Having Renn there was good. Necessary. She didn't need him as she did when they traveled the long miles across the island, but she realized she had needed him in other ways, too. Just the solidity of him, his presence, gave her a point of reference here among the dead.

"Don't touch the bodies yet," Veda said when Kinna moved a few steps forward, knives out.

No one had gotten close enough to identify the dead yet. Unless Arunn had that night, when he was alone. But it didn't take a tracker to note the undisturbed sand around them. He had kept his distance, even in his grief.

Veda glanced at Renn. He was pale but whole. Alive.

I'm fine.

You look tired.

I always look tired.

You always look beautiful.

"Kinna, how long do you think they've been here?" Renn asked, his voice muted in the wind.

Frowning, Kinna tilted her head and squinted toward the nearest corpse. It was the only one by itself, and had remained on a rock. "I've never seen bodies like this before," she said. "Usually they're in a more advanced state of decay. It could be the island. It could also be arcane powers beyond our understanding."

Veda had no doubt these things were all possible. But she was trying to put the pieces together; she felt as if there was something she was missing.

"Don't touch the bodies," she said softly. "Let's walk around them. Observe what we can from a distance." With shaking fingers, Veda took out her field notes and began sketching. The sinews of a dead body, hardened and stretched by the sun, were vastly different than the lines of fronds and stamens, but she found it wasn't so difficult after a time.

She did not observe advanced decay in any of the bodies. There was still hair present; she could still see tattoos on some of their arms, note the wrinkles on their faces. Between the three of them, they were able to identify most of the bodies; a few were unaccounted for, but their suspicion was that they were on the ship.

"People do not simply lay down to die," Renn said, marching back up the sandy bank to meet Veda. "No matter how sick they were. This looks . . . coordinated."

"You don't think they were that desperate," Kinna said.

"I don't know what I mean," Renn admitted.

"Do we know who's on the rock?" Veda asked.

Kinna nodded slowly.

Arunn's sister, Hellaa.

When no one volunteered, Veda carefully stalked over to where Hellaa had breathed her last and, from a distance of a few paces, began her observations and scribblings. Hellaa wore a mix of standard-issue uniform pieces, as well as what could only be some kind of cloak made from the sails of a ship. There was pretty, if basic, embroidery all around the hem, but the design was difficult to make out from so far away.

"Veda!"

But she had already tripped. Her face met the rock and Veda saw the world sparkle and dim around her, but she rallied. If there was one thing Veda Nadiq was an expert at, besides recognizing plants, it was falling. Yes, there was blood, but she used her arms to prop herself up. And now that her hands were in the remains of Hellaa Leftfellow, well, she might as well get a better look at that embroidery.

Holly. Black holly. And little, asymmetrical berries.

"Oh, lords . . ."

"What?" Kinna was there; so was Renn. Their faces marked with concern.

"You're bleeding everywhere," Renn said, dabbing her face with his already-filthy handkerchief. "Veda, we shouldn't have—"

"I'm exactly where I need to be." She fingered the lovingly made embroidery. "I know what killed them."

"What?"

"This was Wintertide. You were right, Kinna. And so were you, Renn. Wintertide would have been a month ago. They came out to the shore, and Hellaa even made herself Holly Queen. They each carried candles. Then they drank what they thought was sweet holly juice, delighted to find something of home here at the edge of the world . . ."

Renn took in a sharp breath then leaned over. Indeed, half buried by sand was a small wooden cup, still stained red inside. "Sweet holly has been used since ancient times in drink . . . but its wilder cousin, the poke vulcha . . ."

"You are quite the historian," Kinna said, regarding the embroidery a moment before turning back to Renn. "What about the poke vulcha, though? Sweet holly juice is just meant for celebration."

"They would have felt elated, happy, at first," Veda said softly, putting her hand atop what remained of Hellaa's. "A few sips would induce slumber and was sometimes used as a sleep tonic. But a glass full . . ."

Renn's voice was rough with emotion. He slipped his arm around Veda's shoulders. "They would have gone peacefully, at least. They would have fallen asleep, likely feeling a little drunk and a little confused. It wouldn't have taken long."

"And it explains the lack of decay. Their whole bodies would have been poisoned," Veda said.

"In some ancient texts, they listed poke vulcha as an ingredient in embalming," Renn added. "But . . . well. I don't think we should burn them. I think we should tell Arunn everything we know. And warn them, as soon as possible, to keep away from anything that looks like a sweet holly berry."

"They were just trying to get home," Kinna whispered, tears now falling down her cheeks again.

"Perhaps they are home, now," Veda said.

They stood there, staring at the face of Hellaa, so brave and noble in life, so tragically twisted now in death. One mistake, and nature had claimed their lives.

No, there were no monsters here on the island; perhaps there never were.

Poke vulcha berries, often mistaken for the sweet holly berries grown throughout all of Aldis, are common in the island reaches of the Barrens. Poke vulcha berries are a relative of the sweet holly, but through years of selective breeding the deadly side effects of ingesting in a cooked state are significantly diminished.

The only significant difference between poke vulcha and sweet holly berries are that the endocarp is dark green in the former and red in the latter.

THE AUTHORS

Natania Barron *(she/her)* is a word tinkerer with a lifelong love of the fantastic. She has a penchant for the speculative, the Weird, the medieval, the Victorian, the literary, and the divine. Her work has appeared in *Weird Tales*, *EscapePod*, *Steampunk Tales*, *Crossed Genres*, *Bull Spec*, and various anthologies. Her longer works run the gamut from Edwardian urban fantasy to tales of the rock and roll world. Most recently, she published the second novella in her *Frost & Filigree* series, featuring monstrous heroes fighting the forces of darkness, called *Masks & Malevolence*. She is also the founder of The Outer Alliance, a group dedicated to queer advocacy in speculative fiction.

Nerine Dorman is a South African author and editor of science fiction and fantasy currently living in Cape Town. Her novel *Sing down the Stars* won Gold for the Sanlam Prize for Youth Literature in 2019, and her YA fantasy novel *Dragon Forged* was a finalist in 2017. Her short story "On the Other Side of the Sea" (Omenana, 2017) was shortlisted for a 2018 Nommo award, and her novella *The Firebird* won a Nommo for "Best Novella" during 2019. She is the curator of the South African Horrorfest Bloody Parchment event and short story competition and is a founding member of the SFF authors' co-operative Skolion, that has assisted authors such as Masha du Toit, Suzanne van Rooyen, Cristy Zinn and Cat Hellisen, among others, in their publishing endeavours. Do follow Nerine on Twitter at @nerinedorman.

Georgina Kamsika is a speculative fiction writer born in Yorkshire, England, to Anglo-Indian immigrant parents and has spent most of her life explaining her English first name, Polish surname and South Asian features. Georgina is a graduate of the Clarion West Writers Workshop where her first novel, *Goddess of the North*, started life as a short story. She can be found on twitter @GKamsika and at kamsika.com.

Rhiannon Louve *(xe/xem)* is a freelance writer of short fiction, video game dialogue, table-top role-playing books, privately commissioned fiction, and the occasional Pagan thea/ology (among other things). In addition, xe has a Master of Arts in Applied Theology and has taught World Religions at the college level. When off work, Rhiannon games (tRPGs 4-evar!), and studies primate psychology as well as French, Spanish, Japanese, Irish, and Swedish!

Michael Matheson *(they/them)* is a genderfluid graduate of Clarion West ('14), with work published or forthcoming in *Nightmare, Shimmer, Nisaba Journal, Augur,* and anthologies like *Upside Down* and *Lost Souls,* among others. Their first anthology as editor, *The Humanity of Monsters,* was released by CZP in Autumn 2015. Michael is also co-founder and co-EIC of *Anathema: Spec from the Margins,* a tri-annual speculative fiction magazine of work by Queer/Two-Spirit POC/Indigenous/Aboriginal creators. Find more at **michaelmatheson.wordpress.com**, or on Twitter @sekisetsu.

Tiffany Trent *(she/her)* is the author of eight fantasy books, including the dark historical *Hallowmere* series and the steampunk *Unnaturalists* duology, which won the 2013 Green Earth Book Award Honor. She has published multiple short stories in anthologies like *After the Fall, Wilfull Impropriety,* and *Corsets and Clockwork.* She is the co-editor, with Stephanie Burgis, of the Locus Recommended anthology *The Underwater Ballroom Society.* She is also adjunct faculty in the online Creative Writing MFA program at Southern New Hampshire University. When not writing or teaching, she can be found out in her garden covered in bees. Find her at **tiffanytrent. com** or on Twitter at @tiffanytrent.

Caias Ward is a thick-wristed HVAC technician with over two dozen publication credits. A member of SFWA and Codex Writers, he lives in New Jersey with his wife and daughter. Find him @caias on Twitter.

Suzanne J. Willis is a Melbourne, Australia-based writer, a graduate of Clarion South and an Aurealis Awards finalist. Her stories have appeared in anthologies by PS Publishing, Prime Books and Tyche Press, and in Mythic Delirium, Lackington's, and The Dark, among others. *Lisette of the Raven, Ash of the Rook* is her debut novella, released in 2019 by Falstaff Books. Suzanne's tales are inspired by fairytales, ghost stories and all things strange, and she can be found online at suzannejwillis.webs.com

GRR6509

ENVOYS TO THE MOUNT
AN EPIC CAMPAIGN FOR BLUE ROSE

BY STEVEN JONES, IAN LEMKE, GRACE LI,
REBECCA WISE, JAMIE WOOD, AND LAURIE ZOLKOSKY

IN THE DEPTHS OF THE SHADOW BARRENS, EVIL AWAKENS

The ancient connections between the nomadic Roamer folk of Aldis and the eldritch folk known as the vata has long been suspected, but never confirmed. When an emissary from the far-off vata stronghold known as Mount Oritaun comes to Aldis seeking a familiar face and a favor from its Queen, a small band of envoys from the Sovereign's Finest are assigned to lend their aid against the sinister power of the Shadow Barrens.

Envoys to the Mount provides four adventure chapters spanning five years and all four tiers of *Blue Rose* play. Together they form an epic campaign that sees the heroes not only facing off against the forces of Shadow, but also unlocking some of the ancient secrets of the world of Aldea.

This epic adventure path and sourcebook requires the use of *Blue Rose: The AGE RPG of Romantic Fantasy*.

SKU: GRR6509 • ISBN: 978-1-949160-00-0

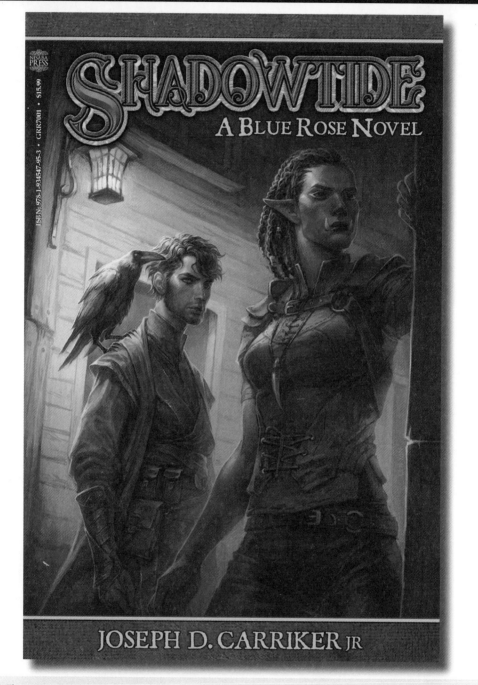

SHADOWTIDE
A BLUE ROSE NOVEL

JOSEPH D. CARRIKER JR